ALL STORIES ARE

LOVE STORIES

ALL STORIES ARE

LOVE STORIES

A NOVEL

Elizabeth Percer

HARPER

An Imprint of HarperCollins*Publishers*

FIRST EDITION

Poem on page 1 transcribed from a photograph by Cheryl Barton
Translation of Latin inscription on page 77 © Kristina Milnor

Designed by Fritz Metsch
Map © 2015 Laura Hartman Maestro

Library of Congress Cataloging-in-Publication Data

Names: Percer, Elizabeth, author.
Title: All stories are love stories : a novel / Elizabeth Percer.
Description: First edition. | New York : Harper, [2016]
Identifiers: LCCN 2015045247| ISBN 9780062275950 (hardcover) | ISBN 9780062275998 (ebook)
Subjects: LCSH: Earthquakes—California—San Francisco—Fiction. | Disaster victims—California—San Francisco—Fiction. | Interpersonal relations—Fiction. | BISAC: FICTION / Literary.
Classification: LCC PS3616.E685 A79 2016 | DDC 813/.6—dc23 LC record available at http://lccn.loc.gov/2015045247

---

16 17 18 19 20   OV/RRD   10 9 8 7 6 5 4 3 2 1

For Maya,
who brings stories to life

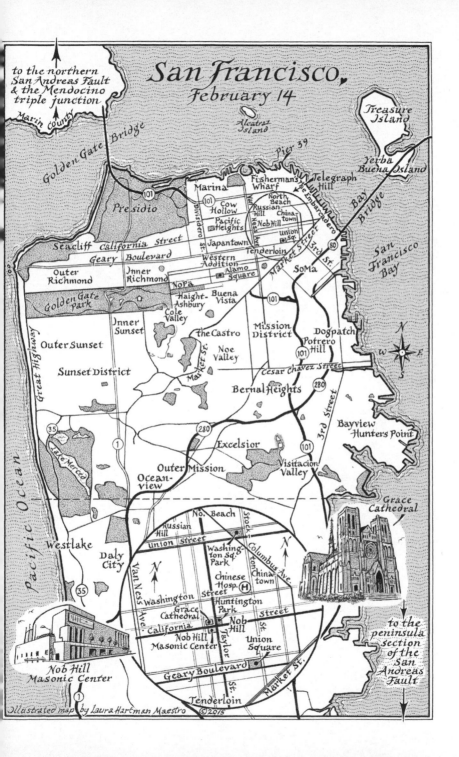

ALL STORIES ARE

LOVE STORIES

Public Service Announcement

~~~~~~~~~~

It may be helpfull to remember that
things have not always been as they are;
this may be obvious as it sounds, easy to forget
walking concrete paths and
perceiving streams of traffic and rectangular shelters.
It may be helpful to keep in mind that at one time
these constructions were non-existant.
It may be of some use to look over
all that you can see now, the
expance and boundries
of your environment, and think how all
of this will be gone
one day
eaten
and reapplied.
It may be helpful to see beauty
in decomposition; because like
the leaves of trees turn brigt and fall
to the ground to replenish
their mother, it is also our inescapable
privilidge to rot.
So now it becomes necessary to
view all items
in the world as reflections, all objects as mirrors,
and then move upon this basis.

—ANONYMOUS GRAFFITI AT THE RUINS OF THE SUTRO BATHS,
San Francisco, c. 1994

~~~~~~

On the morning of February 14, exactly seven hours, fifty-two minutes, and thirteen seconds before the earth's two largest tectonic plates released decades' worth of strain under a busy suburb just outside San Francisco; exactly eight hours, eight minutes, and fifty-three seconds before the energy dislodged from the seismic shifting triggered an even more catastrophic displacement farther north along the San Andreas Fault; exactly eight hours, nine minutes, and twelve seconds before all gas, power, water, cell, and satellite communications were severed from San Francisco and its environs; exactly eight hours and twenty-two minutes before thousands of tiny sparks and larger ignitions got out from under the valiant efforts of a drought-plagued, understaffed fire department and prematurely exhausted volunteers; and exactly ten hours and eleven minutes before the real danger to the old, precariously built, packed-like-sardines city—fire—proved its indomitable hunger, Max Fleurent was on the phone with his mother.

He checked his watch. They'd been on the phone for almost ten minutes and she was still trying, with mixed results, to wish him a happy birthday.

"One of these days we'll have to really celebrate, Max. Do something special. And I *wanted* to get you a birthday present, even hitched a ride"—her phrase for taking the Manor shuttle—"over to that fancy confectionery"—who but his mother still used this word?—"on Hayes. But can you believe the price they put on chocolate these days, Max? Do you people"—a favorite new phrase of his mother's, meaning, he was starting to put together, anyone under the age of seventy-four, his mother's own age—"really eat chocolate with chili in it? Or God, what was it. Bacon!" She tsked, as if scolding the entire chocolate industry in one huffy breath. "It's just revolting, Max. Honestly. If I *didn't* like you, I'd get you bacon chocolate for your birthday." Her voice softened as she remembered herself, "But I *do* want to get you *something*. . . ."

Max, thirty-four as of 5:46 that morning, had no illusions of his mother's ever getting around to the sort of straightforward birthday wishes he imagined some mothers might give their sons. After a lifetime of the kind of closeness many sons might wish to have with their mothers but few would appreciate in reality, Max knew his mother's mind almost as well as his own. He knew that she would never wish him happy birthday in any straightforward way, and he knew that she could not be rushed from one topic to another. He sighed silently, summoning the patience to wait for her to wrap up the current tangent so he could address the odd note he was hearing in her voice.

"Anyway, I'm all out of wrapping paper. I could use old newspaper, I guess, but that's not very special. . . ."

There it was again, a hesitation, as if she were only talking to distract herself from blurting out something she was afraid to say. It wasn't like her to hold back, at least not when it came to the sort of one-sided phone conversations she so enjoyed with her son. In fact, she stored up all her most stinging verbal assaults, vivisections of human nature she kept politely to herself in public, and later rewarded herself for good behavior by expelling them into her son's amiably distracted ear. Usually she prattled along, complaining almost merrily. But there was a hitch in her rhythm today, something off to Max's ear he couldn't quite place.

"Ma, what is it?"

"What is what?"

"You sound distracted, or upset. Did something happen?"

"How could I sound upset? It's your birthday!"

Max stifled a deep sigh. If only she could get on with whatever it was she really wanted to talk about, instead of torturing them both with such a poor performance. Rosemary Fleurent had many admirable qualities, but the fine art of a good lie eluded her. Even when lies might be a kindness, even a social requirement, she botched them hopelessly. *It's not* you, *Max, not you at all, or your looks; it's just those spoiled, ambitious San Francisco women. They all think they deserve the best-looking men! And don't go taking that the wrong way, Max. You know what I mean. The* really *good-looking men.*

Max checked his watch: 8:14. He had some time before his first meeting—an informal sit-down to discuss a one-hundredth-birthday celebration for Jerry Garcia. No need to get there early. As events director for the Nob Hill Masonic Center, he'd worked with quite a few characters in his time, and a 9 a.m. appointment with a bunch of aging hippies in flip-flops was as par for the course as the *Hillbilly Hoo-tenanny West Side Review* he'd be planning in the morning or the meeting he had tomorrow afternoon with represen-tatives from the Sisters of Perpetual Indulgence to discuss their annual Play Fair fund-raising concert. Neither of those were meetings he could prepare much for, either. No need to rush his mother through whatever hemming and hawing she needed to do.

Max sat down to wait her out, leaning over to turn up the volume on the morning news. The weatherman was on the screen now, some guy who didn't fill out his suit, his hair rid-ing a stiff wave. As usual, the weather forecast was the most cheerful segment of the broadcast, despite the grim reports of flooding in the winter, fire in the summer, landslides in the spring, visibility-destroying fog year-round. But it was over in a flash, replaced by a feature report on the increas-ingly sophisticated techniques of online predators trolling social media sites. Typical morning news: an infusion of freshly picked angst to go with your morning coffee. Was that a Mark Zuckerberg interview they'd managed to score?

He heard an echo on the line. His mother had turned on her own set. "Oh, look, Max," she exclaimed, "it's that nice young man with the compound in Palo Alto!" She sounded as delightfully surprised as if she'd spotted an old friend on the screen. "He has such a lovely wife," she continued, "and *he* certainly wouldn't win any beauty contests either, Max! In fact," she added hopefully, "I think he looks a little like you!" Max smiled faintly. What was his mother going to do if he ever did find someone? He'd be depriving her of her favorite hobby: worrying about whether or not anyone else would ever love her son. Maybe this extended dry spell in his love life was for the best. After all, who was he to deny an old lady of such a simple pleasure?

And it was nice to know she still depended on him, even if that dependency took the form of being her pet worry. Two years ago, on the day she moved into Buena Vista Manor (leave it to San Francisco to make a retirement community sound like a Mexican palace), they'd walked into her sun-filled new room with a view of the flowering gardens, met all the well-groomed or at least sufficiently propped-up residents, caressed several state-of-the-art amenities, and, in the careful intonations of a trained and slightly impenetrable staff, were told that they had made the right decision. His mother was settled in by dinnertime, and Max found himself ushered out shortly after, not quite sure if he had been rendered obsolete in the space of an afternoon. It was surreal, after all their years of forced togetherness, to leave her in a place full of people devoted to her individual needs. It felt like his care had been a compromise she'd had to endure until the professionals could take over.

But after she settled into her new home, the steady stream of slightly irritating, slightly endearing demands for his attention continued, minus the sort of terrifying late-night calls she'd made when she was sure of a break-in or wanted to call the police about "hooligans" on the street in front of her apartment, none of which were nearly as frightening as the weak-voiced call after she'd fallen and broken her wrist and hip, injuries from which her spirit never seemed to fully recover. "You might as well face it, Max," she'd pronounced, sitting up in her hospital bed like a queen in her court, the Buena Vista brochure held out like a scepter, "I'm getting old. And no, you *can't* take care of me," she interrupted him before he even got started. "I won't have my future as a grandmother jeopardized by moving in with you. You think it's hard to find a girlfriend *now*?"

But Buena Vista couldn't do everything for her. As it turned out, the subtler needs disguised as wants, the ones that gave the odder parts of her a chance to oxygenate, were the ones only he could meet. Just last week, even her favorite nurse at Buena couldn't get Rosemary to tell them why she didn't take her newly prescribed antacid for three days (with all the accompanying discomfort). It wasn't until Max was summoned that she admitted, shamefaced and only to him, that she was sure the viscous, beet-red liquid would stain her dentures irreversibly. She'd much rather have a little stomach trouble, she confessed, than become a pink-toothed social pariah.

Though lately he noticed that getting off the phone with her was a little like getting gum off his shoe—just when he thought he was clear, he'd find himself entwined all over again. He'd have to ask the director at Buena if they could introduce more early-morning activities. Poker, maybe. His mother had always liked poker. Maybe if they played in the morning, it would seem less cigars-and-gambling and more tea-and-bingo. He was always surprised by how prudish the staff were, as if they had a bunch of easily influenced elementary-school children on their hands. But to hear his mother tell it, retirees were more than a little willing to throw aside the social mores they had been laboring under for decades, not unlike recently de-vested priests. A few lewd jokes or closeted affairs paled in comparison to staring at the end of life as they knew it. Mortality was a funny thing, Max was learning; the closer a person got to it, the more authentic she became.

He had one eye on the news as he listened that morning, vaguely aware that he was missing most of the lengthy story she had just launched into about a friend's poor shopping habits and correspondingly unfortunate wardrobe choices. "I'm not the one to say it, Max, but she really is a size four-teen, and I just can't look *away* when she picks nothing up but tens and twelves!"

She sounded more animated, at least, now that the subject was no longer his birthday. In her own words, she was not "overly fond" of his birthday, though she was quick to reassure him that her distaste had nothing to do with him. On a February fourteenth eighteen years ago, sitting at the plastic table in the kitchen of their new, barely furnished apartment, she'd re-folded the letter his father had left for them and looked up at a waiting Max. "Your father claims you're a man now," she said. Her fingers, hovering at the edges of the letter, were shaking with fury. She stood up. When she spoke, her voice was pre-ternaturally calm. "Take his plate off the table." As soon as

Max did, his mother tore and tore at the paper, the tiny shreds falling to the ground, making him think of a hectic, feathery swirl, a bird fighting for its life. Later that night, she hunted down every last speck with her broom, as though sweeping up the last remains of the man himself.

Max turned the volume down as his mother guessed aloud that he hadn't been listening to her. Too late, he tried to recall the turn the conversation had taken. All he knew for sure was that another friend—a new friend, Alma—was the subject.

"Isn't Alma the one who stole that last boyfriend of yours—Clifford? No, it was Craig. Alma went after Craig. Aren't you two mortal enemies now?"

She exhaled her irritation. He'd missed the important points of her story and ended up trying too hard to sound as though he hadn't. "It was *Clarence*, Max. And we moved past that months ago. These kinds of things happen with new widows. A little bed-hopping is to be expected. We have a certain understanding." She sniffed fiercely and was quiet.

Yup. There was definitely something else still there, lingering on the edges of her voice, like a stray waiting to be invited in.

"Ma."

"What?"

"Is it this Alma person?"

A telling pause. "I'm not upset, Max."

"Craig?"

"It's *Clarence*, Max, for Christ's sake!"

Max heard a rumble of thunder, or felt one. He was about

to comment on it when all of a sudden the thunder was slamming into the walls around him, rattling the glassware in the kitchen and setting the blinds to trembling. "Oh God!" his mother exclaimed, confusing him further by making it seem as though she were in the same room with him. The newscasters on his screen looked shaken, too.

"Ma?"

"I'm OK, Max."

Well, talk about the earth moving on Valentine's Day! the anchorman joked. He was smiling insecurely at someone beyond the camera. *Hope I'm not the only one who felt that!* A wavering doubt skittered across his expression, followed by an almost instantaneous recalibration, a victorious return of the ubiquitous smile. *We should have a reading momentarily on that big bump I suspect most of us felt. And here it is!* He grinned into the camera, a surge of relief illuminating his face. *A respectful 3.8. Now if only the Niners had bumped the score up that much last week, we'd be Super Bowl champs!*

His colleague, a stony beauty with a head of precisely highlighted hair, laughed dutifully. *We'll be back in a few with more news on any damages this temblor might have caused and the latest in morning traffic.*

"Max?" his mother's voice seemed to come to him from far away.

He took a deep breath. "That wasn't anything, Ma. We want those big bumps; they let off some of the pressure," he recited, the San Franciscan knee-jerk response to living with earthquakes. He sat down, letting the temporary fear flood from his body. It felt good, he thought, stretching out his legs before him. The newscasters were now laughing for real, the tremor having shaken some of their falseness free.

"That poor man. What have they done with his hair? Is that a toupee? My word. What an unfortunate choice. Can't they do hair plugs now, Max? I thought we'd seen the last of the toupees years ago. There should have been an ordinance. A public burning."

Max smiled in spite of himself. "They must have all been fire retardant." She laughed, the sound unexpectedly light-hearted. Max felt himself grinning in response, disarmed, staring out the window; her laugh had suddenly thrown open an earlier picture of their lives. When they were both much younger and still living in upstate New York, he would entertain her during those endless afternoons waiting for his father to come home from his latest trucking gig or prayer service, helping her with the warm work she made of keeping house by telling her embellished stories he'd heard at school. He'd dance, too, and sing, if it made her laugh—acting the willing fool to ease the somber disappointment his father's long absences stiffened within her. A Max he'd long forgotten bubbled to the surface.

"Let's have dinner together," he declared spontaneously, "anywhere you like. My treat." It felt good to offer such a treat to her, better than a birthday present.

"Dinner?" she squeaked. "On your birthday?"

Damn. He'd walked right into that one.

"Oh, Max," she whispered, as though neither of them could bear the answer, "don't you have someone else to go out with tonight? On your birthday? There must be someone you've been meaning to ask out. . . ."

"No, Ma. I don't."

A weighty silence settled between them, each struggling to stave off disappointment.

His mother was the first to find a way back into the conversation. "We both know thirty-four isn't old, dear." Her voice was awkward with cheer. "But it isn't young either." Said as if one's advancing age were simply the result of making poor choices, as if discovering love could simply be the result of making better ones.

"No, it isn't," he replied briskly. "You're right, as usual."

He didn't need to hear her huff on the other end of the line to know he'd irritated her. He knew she hated it when he humored her, but it was one of his only defenses against her increasingly vocal disapproval of his lack of a viable love life. The fact that he refused to talk to her about it only irked her more. But he doubted it would bother her less if she knew that he felt as desperate about it as she did, that after so many years, his heart was still stuck on its singular fixation—one that was at first beyond reason but now beyond hope, probably even beyond sympathy. He'd rather not think about love, never mind launch into a full-scale discussion with its most agitated fan. How did thinking about love help it along, anyway? If thinking did the trick, he would have taken to it long ago instead of standing to the side as others stepped bravely into its current. Heck, by now he would have sprouted gills.

Max muted the TV and sat down by the window watching

the rain, a pleasure he knew he shared with other residents citywide, the lot of them so shell-shocked by the lack of water that three days of slippery streets and flash flooding and mud slides were cause for celebration. Down the street, the kids on the corner set out toward school, splashing through the cold and wet, their heavy book bags bouncing against their backs. He felt pleasantly lulled by his mother's voice, which had moved out of the range of high drama to settle on calm with a hint of future disturbance. What *was* that? It was still there, even clearer than before. Was it this nonsense with Craig or Clarence, whatever, that he heard in her voice?

"Ma." He stopped her midsentence.

A beat. "What?"

"What's going on with you?"

"Nothing, Max."

"Doesn't sound like nothing."

She clicked her teeth and didn't answer, shutting him out. He sighed. She had her own clocks to consider, and his curiosity could not rush them. He continued to listen with only half an ear as she launched into a report of the appointments she'd need him to take her to: the dentist tomorrow, a visit later in the week to the verbally abusive hairdresser she was devoted to in the Inner Richmond. Max pressed his face to the cool glass, hearing a few muted horns in the distance as the rain seemed to redouble its efforts. He closed his eyes, remembering that first winter in the city eighteen years ago, when it seemed there was nothing but rain, an endless sheet of wetness that made him feel he'd never find his way home.

But the year after brought stolen nights in bed with Vashti, the sweet, musty smell of her windblown hair as she came in through the window, the nights they'd slept together so peacefully, the peace all the more satisfying after the thrills that came before it.

"And you'll have to take me to the post office when you visit next Tuesday. I need to pick up stamps, Max. You know how I like to write my compliments and complaints in my own handwriting. They pay better attention that way. Oh," she said, "that reminds me." Her voice dropped suddenly to an oddly timid, nearly inaudible tone. He'd have to rush to catch it.

Max snapped to attention. "What?"

"Hold your horses, Max," she spat out, still refusing to be rushed. "It's just . . . well . . ."

He forced himself to take a deep breath, letting her fumble toward it.

"I've had a letter."

A letter. Not an e-mail or a note? "A letter?"

"Yes, Max."

He turned off the TV. The steady rain outside was calming now, though his chest had constricted. There were very few people in his mother's life, present or past, who would actually send her something through the mail, never mind the out-of-date, out-of-touch intimacy of a letter.

"From who?"

Rosemary cleared her throat. "Would you look at that? *Now* they tell us the BART strike is on again. After distracting us with news that doesn't matter. I swear. They're all just talking heads. With fake teeth. And fake hair."

"Mom. Who sent you a letter?"

He heard his mother sigh, then turn off her own TV. An unnatural quiet settled between them. "Well, if you must know, it's a letter from Guy." Her voice faltered but she caught it, suddenly determined to forge ahead. "It's a letter from your father, Max. Well, not so much a letter as a card, really. Anyway. I guess it was delayed a little—he sent it around Christmas, looks like. That nice super at my old apartment building held on to it, finally got around to dropping it off."

The rain continued its downpour, the sound a solid block now, like the sound of static, some kind of misguided connection.

"From my father." He heard the words leave his mouth in a monotone, but inwardly he tried to regain his balance, thrown by the sudden, violent jerk backward. And then, just like that, he was teetering precariously over the edge of a past he thought was over.

His father.

It didn't make any sense. Did it? His mind spun, disoriented. His father was as good as dead. Max envisioned his father rising from the grave and taking pen in hand, sitting down in his thin gray clothes to write. But he wasn't dead. Just because you don't hear a voice for twenty years doesn't mean it hasn't spoken. Suddenly, Max realized that he'd thought of his father's life as worse than over. It had been unimaginable.

His mother's voice sounded like nothing more than an echo on the line. "Let's just talk about it later, another day. Max. It's nothing. It says nothing. I wasn't even going to tell you, but then I figured, why not tell you about nothing? No reason to keep nothing from you!"

2

〰〰〰〰〰

Senior lecturer Eugene Strauss walked out of his eight-thirty lecture on plate tectonics and into the oncoming stream of bicycles and pedestrians on Lasuen Mall, not bothering to raise his umbrella. He lifted his face into the cold and the wet, squeezing his eyes shut, letting it take his breath away.

A frantically rung bell brought him back to the present with just enough time to dodge a careening bicycle. But the student's glare didn't puncture the bubble of nearly hysterical excitement rising in his chest. Instead, it made him laugh aloud. He had been that student once, hadn't he! Not so long ago, really. He stared after the boy, wishing him well with the magnanimity of a man in the flush of spectacular news. Academia wasn't easy for anyone, he reminded himself, not even for golden boys. It pulled you in, rubbed you raw, then threatened to spit you out at any moment. He smiled generously at the thought, newly freed of it as of that morning. Because tenure—the holy grail, one of the few true signs that your faith in the nameless, mercurial god of academia can find confirmation—was finally beginning to shine its light in his direction.

Making his way east toward the department meeting at the Stanford Faculty Club, he dodged the onslaught of pedestrian traffic as lightheartedly as he might a crowd at a dance.

Screw tight-assed, Oxford-reared, stiff-upper-lipped-and-God-knows-what-else Smythe and his infuriating insistence that they risk all their necks on a premature and shaky—no pun intended—earthquake prediction system; the assistant professorship was going to be *his*.

Soft-shoeing down the mall, Gene was already replaying the conversation he'd just had with the dean in all its glorious minutiae, paying particular attention to the details Franklin would love: the dean's old-boys'-network clap on his shoulder; Gene so nervous in the wake of recent firings that he began to sweat so copiously that by the time they reached the dean's office, he was practically walking like a penguin to keep the telltale wetness from showing; the dean's exact wording after several minutes of agonizing, meaningless pleasantries. Gene half closed his eyes as he walked through the rain, recalling every word as one might each flavor of an all-too-fleeting, unforgettable meal: *I'm sure you know there's an assistant professorship opening up, Dr. Strauss. We like you for it. In fact, I'm personally rooting for you on this one. It's not every day we come across an academic as talented and likable as you. You're good on your feet, young man. And God knows it wouldn't hurt the department to have a few level-headed ambassadors out there in the world.* A not-so-veiled reference to Gene's recent coup in the department battle over rolling out the NCEPT (the New Center for Earthquake Prediction Technologies), a developing Stanford-based earthquake prediction system that might actually trump the thorn in their side that was UC Berkeley's ShakeAlert.

But of course Gene's departmental rival—the insufferably

English, snub-nosed Sam Smythe—had argued in his perfectly nasal, thin-lipped accent that they move ahead immediately (*im-MEE-dee-at-lee*, in the dialect of snobby Englishmen). But as exciting as their research was, it just hadn't been tested thoroughly enough, and they wouldn't get the kind of support and funding they needed until that happened. Sam had kept his mouth shut after the dean took Gene's side, but he was obviously seething. Gene had been too relieved to savor the schadenfreude. Looking over the project files the morning before the meeting, he'd suddenly been sure Sam would win this battle. And if he did, that'd be one more departmental vote for Sam, one less for Gene. Sam was brilliant—more brilliant than Gene, by most accounts—and it was his work behind the scenes that really made up the meat of their shared research.

But it was Gene who knew that although the project outline was revolutionary and their earliest tests had been promising, funders would need more than just potential to fork over anything substantial—and the Department of Earth Sciences needed a good, sexy hit like this. Politically speaking, they definitely flew under the Stanford radar, a knee-knocking place to be in the competitive world of academia.

As he ducked under an archway and dialed, Gene was already rehearsing what he'd say to Franklin. *I swear, my heart stopped when he walked in. Totally unannounced, and then he goes and takes a seat in the back row! You should have seen the kids trying to sleep back there suddenly sit up at attention.* He smiled to himself as he selected the most savory bits to share with Franklin, the way a chef might select the best cuts of meat for the person he most enjoyed feeding. And not only did they have this morning's news to celebrate, but they might soon be looking forward to a dinner at The French Laundry, thanks to the bet he'd placed with Franklin that he'd become a Stanford professor by the time he turned thirty. Well, not so much a bet as a way for Franklin to boost Gene's competitive edge, to enhance that resolve he knew a little friendly wager would only fuel. Just under the wire, too, with the milestone only five months away. Ah, The French Laundry in late July. Summer squashes would be at their peak, the butter that graced them tasting faintly of the summer fields down the street, thick with smoke bush and sage. He shook his head as the phone continued to ring, still smiling in anticipation of the conversation he was just about to have.

No answer.

The flutter in his stomach was easy to ignore. Franklin hadn't had an episode for weeks. And he'd said he'd be shopping for dinner this morning: "lots of flesh and chocolate" had been his opaque description of the evening's meal. Now they'd have to add champagne. Gene toyed with his phone, trying not to redial immediately.

Who knew what kind of possibilities might open up for them? Maybe this assistant professorship was the tipping point, the first in a line of personal miracles heading their way. Heck, even the doctors admitted that strides in medical research were being made on an almost daily basis. He curled his fingers around his phone, wanting to grasp joy as tightly as he could, wanting it to stay, wanting to embrace and trust it as the devoted might their faith. But it began to slip away as if it sensed his clumsy pawing, his virginal awe and fumbling hold.

Until Franklin, Gene had known joy only tangentially: a shooting star of emotion, a distant, too-brief-and-brilliant-to-be-believed sign of life on other planets. He'd learned to be happy, even content. But joy, that rush of full abandon in the face of life rising up to meet you . . . only Franklin had given him the courage to reach for it.

He dove back into the rain, promising himself he'd wait at least five more minutes before dialing again, rebuilding his story as he hurried along. *I had no idea what he was doing there, so of course, halfway through, I almost passed out worrying about the worst possible reasons*—having the dean in your classroom was like an appearance by God himself; it either meant death or sanctity—*but then I had the most brilliant idea, which was to shut up and pass the ball to my students, who somehow managed to start a surprisingly rousing conversation about electromagnetism! Surprising at any time, never mind before breakfast on a rainy February morning. A-pluses all around.*

And sure enough, Gene's first sign that all was well—more than well!—was the expression of wry concession on the dean's face when he approached after the class cleared out. "Never could quite drum up enough interest in that one myself," he admitted good-naturedly. "Not even way back in the day, before they all had every bleeping goddamn thing on Earth to distract themselves with, and the audacity to look at them while you're talking. Well done," he said, and smiled as though they were both already in on an enviable secret.

Then, after a few more agonizing moments of chitchat,

came the seemingly casual insider tip about the assistant professor position opening up in the spring. Gene had to watch his feet to keep them from leaping into the air with joy right then and there. It was one stroke of good luck to have that kind of tip from a senior faculty member, and another kind of luck entirely to have it come from Dean Abernathy. Everyone knew that Abernathy had the ear of God when it came to choosing new department members. This was like a blessing from the pope himself.

Nearing his destination, Gene shot his forearm out of his jacket to glance down at his watch: 9:48. Shoot. No time to get coffee before the ten o'clock monthly departmental research meeting, but they'd certainly have coffee there—the good Faculty Club coffee, too. Not Wichita Water, as Franklin called the stuff Gene occasionally tried to make at home.

At the Faculty Club, Gene ducked under the courtyard overhang to try his call once more, but Franklin still wasn't there. "It's me," Gene said, his voice suddenly drowned out by a surge of rain overhead. "Call me. Now." Oh God, he couldn't wait until after the meeting to talk. He chanted silently, half-mindedly reaching out to nothing in particular: *call, call, call, call, call.*

But Franklin didn't call, and he still hadn't when the meeting ended. Nor had he responded to Gene's texts. Gene, after everyone else left, ordering another coffee. His heart dropped into his stomach as he dialed once more, the phone ringing again and again. Still no answer, no matter how sure he tried to feel after each ring that one would come.

The pit in his stomach widened, turning joy into its

inverse, that all-too-familiar vacuum of fear threatening to burst open within him.

"There are a few conditions to this ongoing relationship," he had announced several months earlier, trying to cheer them both up. As if anything would put a condition on the relationship they'd poured the best of themselves into for nine years. Bests each didn't even know he had before meeting the other. But Franklin was worried—picking fights and walking around with his shoulders hunched and his brow wrinkled— and Gene couldn't blame him. They'd both seen their own fair share of husbands dumped after a few tense months and extra pounds, never mind a debilitating disease.

But at least now, after almost a year of imbalance and weakness and fatigue, they had a name for their trouble, had forced it into the light. Though the name itself was awkward and ugly: multiple sclerosis. Gene said it sounded like the postural condition of a Victorian child lurking in a factory. Franklin had thought it was something only plump, middle-aged women were affected by. Some kind of side effect of wearing frumpy sweatpants. Thank God for its snappy nickname, easier to share with their friends: MS. Lying awake at night, staring at the ceiling, Gene heard it more viscerally: the hiss of a snake, the muted warning swell of bees.

A week after the diagnosis, they'd been sitting in bed together hours after leaving Franklin's new team of doctors (a phrase heart-stopping enough in itself) at UCSF: Franklin in his silk pajamas, leaning against their reclaimed-wood headboard that he'd had to buy from Restoration Hardware when Gene wasn't looking (*it sort of cancels out the "reclaimed" bit if you buy it from a three-hundred-page glossy)*; Gene in his form-fitting organic cotton T-shirt and underwear, resting on his elbow, done crying. Gene felt fortified by how civil it all was still—their life, their relationship, their approach to even the most terrifying news. It seemed almost hard to believe that such a base disease could worm itself into all their layers of elegance: their home on the top floor of Fin de Siècle, the intimate boutique inn overlooking Washington Square Park that Franklin had owned for almost two decades; their social calendar full, save for regular weekends in Napa and lazy Sunday afternoons; the easy and steady way they'd slipped into each other's hearts and then, to their mutual astonishment, somehow stayed there.

"One"—Gene grabbed a pen off the nightstand and pulled his lover's arm toward him—"I shalt not withhold medical information from my spouse."

"Are these commandments or conditions?"

"Call them whatever you like."

"I knew I shouldn't have married a Catholic."

"Protestant, Franklin."

Franklin shrugged, finally well enough to jab, "Christian Shmistrian."

They watched as Gene continued to write on Franklin's forearm, the pen drenching the beautiful, unmarked skin. God, the man had such skin! Olive but pale, the color of an eggshell protecting the most delectable yolk. "Two: I shalt not prematurely bury myself, even in my own head."

Franklin didn't look up.

Gene would let that slide. For now. "Three: thy spouse

shall allow at least thirty minutes for the return of phone calls. After that, he's allowed to hunt you down."

Franklin snatched his arm back, rolling the sleeve down punitively. "I'm an invalid, Gene. Not a prisoner."

"You're neither, actually," Gene insisted, not bothering to step delicately around these melodramatic characterizations. After all, if Franklin died, wouldn't Gene be the one living with his story? Wasn't his version of it just as important, given that it was most likely to outlast any other? "But instability and falls are a possibility." As were blindness, paralysis. They had both swallowed this unspoken litany and were bloated with it.

Gene loosened his collar, feeling his temperature rise. He didn't have time to run home before his next class. Listlessly, he tried FaceTime, then Skype, even though he knew Franklin never picked up either one unless he was freshly groomed and cheerful. *Damn*, he swore silently to himself. The rain picked up, drumming loudly on the roof overhead. The Faculty Club was almost vacant, the lull before lunch fully in effect. The waiter attending him had taken a seat in the back of the room and closed his eyes. In the quiet, Gene allowed himself to wonder what it would mean if he suggested that Franklin sell the inn, that they leave their beloved San Francisco and move down here. Palo Alto wasn't all that bad. Maybe they could get their hands on a nice little Eichler, restore it themselves. Then Gene could be home at almost any time of day in a heartbeat.

He swallowed the last of his coffee. He wasn't sure he was ready to kill Franklin's spirit just yet, even if all signs pointed toward a future in which keeping him alive might mean killing both their spirits just a little. He fished out a generous tip and put his wet jacket on, trying to step back into the joy that had so recently washed over him. Things would be OK, he told himself, dashing back outside and into the rain, darting through Tressider and back toward the Main Quad, passing clusters of people who had decided to wait out the storm under meager shelters along the way. But Gene only hurried more. His class was about to begin.

~~~~~~

3

A few moments later, nine hours into her ten-hour graveyard shift, Vashti Shirah—night baker at Sucre, the Zagat-
rated, hipster-hounded bakery on a gently edgy block
between NoPa and Alamo Square—woke from a nightmare, drenched in sweat.

She sat up quickly. The oven alarm was going off, and for
God only knows how long. She leapt off the baker's cot in
the room behind the main kitchen and threw open the door
to the oven, rescuing the cakes just in time, slamming them
on the counter in her unbalanced rush to save them. Damn.
She rubbed her shoulder where she'd banged it on the wall,
surveying the cakes' edges for signs of overbrowning. *A lesser
baker would let these slide*, she thought, assessing the burnt gold
at their rims and shaking the oven mitts off her hands. *Stupid heart-shaped cakes*, she thought, grimacing at them. She'd
hated them while she was making them, and now that she'd
ruined them she hated them more. She pressed the edge of
one lightly. It sprang back dutifully. Maybe she should try to
pass them off anyway. They were only Valentine's Day cakes.
She could fill in what she didn't shave off. It wasn't as if the
ridiculous shades of red and pink icing waiting for them were
designed for the subtleties of a perfect pastry. But still—she
had standards. Or was everything about her falling apart?

Vashti sat back on the baker's stool, her pulse still racing from the adrenaline of waking suddenly from a restless sleep. She should have expected the dreams to worsen around Valentine's Day: it was his birthday, after all. *You never forget*, he always said, his voice in that gentle, low region that reverberated in her own chest. *Like tigers chuffing to each other*, she told him in the dream, just as she used to tease him. She could still hear it, more the noise of affection than its words. She tried to squelch the insistently rising details of the nightmare that had woken her—they'd dropped their clothes; no, they'd never had them; and then they swam in a dark lake past the body of her late husband, the light snowfall dissolving on her skin and collecting on his lifeless form.

She hated remembering the dreams almost as much as she did having them. Yet try as she might—sleeping pills that would fell a horse or, when those only made her dreams deeper and more vivid, loud music or the TV to keep her awake—they persisted. And recently, they'd become more frequent. Six months ago, when they began, they were intermittent, mingled almost politely among the far more prominent dreams of caring for Dale just before his death. But now, her mind persisted almost every night in dragging her into some new, lustfully macabre terrain with Max and Dale, the three of them playing out some stupidly obvious version of the tale her subconscious insisted on repeating. She as villain, Max as hero, Dale as victim. Or was it Max as victim, Dale as hero?

She wiped her eyes with the back of her hand, regretting it instantly. God, she was a mess! She sighed, wishing the bakery had a shower. Her arms and face were caked with a fine dusting of flour, and the sweat from her nightmare still clung to her. Abruptly, the stool she sat on wobbled beneath her. She cursed herself silently; such a mess, she couldn't even sit straight on a chair.

Vashti set the timer for the cakes to cool, knowing she'd have to start frosting before she left at eight. A quick glance at the window told her that it was still as dark as night outside. Her circadian rhythms were hopelessly off. They always were when it rained like this for so long. *Maybe that's it*, she lied gladly to herself, *the run of bad weather*. She wasn't obsessing about a man she hadn't seen in more than a decade because her poorly beloved husband had just died and she was losing her mind from guilt and grief. She was simply tired from the rain.

Her love for Max—or, it might be more accurate to say, her memory of her love for Max—had become like a chronic disease, something she'd tried to deny at first, then wish away. But she had found more peace with it over time, glad for the months or even years when she was asymptomatic, soldiering through the times when his image occupied her mind so often that she could think of little else.

There were times, especially when Dale was sick, that she'd imagined she was cured. Those long, summery months when he was dying at home, the lavender breezes coming through the windows he asked her to open when the baking Sonoma heat had passed and the night crept in, cool and inviting, as tender as what was suddenly between them once the doctors told them that there was nothing they could do to stop Dale's heart from failing. Although she did not fool herself into thinking that the sort of love she had once hoped for was finally blooming between them, she was pleasantly surprised to find they were developing a new friendship, a deeper, less guarded bond than the stubborn fondness they'd built their marriage upon until then.

Before Dale got sick, any affection between them had been strained and convoluted, as affection in a marriage without passion so often is. She entered the marriage guiltily and never lost her sense of shame, the sense that she didn't deserve what he gave her or that she'd somehow come by it dishonestly. Odd, since the relationship she had with Dale was probably one of the most truthful she'd ever enjoyed.

Still, she kept to her role as a wife on the periphery, tending to Dale's operational needs assiduously, monitoring the edges of the life she couldn't bring herself to enter fully. But once the home grew quiet and all but those charged with guiding him into death had gone, something shifted. Instead of watching as others cared for her husband, now she sat at the edge of his bed, sorting through the simple cotton things he preferred against his thinning skin or lowering and lifting the shades throughout the day so he'd get just the light he wanted. Their conversations remained minimal, but they were now threaded through with an openness they hadn't enjoyed when they thought they had an indefinite amount of time left to figure out how to keep living with each other. Vashti found herself smiling unself-consciously in Dale's presence, spending hours around him without feeling the need to exchange words.

The unavoidable wonder of a nearing death made it suddenly easy to be vulnerable, knowing it wouldn't last long enough to demand more from either of their heartstrings than they had to offer.

After he died, the spirit of that vulnerability lingered for a few precious weeks. It helped her cope with the interrupted sleep, the exhaustion of putting someone recently alive into the earth, then recalibrating to life without illness. She was even good to herself, unusually so. *It's to be expected*, she reassured herself when the dreams kicked in, *that a new widow's sleep would be disrupted and disturbing.* And at first she delivered only manageable nightmares to herself: dreams of Dale that were memories of his pain, haunting images of how he looked just before he died—blue eyes paler than ever, the skin waxy across the forehead. Part of her was glad—nearly triumphant, in fact—that her nightmares immediately following her husband's death were of her husband. *Maybe*, she told herself eagerly, *I loved him more than I realized.*

But those dreams faded quickly.

After just a few weeks, she was dreaming again—despite her best efforts—of Max. She remained properly somber and thoughtful during the day, conscientiously—even sincerely—grieving, but at night her subconscious swept in and took her best intentions hostage. As soon as she let down her guard enough to sleep, another self emerged: a child laughing at the chatter of a squirrel during her mother's funeral; the young adult who denied her baby's doomed genetic code, drinking in the smell of her and marveling at the thin silk of her hair.

Vashti pulled off her apron and splashed some warm water on her face at the sink. She had been stupid to think that taking the overnight shift would mean less sleep, fewer dreams. The half-rested mind, she was now discovering, loved nothing better than to dream, to blur the lines between being awake and being asleep. It was just grief, she told herself, the extreme lurches of the heart dredging up old memories.

Her phone rang. She pulled it off the counter and looked at the caller ID, though she knew who it was: Javi. She never missed Valentine's Day. Vashti answered, eager for a sympathetic ear, already resenting the note of pity that would accompany it. *Wasn't it Javi's fault, too*, she found herself thinking, *at least a little?* Falling apart alone was one thing; having a sister who was kind enough to recognize and worry over it was another.

"Where are you?" she answered. She looked up at the clock on the wall. "What time is it?"

"Paris. About to board a plane to Istanbul. We were late to the gate, so I have, probably, almost ten minutes." There were some garbled sounds in the background before her voice came through again: " . . . sad to say that Parisian airport food is as much of an oxymoron as you'd expect."

Vashti closed her eyes, the sting of tears threatening to return. *Thank God for modern technology*, she thought, savoring the familiar sounds of her sister's voice. If she kept her eyes closed, she could imagine Javi was right there, maybe sitting right across from her, her elbows on the counter and her hands a folded shelf for her chin, her eyes searching her sister's face for a way to understand what Vashti felt but couldn't say.

"How are you?"

"Fine."

Javi was silent, waiting for the real answer. More garbled noise. Vashti hated these snatched phone calls, the threat of an abrupt ending always humming in the background. She couldn't remember the last time they'd talked unhurried. But then, hurry was her sister's favorite drug, a sweet distraction from a deep loneliness that was as frightening to her as a child's underbed monster, the sort of loneliness that arose from a loss that could never be recouped. Years ago, Javi could go on vacation for a week or more, but her dependency had gotten the better of her. Now even a day off from work made her shaky and nervous. If only she would come home, just for a little while. Maybe if she could see and touch her, Vashti could make her sister see how far she'd run away. But maybe that was why she didn't come home.

Javi's voice broke through her thoughts. "What is it?"

Vashti focused on the mess of flour on the counter, sweeping it into piles with the side of her hand. "Just not sleeping well."

Javi raised her voice into the next ripple of static. "Vishy? Are you there?"

"Yes, yes!" she called out, the note of desperation in her voice taking her by surprise. "Can't you hear me?"

"Lost you for a second. You're not sleeping? Is it more dreams?"

Vashti nodded, unwilling to speak. The interference was too loud, Javi was always too far away, she could barely contain the sadness suddenly swelling in her throat.

After a moment, Javi's voice broke in, oddly raspy, almost hoarse. Had she started smoking again? "Listen, Vishy," she said. Vashti squeezed her eyes shut to conjure up her sister's face: narrowly beautiful, with a long nose and chin, intelligent eyes. "I've been thinking."

When is Javi not thinking? Vashti thought irritably. *At least about how to fix her sister's miserably thwarted personal life.* But she listened anyway. This was the implicit arrangement between them: Vashti could complain endlessly about unreasonable romantic desires as long as she spent just as much energy listening to her sister's critical advice. Of course she should *start dating again, just put herself out there, see what happens.* And of course, her sister was right. Vashti was primed to step over that invisible but all-important line between being a callous widow and a cautiously available one. And of course, *Dale would understand.*

But Javi knew it wasn't about Vashti's dead husband. Or at least not just about him. Her sister couldn't exactly read her mind, but sometimes it seemed like she could hear Vashti's thoughts, just as whales can understand each other by calling out into the spaces between them.

"You should just go see him."

Vashti's heart slapped once against its cage. "I can't."

"Why not?"

Vashti didn't answer. She leaned over and fumbled a little to open the window over the sink, stretching her neck to catch a face full of chilly, damp air. Had the rain not been blocking her view, she would have been able to see a few crates and a crumbling brick wall, but not much else. Some might feel too hemmed in down there, but she liked the co-coon of it, the old basement comfort and the warm ovens.

There were a thousand reasons why not—why she couldn't or shouldn't or wouldn't go see Max—most of which they'd discussed as many times.

"If he'd wanted to see me, he would have said."

"Why? Because you exchanged a few meaningless hello-how-are-you e-mails a few months ago?"

Well, yes. Because she'd hoped he would send out some kind of smoke signal when she reached out. Something other than the miserably chaste politeness. *What a pleasant surprise. Glad you've moved back to the area. Nice to hear you're doing well.* "I just can't, Javi. You know why."

"Not really, at least not anymore. Maybe ten years ago, I knew. Now I'm not sure *what* it is, exactly, that's holding you back. Are you?"

"I was the one who walked out, Javi. I walked away," Vashti said under her breath, the memories flying across time and distance to pierce her as painfully as ever.

There was a pause on the other end of the line. "You did. But that was a million years ago, and you walked away for the right reasons."

"Maybe. If he actually knew the truth, maybe he'd agree. Or maybe he'd hate me even more."

"Maybe. But that was then. And he doesn't hate you. I sincerely doubt he ever hated you, Vishy. Anyway, there's really only one way to find out."

Vashti bit her lip. She wouldn't even know what to begin

to say. Each time she thought about seeing him she remembered her guilt, and the hot shame of even hoping he might be open to seeing her flooded her face. "He could never forgive me."

"Yes, he could."

Not after what she'd done, and certainly not after what she'd kept from him.

"He *could*," Javi said gently, knowing and arguing with, as sisters do, the hidden contents of Vashti's heart.

Maybe. To someone else, what she had done might be forgivable. A sister, for example, whose forgiveness is easily won. Even someone like Dale might have forgiven her. A person who was levelheaded and experienced and—they all knew it— rich enough and lonely enough to believe that he could change the heart of a woman who didn't love him, save the heart of a child unlikely to live. But Max, whose young and inexperienced heart she had, in her confusion and pain, so abruptly broken, could not.

"Are you traveling alone?" Vashti asked. The ache for her sister rose again in her chest, riding the wave of old anxieties about love and its aftermath. What if her plane crashed or was hijacked? What if the hotel in the next city was unsafe, populated by foreigners whose curiosities were aroused by a pretty young executive traveling alone? "Is it just you again?"

"I'm meeting colleagues there."

Vashti didn't bother asking who such colleagues might be. She could never keep track of them anyway. Her sister's professional life was as mysterious to her as the moon. She resented not only her sister's preoccupation with work, but also the opacity of international business law itself, how its purpose was encased in a lingo that made sense only to the ones who used it, how it stole a part of her sister's consciousness and rendered it unfamiliar. In her darker moments, Vashti thought that it wasn't enough that Javi had to be busy all the time; she needed to be busy with something those who loved her couldn't possibly dismantle.

"You've ruined me for Valentine's Day, you know," Javi was saying, the efficient French voice over a microphone in an airport more than five thousand miles away making Vashti strain to catch her words, unsure if she'd heard what she thought she had. "I could be sipping champagne and prepping my coiffure for a candlelit dinner for two over the Seine."

"You mean the Bosphorus."

She could hear Javi's smile in her voice. "Just call him. Wish him a happy birthday. Who doesn't want to be wished a happy birthday?"

They both listened to the next warning. Javi had five minutes before she would be swept away, again, into the anonymous international sky.

There was a long pause on the other end of the line. They both knew their time was nearly up, and there was too much to say that would go unsaid. "You're OK, Vishy," Javi said. It was what she said when she worried that neither of them was.

You're OK, a ten-year-old Javi had told an eight-year-old

Vashti after discovering her sister shoveling dirt into her mouth on the morning of their mother's funeral. She'd taken one of her sweaty, tear-smeared fists in her own and kissed it. *You're OK*, she'd said in the days and weeks of Vashti's ongoing compulsion to eat from the earth as if it really were a mother whose soil could nourish her. Javi always knew where to find her, always tucked a tissue into her back pocket to wipe her sister's blackened mouth. In those moments, it didn't matter as much that neither of them was OK, because if they leaned into each other, it felt like they could both stand up straight.

Vashti nodded, choked with memories. "I miss you." Her voice sounded thin even to her own ears.

The flight attendant's voice grew louder, the squawk of meaningless orders, as self-important as they were hollow, flying up and into the spaces between them: where to be and when and never why.

"Listen," her sister began cautiously, "how about this?" Vashti strained to catch what she was saying over the background noise. "If you go to see him, I'll come home for Passover."

Vashti sat up straight, fully awake for the first moment in weeks. "You're coming home?"

"I said I'd come if you went to see him."

"But why wouldn't you just come home, if you can?"

"I'm supposed to be in New York for partner meetings, which I really shouldn't miss. But just this once, I *could* invent some family emergency."

It was better than nothing. Unless—"Passover *with* Dad?"

If only there wouldn't be a Passover. Javi could come home just to visit, without duty and their father's watchful eye weighing them down. But they were adults with responsibilities to consider, no longer children scheduling play.

"Just go see him."

"We'll talk about it later. You'll miss your plane."

"The deal only lasts until I hang up this phone."

Jesus, Vashti swore silently. *Blackmail. Going-for-the-jugular sisterly blackmail. Damn her.*

"I can't."

"You can."

Vashti dropped her head into her hand.

"Vishy. Just do it. You're going to make yourself crazy unless you do *something*. How long can a person go without sleeping?"

Vashti didn't answer.

"Let me ask you this: would going to see him be any worse than the dreams?"

"The dreams will stop eventually," Vashti tried, halfheartedly. *Oh God.* She felt her heart in her throat. *What if they didn't?* "They couldn't possibly last forever," she tried convincing them both.

"I hope not. But how much longer?" Her sister chose her words carefully. "Just go. Please, Vishy, I can't bear to hear you this upset for much longer. It's time you restarted your life, yourself, something. Go for me, if not for you. So you get a good night's sleep. So I can."

She hated when Javi worried about her. If anything confirmed her worry about herself, it was her sister worrying about her, too. She was worrisome, wasn't she? Stuck. Had she always been this way? She couldn't quite remember.

"OK," she said quietly.

"Really?"

Vashti couldn't quite believe it either. Then she heard herself speak again. "I said OK."

"OK," Javi confirmed, unable to keep the surprise out of her voice. "I'm hanging up before you can change your mind. I'll call you when we land."

Vashti stood with the phone still in her hand, gazing at the condensation on the windows over the sink: still raining. No rain forever, then nothing but rain. She felt wearied by extremes. Devastating loss followed by miraculous gain, the pendulum always threatening to swing.

Fear poured into her belly, already stiffening into regret. There had to be a way out of it; something taken on so easily could surely be dropped just as easily. Javi wouldn't really stay away if she didn't go see Max. Would she?

Vashti's heart leapt to a Valentine's Day years earlier, her mind too slow to catch it. After six weeks of dry rounds and grainy frostings, she'd perfected her mother's recipe for Persian Love Cake right down to the sugared rose petals, which she and Max found too lovely to eat at first. Vashti saw herself at sixteen, her face flushed from the hot kitchen, her apron smeared with flour, the pride and light from the birthday candles on her face. Max had loved it. She had never been more proud of herself, or happier.

She could just go *see* him. Get a glimpse of him somehow. He didn't have to see her back.

4

~~~~~~

Max strode out of his apartment on Filbert and was down the block in seconds, glad for the wind tunnel around the corner at Taylor. He let the air take his breath away as he leaned into it, trudging uphill. Around him swirled the sounds of foghorns from the bay and early-morning children shouting from a passing school bus, the calling tones popping up like flowers as they passed. Every morning in San Francisco was a bit like waking up on the edge of the earth: beautiful and damp and wild, full of the strange music people make, open-armed, into the wind.

He passed Bernie, a fixture of a man covered in so many layers of filth and clothing that they were no longer distinguishable from one another. Max lifted a hand in greeting, but Bernie was thoroughly absorbed with the contents of a Folittière takeout box. His pet parrot, which on good days he liked to claim was one of the wild ones from Telegraph Hill, sat on his shoulder, peering in at the food, snatching the few scraps offered him. They were always together. Though on some days, the parrot tucked its head into its feathers while Bernie insisted to anyone who walked by that it had once been a cat that grew feathers and wings and painted itself.

Had Bernie left his family, too? Or had he been left? He was sockless again, wiggling his toes in the wet and rain because, with the rueful delight shared by many of his fellow transplants, he figured that if he was going to be homeless in San Francisco, he might as well enjoy the weather.

Max put his head down and hunched into his jacket, bracing himself as the wind grew fiercer nearer the summit of Nob Hill. His chest burned as he climbed harder, his breath in his throat.

A letter. After eighteen years. Not even a letter: a card. Had his father just gone to the drugstore card section marked "Regrettable Life Choices" and plucked out the right mix of wit and chagrin to sign and toss into the mail, expecting his mother to receive it as casually on the other side? Or maybe it was a notification card: news of a slow death by a horrible disease. An inheritance he'd forgotten to mention, a sudden windfall that his life as an ascetic prevented him from accepting.

Trying to calm himself—to rid himself of the old unresolvable feelings threatening to rise like so many foolish, graveyard fears—Max stopped and took a breath at Ina Coolbrith Park, allowing for the voiceless protection of its lanky trees, grateful for the distractingly steep grade flanking it that made his thighs ache in protest as he resumed his march up Taylor, the peaks of Nob Hill's majestic buildings starting to make their appearance on the horizon just when you felt you were reaching the empty top of the world.

It was lonely to be faced with so much beauty and still feel bereft. When he was unhappy as a child in and around the dark fields and forests of upstate New York, he'd always felt he was in good company. But San Francisco corralled its unhappiness to corners easy to avoid and neighborhoods easy to circumvent, encouraging the unhappy to stay small and keep to themselves. Even the current dismay over how new money was changing the city didn't stop people from lying down like children in parks during their lunch hours, talking about the future, identifying superheroes in the city's politicians who might save them all while dining on the latest artisanal fad. And sometimes—and here was where things became truly unbelievable—the politicians came through. Mayor Benioff's tax-break measure for working artists and 501(c)(3) employees had somehow miraculously passed, and over the past several months, it seemed that every political discussion had been underscored by the breathless hope that the city could, once again, claim its status as the only conscientious utopia in the country. Certainly, here on Nob Hill, watching the rain drip from the eaves of so many view-capturing windows, no one would guess that it was anything but a snow globe of a town, willfully picturesque, even if trapped in the invisible bubble of an endless storm.

Not that Max didn't love the city's warmth and spirit, its joie de vivre that waned occasionally but never faded. But before it was home, when his father had essentially dropped Max and his mother off there on his way toward a life without them, Max's sadness had only enhanced his sense of displacement. He ached for cold weather, months of being iced in before anyone expected him to walk around in public, skin exposed.

He used to fantasize about going back. Taking a bus or a train or even scrounging up enough airplane money to return to Altona, the last in a line of small towns where they'd landed in their nomadic search for the most affordable rent. They'd moved too many times to know many people in any one place, and neither of his parents maintained much in the way of family ties, but the surroundings themselves—the woods and the green mountains, the cold streams and dusky gardens—would bring far more comfort than days filled with either dense fog or a piercingly bright sun, blocks and blocks of stucco houses washed pale by drought and salty air.

But he never did. Even in his worst moments—the ones when he thought that he, too, could leave his mother if it meant finding his way to a world that felt even a little more familiar—Max knew that he wouldn't find what he wanted there, that he wanted to return to more than just a place. His true wish was to find his way back to the old life they'd had, the last moment he'd felt sure that he and his mother were part of his father's future. Which probably would have been the night Max had helped him burn his rank, oil-stained trucker's uniform: a Yankees cap and a Coca-Cola T-shirt older than Max, heavy jeans shiny at the knees from wear. His father had always hated the dirt, coming first to the sink whenever he came home, scrubbing at the black stains in the creases of his knuckles. Yet even at the time, it seemed miraculous—and rightly so, as miracles are always tinged with suspicion—that all those things his father hated could simply be burned.

It was ceremonial, his father had declared, his face shining in the light of the backyard bonfire. They'd camped out beside it the night after he quit his job, and Max's father had told him about their new lives in San Francisco as if they were already living them. He was never more open than when talking about his dreams. They would be living in the Sunset, a nice, family-oriented district where rents were cheap and the streets were wider and quieter than you'd expect in a city. The bustling, brilliant downtown was only a bus ride away, and they could go in on school breaks or the weekends his father had free. His father's stories had inspired a vision so clear, Max could almost see the little church where he would actually make a salary as a deacon instead of having to drive for YRC Freight to make ends meet; the high school within walking distance; the peeka-boo view of the ocean from their new apartment.

But it hadn't been what his father had described. The salary that had been more than enough to cover the rent in small-town New York barely covered their tiny apartment in San Francisco, leaving not quite enough for food, never mind the sort of expenses that make life a little easier to live. His father grew demoralized fast, collapsing in on himself as if the air of his dreams had kept him whole, and without it he was unable to draw a good breath. Just a few months after they arrived, on Max's sixteenth birthday, his father wrote a note, left the rent money, and was gone.

There had been a time when Max thought he'd get over his father's abrupt departure—eventually. But that was when he was with Vashti. Loving someone that much led him to believe that the people you are born to are not always the ones who make you whole. Then, after he lost her, too, it seemed that the kind of pure recovery he'd once hoped for—to a certain extent, hope itself—flattened into something two-dimensional, an abstraction, like a philosophy too beautiful and clean to apply to real life. Certain losses must be lived with, even if assimilation is too much to hope for. Once Max learned to live with it, the loss of his father gradually drifted to a place within him that he simply did not visit.

But his love for Vashti hadn't been so easy to corral. It behaved like a live and wild thing, impossible to tame or break. And unlike the dull and painful attachment he'd had to his father, his feelings for Vashti had lit him from within. For a while, Max wanted nothing to do with the bites and stings of love, and then he could think of nothing but them. He began to date again, but only in the manner of someone looking for something he'd misplaced. Coming home from the rare evening out at a bar or after an inexplicably poor date—during which nothing had gone wrong and nothing had gone right—he walked the city's streets, sure of an insistent, sinister drumbeat beneath the surface of his adoptive home, a foreign pulse driving him to seek what he couldn't have.

But time passed, as it does—eighteen years since he last saw his father, fourteen since Vashti had walked out—and its passing had brought far more contentment than he'd ever expected to have. He had learned to understand the city as his own, to live in a version of San Francisco that made sense to him; learned that one reason why the city was so magical was that it allowed so many versions of itself to coexist. In the quiet Sunset, Max and his mother rebuilt a life together, and after a while his father's absence mattered less. In the job and apartment he'd secured when he still hoped Vashti would stay, he learned to make peace with the fact that he would never have the life he once thought he'd have there, and he somehow cobbled together another in its place. More than a decade later, he still had the same apartment he found after he was hired at the Masonic, and had advanced in his job enough to be able to get his mother the kind of care she deserved. A jolt of protective rage ran through him as he thought about her receiving that letter.

What an entitled, selfish ass his father was, thinking he could dash off a few lines and pop them in the mail. No one gets to leave that completely, that definitively, and then just decide to come back eighteen years later. What made him think he had the right to resurrection?

Now jogging downhill toward Broadway too fast, Max felt like his feet might fly out from under him. He forced himself to stop at the bottom to take a breath, surprised by the white-hot fury in his chest. He was no longer that child, he reminded himself, no longer in need of his father's care. What his father did or did not do hadn't been his concern for some time. But his heart was still racing—he wanted to kick himself, but it was still racing. Because while Max might have been pretty good at getting over things—the prospect of a more fulfilling job, maybe better money—he was never very good at getting over people. God, if this was the reaction he had to the father he was sure he had moved beyond, it was no wonder he didn't trust himself to get anywhere near Vashti.

What was she doing back in the city, anyway? Surely there had been plenty of great bakery jobs in Sonoma or Napa. He sighed. As angry as he was with his father for leaving him, the worst he could muster when it came to losing Vashti was an old, deep sadness. If his father was the trickster of his heart, Vashti was its ghost.

Max took in the view to the east, the narrow spear of the Transamerica Pyramid barely visible through the mist, the smear of the Bay Bridge just beyond a blurry line of tiny white dots parading into the city. He pretended not to notice the curvy blonde in the yellow pants with the matching yellow spaniel coming toward him, even as he thought, *Why not notice her?* And just after she passed, *Maybe ask her out?* When was the last time he'd found a woman he liked well enough to ask out?

It's my birthday, he thought, watching her climb the impossibly steep steps up Broadway, displaying strong calf muscles and a determined stride, the short-legged, long-eared dog keeping faithful pace at her side. He sighed to himself, the sense of countless moments he'd missed weighing heavily on his mind. The sky was so strange today: gray, but purple, too.

A bus drove by, splashing rain onto Max's trousers. He looked down ruefully. Not for the first time, Max found himself wondering if leaving them had been his father's plan all along, if all that noise about an old theology friend holding a place for him in a church across the country was only a ruse, if he were just waiting for Max to turn sixteen and "become a man" to walk out on them. A man. What kind of idiot saw a boy of sixteen as a man? The same sort of idiot who would leave his wife and child to take a vow of Benedictine silence in the twentieth century.

He had to get to work.

But for just a few minutes more, Max stayed staring out into the rain, into the city's freakishly stunning beauty, the view he glimpsed through the downpour a panorama of muted colors, tiers of quaintness and crowding and creative living. It was beautiful; he could enjoy this beauty. It could still be a great day, a good birthday. He had the San Francisco Children's Choir today, a gratifying afternoon of kids and music after being a good adult and finishing the work he was actually paid for. And he could call his mother back, insist that she at least go to lunch with him if dinner was too much to bear. Maybe a bar for dinner—no, a jazz club. Perhaps this birthday could even be the start of a new chapter in his life, one in which his father was available but no longer desirable, maybe one in which he finally reached that point where new desires could take the place of the old ones. He thought again of the woman climbing the hill. Maybe he'd hesitated just a moment too long. It was entirely possible that he had hesitated a moment too long lots of times, which meant that not hesitating might be the work of a moment, too. The thought inspired him, and as the rain picked up again, he took the last few blocks to the Masonic at a run, eager to reach shelter and begin the day anew.

〰〰〰〰〰

5

"It was the silliest thing, really." Franklin's voice sounded tinny and far away, as though he were calling through a tunnel. "Muppet just went completely off her rocker. Did you walk her last night?" They both knew he had. "It's the rain. She hates it when her bows get wet."

"She tripped you?"

"She didn't *trip* me, Genie," Franklin huffed. "She's not a seventh grader."

Gene tried to stay calm. "So you tripped yourself?" He was clenching his fist so hard that the whites of his knuckles shone through.

"No one tripped anyone. There's no one to blame. She was yanking the leash from the moment I snapped it on her, and she just got away from me. Under me. Oh, I don't know." Franklin suddenly sounded tired. Gene bit his tongue. They both knew that a few successful days on a medication didn't mean that Franklin had any business walking the dog alone. "I just fell, OK?" A beat. "But I want to talk about you!" His voice teetered on the edge of pleading, eager to refocus. "Such news! Start from the beginning. And go slow."

Gene pictured Franklin sitting at his desk overlooking Union Street and the church across the park, worrying over the books because the staff would have kicked him out of the inn's kitchen, rubbing their dog in that spot between her silky ears. He wanted to cry out in frustration and residual fear. "How bad is it?"

"It's nothing! Just a mild sprain."

He had been happy. Franklin wanted him to be happy, to be happy himself. Gene *was* happy; he'd be happy again in a minute. But he was still sick with that initial rush of fear. The news—while not the worst—was just the sort he feared the most.

"What were you doing walking the dog by yourself, anyway?" He knew he sounded like a scold, but he couldn't help himself. "Where was Esmerelda?"

"The woman is entitled to a coffee break," Franklin shot back, "and Muffin had to *go*. There's no reason why I can't handle a few stairs, especially if the welfare of my Turkish carpets is at stake."

Gene stifled a sigh, gathering that Franklin had orchestrated an unscheduled furlough as cleverly as usual.

"Stop fussing over me!" Franklin continued, his voice growing more insistent. Like a ripple going through the coat of a dog, the ground shuddered lightly. Muppet, low to the ground and the unlucky recipient of ominous, invisible vibrations that all but the dullest of creatures know too well, leapt from her master's lap and began yapping, annoying them both.

"Did you hear that truck go by? Jesus, it shook the entire house!"

"I don't think it was a truck," Gene observed. He'd felt something, too. At least they were connected on some level.

"Muppet!" Franklin had covered the phone to yell at her, as if they both weren't familiar with the everyday ways in which the other lost his cool with the dog, or was unsteady on his feet, or worried too much. "Jesus! That dog. God! It's been such a weird day. Hey, did you hear about the sea lions?"

"What?"

"They're on the move. Migrating, apparently, down Third Street."

Gene didn't answer. He was standing under a dripping overhang, realizing how cold he suddenly was. Tired, too.

"I can come home."

"Don't come home. Smelsmerelda's here until five. She promised not to leave my side for a minute," he grumbled.

Gene tried to smile but couldn't. Poor Esmerelda. Franklin had objected to her sight unseen, and he'd practically preened with self-righteous indignation when she turned out to be even worse than he'd thought. Weighing in at a hundred pounds more than Franklin's Queen Anne chairs could safely take, Esmerelda Duchamp had materialized in November shortly after his diagnosis and their insurance company's noxious and formidable response to their need for part-time home support, at least until the doctors found the right cocktail of meds to keep Franklin from overly aggressive relapses. He could complain all he wanted about letting the "obsequious, entirely too fresh-faced" Ernie manage the inn while he was stuck upstairs in his "sulfurous reality" with the "unfortunate spawn of a French-Mexican union"—though, to be fair, Franklin was generally disgusted by any hint of heterosexual passion. Still, despite Franklin's misgivings, Esmerelda won Gene's heart her second day on the job, when Franklin decided he'd sneak downstairs to the kitchen while she was in the bathroom. He made it all the way to the first-floor landing, only to lose his balance and fall down the last six steps. She carried a squawking Franklin back upstairs, cleaned him up, closed the gash on his forehead with Steri-Strips, and called the paramedics and Gene. Gene rushed home to a grudgingly beatific Franklin resting in bed, his caretaker as unruffled as she had been when she rolled in that morning with coffee and croissants for the two of them. Gene could have kissed her on the mouth, her Gallic taste for raw garlic and her equally Gallic insistence that she have it every day for lunch be damned.

He suddenly couldn't wait to be home. *Even red-roofed buildings and manicured courtyards look gloomy in this weather,* Gene thought, watching dripping undergraduates run by and thinking of the inn and the rain running off its gables; the woodsy, sweet smell that permeated it ever since the day he'd walked in there almost a decade ago. Especially on cooler afternoons, when the heat was on and maybe one of the guests had a fire going. It was hard to get warm when it was cold in California. But the inn was draft free, full of blankets and inviting landings. Sometimes Gene wondered if he'd fallen in love first with the man or the beautiful house he'd created. Franklin would have fresh flowers there as he did every day, thanks to a twenty-year business friendship with the florist across the street, and the sight of them would relieve Gene's anxiety in a way no reassurances over the phone possibly could.

"Tell me about the sea lions."

"Well . . ." Franklin launched eagerly into a long and muddled news story he'd been following about weird sea lion behavior and relocation, which told Gene that he'd been feeling bad enough not to go out all day and was stuck watching local news on a loop. "The last time they left Pier 39 was in '89, right around the time of the quake. Hey, we should go see them! Do you think they're proceeding one by one, or in pairs?"

"Definitely in pairs."

Franklin laughed. "Always the scientist, ready with a hypothesis."

Gene felt himself smiling. "True." There was a pause. "Are you really OK?"

"I'm fine," Franklin insisted too quickly. "How are *you*? What was that 'Call me now!' voicemail all about?"

"I'll tell you later. Right now I'm worried."

"Stop it. Tell me. We could both use some good news."

"I'll be home after my next class."

Franklin swore at no one in particular. "It's just a sprained wrist, for Christ's sake. Nothing's broken." But his resistance was waning, meaning he really was badly shaken. Gene wished he could go immediately. He wracked his brain for the right thing to say. There must be some kind of comfort he could offer.

"You tell that little rat that she's in for it when I get home," he said, picking up the ball Franklin had tried so hard to put into play and lobbing it lightly back. "Tell her I'm stopping at the muzzle store on the way." He kept himself from urging

Franklin not to worry about the special dinner he was all set to prepare in the painfully narrow galley that passed as their upstairs kitchen—it would ruin Franklin's day if he did. Still. "And I wanted to surprise you, but I got us reservations at that new place on Green, Chez Turtleneck or whatever it is."

He could hear the delight in Franklin's voice. "How could you possibly?"

Well, he hadn't. But he would, even if it cost him a few hundred dollars in bribe money. It was worth it. "News of my greatness has reached even the farthest corners of the city."

Franklin laughed again, enjoying it this time.

They chatted excitedly about the restaurant and the tease of good news until, a few minutes later, Gene could bear to end the call.

He ducked into the CoHo for a quick lunch, though he wasn't all that hungry. Franklin wanted so badly to feel normal, to not live his disease. Although Gene felt the devastation of it as keenly as if it were in his own body, it wasn't. It was Franklin's body and Franklin's sickness, and Franklin's choices and desires directed how they dealt with it—at least when they were together. Alone, Gene supposed he was free to react as he wished. But there was only so much crying in very public university bathrooms that a lecturer hoping for a more permanent job could do.

The café was warm and smelled comforting, despite the press of young bodies in dampened layers. He smiled at the girl who took his order at the counter and tucked a bill and change into her tip jar before spotting an empty seat against the wall. He wedged himself into it with his mug of hot soup and baguette. He was never going to get through his afternoon class. He took a swig of the steaming liquid and burned his mouth.

He was no good at this.

Franklin was the caretaker, the sensitive one, the one who tended to every manner of guest from every corner of the world and found the one little detail that would make each of them feel comfortable enough to sleep away from home. Gene was the cerebral one: the distracted, obsessive scholar who for months at a time came home only to fall asleep over his books or papers, his coffee always in close proximity, half-drunk and cold.

In recent months, he'd learned to make a decent breakfast for two—a developmental milestone, Franklin called it—change sheets, help Franklin to bed. But while Franklin allowed that it was high time someone waited on *him* for a change, without his usual bustling rhythms to energize him he'd grown pale and petulant, irritated all the more when Gene tried to distract him. It used to be that Franklin would wake nearly buzzing with anticipation for his day, chatting with a dozing Gene about who was staying with them and from where and why before going downstairs to lord over his domain. These days, Franklin slept through his alarm more often than not, and if he lasted through breakfast with guests, he'd be crawling up the stairs before lunch, facing an afternoon of total exhaustion. *If only*, Gene thought, and not for the first time, *I'd turned out more like my mother*, a woman who turned her keen intuition and patience into a career as a highly skilled nurse. Unfortunately, he was his father's child through and through: inward and inflexible. Gene gulped down more scalding soup, so lost in thought that he felt rather than tasted the hot liquid go down. His father had regretted how much his son resembled him, too.

Hans Strauss—or Harry, as he insisted his American neighbors call him—had fled his native Bavaria to avoid the sort of social stigmas he found intolerable. Hans rarely spoke of the home he'd left, but from what Gene could gather, his father had been the older of two sons born to traditional Bavarian Catholic parents in a traditional Bavarian Catholic home. Hans was the typical older brother: straitlaced, hyper-responsible, and orderly to a fault. His younger brother, Georg, had been everything Hans was not. And, after a lifetime of taking advantage of their meek father and his minor fortune, Georg had squandered the last of the family funds in a final drunken frenzy that ended in his drowning in the pond behind their parents' home. Instead of enabling his family to bury the shame associated with Georg, along with the man himself, his death seemed only to seal off any chance he might have had to redeem himself. Very quickly, the family's sense of disgrace over his life became inescapable. As Gene's father put it, "There are certain acceptable ways to live"—meaning, of course, that there were also certain unacceptable ways to live—"and a soul who does not adhere to them is damned forever." His father was one of the only people Gene had ever met who truly believed that a person could will himself to lead another life, if he just tried hard enough.

So Hans fled his homeland and disconsolate parents for

the kind of dream of perfection one can only hatch from afar. He landed on American soil with a student visa to study engineering at Kansas State, and from that moment turned his back on anything and everyone who reminded him of the self-indulgent, irresponsible brother whose actions hung over Hans like a ghostly malediction. He met Gene's mother, Anna Linder, while they were both still in school, and it wasn't long before he had a family to suit the life he created: a good wife and a smart son. There was no alcohol in their home, no hidden pornography. Every night for the seventeen years they lived together, Gene watched his father walk in from his job as a quality engineer at All American Autoparts by six o'clock every night, and, until she died of ovarian cancer when Gene was thirteen, give his wife a single, somber kiss on the cheek by way of greeting. Every meal was planned ahead of time and included a modest amount of meat, microwaved vegetables, and boiled potatoes or sliced bread. The soul-soaring joy of Gene's favorite dessert—chocolate layer cake with fine crumb and inches of frosting—was something he rarely got to enjoy. Gene's mother usually served canned fruit or made fruit-sweetened apple pies, the bottom crusts drenched in their own unabsorbed juices. His father ate them methodically and cleared his plate, as he did with anything his wife served, and in his spare time he joined the Knights of Columbus and taught woodworking classes at the local hardware store. Until Gene hit puberty, the three of them lived like dolls in a house whose front wall had never been built, their perfect American family always readied for inspection. It seemed that his father had achieved the impossible: left his worst secrets behind him on another continent, as if they were physical things that could not travel.

When his mother died, Gene watched, devastated and fascinated, as his father went back to work the Monday after her funeral. He held down the same job, returned home every night at the same time, and managed to keep the shell of his former life intact. On the night Gene left home for college, scheduled to be on a 9 p.m. flight to Northwestern University by way of Chicago, his father had still come in at six, hung up his coat, ate his dinner, and changed his shoes before driving his son to the airport. Four years later, when Gene related the news that he would be going to UC Berkeley for graduate school instead of returning home, Hans had simply asked if he needed any money. Gene hadn't. He'd been on full scholarship since his freshman year, and his doctoral work would be subsidized. Hans had seemed relieved. Not because he didn't have any money to offer, but because his parental obligations seemed, finally, to be over.

That was what Gene knew of his father up until the last three months of his life, when a terminal diagnosis inspired Hans to make a series of bizarre phone calls to his son. They hadn't spoken in years, but the sound of his father's voice on the phone struck Gene with a familiarity so acute he was immediately transported to a younger version of himself and their gray-shadowed past. He had thought, perhaps stupidly, that redemption was possible, wasn't it?

But per usual, his father had something completely different in mind: a sort of detached deathbed confessional the likes of which still baffled Gene. In several conversations during which he learned his father was refusing chemo and allowing only a professional nurse access to his home, he also learned that Hans had been the one to find his brother's body in the pond on the land that was supposed to have gone to them both. And that the evening before Georg drowned, he'd come to his older brother begging for money.

Hans never spoke to what most might expect a dying man to tell his only child: that he loved him—or, if that were overly generous, that he at least regretted that he didn't. Instead, just as other fathers might pass along a treasured keepsake, Hans seemed hell-bent on passing along his worst memories. Gene couldn't figure out if he was the recipient of these urgent confessions because his father felt he could be absolved of them by leaving them with his son, or because he wanted his son to know the pain that had shaped him into the hard shell that he was, rotting from the inside out.

Even so, the telling itself was an undeniable act of trust that Gene couldn't help marveling at. And he did hold on to his father's memories as receptacles for the older man's bitterness, as warnings for himself when his own perfectionism reared its ugly head. He attended the funeral only because he feared no one else would, though he flew in that morning and left on the red-eye, as if his childhood in Kansas were a contagion he was still in danger of catching. Early the next morning, Gene crawled into bed with Franklin, who couldn't sleep either.

Franklin—who had been raised by tolerant Jews, who had already sent both parents to the grave and mourned them genuinely, who could not imagine such coldness between parents and children, who had once wanted children himself before a young lover with no tears for his own father came into his life—lay awake and listened as Gene wondered aloud why the last words he heard from his father, while seemingly inspired by some desire to depart the world unburdened, were dripping with hostility. How could a man think that speaking his sins aloud was enough, if the words weren't tinged with regret? Had he really been so self-righteous that he couldn't even let go of his own defenses when doing so might have been the only way to find the peace he must have craved? Reading Gene's mind, Franklin ran his finger along his lover's jaw in the dark and promised him that the similarities between father and son ended at their looks, and that it shouldn't surprise Gene in the least that his father, a cruel man, would leave the world with cruel stories. But Gene knew his father wasn't cruel, though he'd done cruel things.

No, he hadn't been a cruel man; he'd been a terrified one.

And what would Gene do, now that he was facing his own terror? Dive under the shield of work? Or come up fighting for himself as well as Franklin? Gene sighed. Only time would tell. At least for now, he could still enjoy the morning's great news and the rest of his day, couldn't he? He *would* leave early, get home before the worst of the traffic, surprise Franklin before he could raise any more objections. He didn't really have to spend the afternoon reviewing his notes for the next day's classes. It was a day of celebrations, after all! He checked his watch—if he left after his last meeting, he could be home by three o'clock. He nodded to himself decisively. It was a plan.

~~~~~~

6

Vashti was wrist deep in dough again, desperate to lose herself in blissful devotion to the four gods of pastry: Flour, Butter, Sugar, and Water, elements in whose purest forms she believed as devoutly as some believe in divine perfection. But her prayers were not being answered. As deeply as she wished to find communion with her simple devotions, she could not be distracted from her anxious heart, the beads of anticipatory sweat collecting on her forehead and lip.

What had she gotten herself into? Somehow she'd helped her sister cajole her into doing the thing she most wanted and most feared. And she'd done it all before lunch, well before the blessed darkness of evening could drift in and help her put it off, maybe even renegotiate in the morning. She'd thought it was a blessing in disguise when Jesse asked her to stay a few extra hours to help manage the holiday rush, but all it had done was give her more time to think.

She tried anew to become absorbed in preparing the next day's croissants. Thank God for the rich reward of pastry, its even demands. She pulled a rectangle of cold butter from the refrigerator and placed it on her freshly rolled dough, standing back to adjust and admire the symmetry of her work. Fourteen ounces of butter: an astounding amount, and just enough. It never failed to give her a little thrill. Reverence for butter was a job requirement, and one of the first things that helped her stand out from the stylishly aproned young women who could frost a pretty cupcake but whose svelte figures quaked at the undeniable lead role that sheer, unadulterated butter played in the making of French pastry. Svelteness had never been Vashti's problem. Her roundness was as much a part of her as her taste for the things that contributed to it. It might be written on her tombstone: *Here lies Vashti, who was not afraid of butter.*

Over and back, palms across, wrists twisting, the dance of dough. She began to breathe into it, borrowing the rhythms of its transformation. *Every dough must contain life*, she thought to herself. *It takes a little and it gives a little back.*

How long ago had it been, exactly? She pretended it took some effort to recall that it had been fourteen years and three weeks to the day. Just as he had pretended throughout her marriage that she had made the right choice to leave Max; that she was investing in a better, sturdier love by leaving San Francisco for the expansive shelter of Dale's Sonoma estate; that she could forget what true love really felt and tasted and looked like. But instead of living the sort of inspired life she'd once wished for, she found herself trying to live someone else: Dale's, or the life she and Dale tried to fabricate together. The truth was, and it didn't bother her as much now to admit it as it once had, she'd been acquired, just as Dale had acquired his wealth and his stature and his land and success. It was not a callous acquisition—Dale never acquired anything he didn't want unequivocally—but she walked into the terms of someone else's world when she did, and she knew it would no longer be hers once he was gone. The ranch and the wealth and the great big house with its wide-open spaces were where she had lived, but they did not belong to her the way San Francisco belonged to her, the way a place echoes of who you are no matter how long you've been away from it. She had loved Sonoma, but it was the sort of love one has for a favorite vacation spot, where everything new and wonderful is held up to everything old and loved. Objectively, Sonoma's lush harvests and violet dusks and bee-and-blossom-choked fields were more beautiful than the city, but Vashti lay awake at night thinking of strange eucalyptus groves and narrow hills and distant sirens and houses with windows larger than their doors. When Dale died, she used part of the money he left her to buy an apartment at the top of Liberty between Noe and Castro and buried the rest of the funds in accounts she never intended to touch. Freed from his world, she returned to hers, happy despite its changes. She secured a job at Sucre thanks to a great deal of luck, her not insignificant talents, and the Culinary Institute of America degree she'd earned in record time after her daughter died and she found herself too shattered to do anything but work.

Dale knew when he married her that she had been in love with another man. In fact, if she hadn't been, she might never have taken him up on his proposal. If she hadn't loved Max so much and hadn't been so desperate to leave him, she might not have been so willing to flee the city and take a chance on marriage with a man she did not know very well but who promised her a new life, stability for the baby she was carrying.

Yet even though Dale had offered love, the sort of steady, protective love she'd probably have been better off with, she hadn't been able to receive it. Her sense of love had been indelibly shaped by the impressions she'd made with Max, and as good as Dale's offer of love was, and as much as she wanted to accept it, it was a poor fit. And not only for her. She knew Dale wanted to believe that love could be managed just like money or property, but Vashti knew it couldn't. She knew after Max, and was only more convinced after the brief, bittersweet joy of their daughter's life. She knew rumors abounded that people made practical choices in love, but she'd never met anyone who had. Love was a disease, not a controlled substance. Though maybe it was a rare disease, at least when children weren't involved. Maybe the degree of unqualified adoration she'd had with Max was doomed to consume everything in its path from the start. Sometimes she wondered if it had ever existed, or if it might have been a trick of the mind or the heart.

She could hear the continual ringing of the bell on the door in the other room, so many insistent lovers coming into the bakery, a daylong line of them demanding sugar and sweetness, their right, their fill of the kind of food that matched the kind of love they either hoped they had or yearned for: an immediate, overwhelming, heady connection.

"Vashti." Her boss at the door startled her.

She looked up. "I know, I know. I'll leave when this dough is done."

"I can finish that." Jesse elbowed in close enough that the good, warm smell of him was even stronger than the bread dough's. He was wearing a "Kiss Me, I'm Irish" T-shirt and a white apron with hearts on it tied around his waist. Somehow the combination of these two things served only to emphasize his biceps. She stepped chastely to the side.

He smiled at her, his deft hands already taking over. "The offer still stands, you know."

Vashti nodded. "Actually," she said, "I have plans. But thanks."

She read the skepticism on his face, but he was too sweet to speak it aloud. God, was she that obvious? If only she were the type of girl who could play games, who could lure and trap and shift and dodge her way suavely through the pitfalls of love. She plunged her arms up to her elbows in a stream of warm water, washing up for good, letting the water grow hot on her skin, suddenly angry and frustrated with herself. She didn't deserve this, this kind, handsome boss looking away while she lied to his face, shutting out the very person responsible for the wonderful job she'd only imagined she might one day have. She was so good at shunning available men, she might as well throw in the towel now. Go home. Go to bed. Die alone.

"But if they fall through, you'll come, right?"

She turned off the water. Her back was to him, so they couldn't see each other's face. She looked up, sighing at the wall. What was wrong with her? Maybe anyone actually available was the problem, proximity as deal breaker.

"Heck, bring him with you! The more, the merrier."

She nodded, drying off, then tried to smile at him, tried to express her gratitude at his kindness, his interest in her, his beauty. "I'll see you tomorrow," she said a few short minutes later, already in her jacket and heading out the door.

She lifted her hood and strode down the street, racing to catch the 24 bus as she rounded the corner, seeing its doors already open.

"Why if it isn't the Queen of Sweets, the Princess of Sugar!" crowed the driver, a squat man of indeterminate grandfatherly age. She had an ongoing debate with herself as to whether his cheer was real or canned. Today it was real, she decided. Was that a good sign? He smiled at her. "Working late, I see."

She smiled, handing over the box of pastries she'd tucked under her arm on the way out. "We're busy."

He opened the bag and inhaled deeply. "Hoo-wah," he said. "I'll bet you are."

The bus was too warm, the air damp from the morning's stream of soaking passengers, a mobile furnace making its bright way through the rain. She stared out into the streets. Everywhere she looked, signs of love bombarded her. Down Divisadero and well into the Castro, store windows were filled with everything from winking Burmese rubies to paper castles with a million tiny heart-shaped windows filled with light to copies of *Chicken Soup for the Transitioning Soul* and red dildos with heart-shaped scrotums. She loved that on Valentine's Day in particular, she could look almost anywhere and know she was in San Francisco, its whimsical, unapologetic genius on full display. Even the newscast playing on the bus was almost childlike in its cheerfulness, as a few of her slightly soaked, slightly irritable fellow passengers watched the screen halfheartedly.

Well, it sure has been a bumpy ride this morning here in San Francisco! Ahead on the KSFA midday news, we'll be taking a look at some recent activity on the San Andreas Fault and bring you up to date on the latest in the BART strikes. Also, Dr. Wyatt will share surprising ways that root vegetables might help protect our kids from a devastating childhood illness, and our own Chuck Lorrie will be visiting us live from the parking lot of the Marina Safeway for the Ninth Annual Love the One You're with Fest. Join us at noon.

Vashti's stop was at Twentieth and Castro, and even though she dashed up Liberty to her apartment at the top of the hill, her feet were soaked and her fingertips freezing by the time she fumbled open the door. Six months of living there had helped her master the order of letting herself in: equal parts jiggling of key and knob, one perfectly timed jab with her hip.

She was out of her dripping clothes almost as soon as she closed the door behind her, in the shower not long after that. The cold and rain had given her a short-lived burst of adrenaline. Vashti rested her head on the tile, letting the steam fill the air and soften her breathing. As much as she'd tried to avoid it, she suddenly realized she'd found herself in a place without distraction. Her apartment was quiet as a tomb. She should get a roommate. If it weren't for Dale's money, she would never have thought of living in the city without one—or six. If wealth bought you anything, it was the ability to isolate yourself comfortably.

The pipes shuddered and moaned, announcing the imminent loss of hot water. She couldn't put it off any longer.

But what would he say? What would he do? She shook her head, trying to curtail her growing uneasiness. It was better to avoid questions and answers of any kind than it was to come to the very likely conclusion that he might not want to see her at all, or that he might ask her to leave. Or that maybe he'd be indifferent. Or, worse yet, that maybe he'd try to pretend he was indifferent.

Good God. She was exhausting herself. Javi was right. She had to just go and get it over with.

No matter what, there was the consolation prize of her sister coming home. When had they last been together? At Dale's funeral, of course, ten months ago. If that could be thought of as togetherness. It was really only an emergency, with Javi showing up to make sure Vashti's dams didn't dissolve entirely. Then she was gone, whisked away again by the siren calls of professionalism and a compulsive need to earn and achieve that began long before she'd seen the inside of a courtroom. Vashti traced it back to the maelstrom that followed their mother's death, when their father's intensely silent grief inspired his eldest daughter to try desperately to take her mother's place in the store—running the register, answering the phone, dealing with adults burdened with half her maturity and ten times her arrogance—so professionalism became both her armor and her crutch, a way to leap around the world and keep her carefully protected heart from prolonged exposure to any one place or person.

"Here," a ten-year-old Javi whispered into her sister's ear, "try this." She held out a pail filled, to Vashti's aching delight, with crumbled earth. Like a bear cub, Vashti cupped her hand and reached in, shoveling the welcome filler into her mouth. Only Javi could be trusted with Vashti's compulsion to fill her mouth with dirt, joined as they were in the mystifying, terrifying aftermath of life after their mother's death. They were both doing whatever they could to keep from caving to the pressure of crushing grief, whether that meant Javi's staying awake late into the night with her back against the wall and her sister's head on her lap to avoid the despair of further nightmares, or Vashti's eating dirt. That was, until Javi changed the rules of the game.

Javi smiled over the bucket between them, her eyes winking down and her mouth lifting up. A smile as wonderful and frightening as the man in the moon's.

"You've got to eat something, Vishy," she explained.

But Vashti just held the strange taste in her mouth, shaking her head, stuck between the desire to swallow the sweet, spicy impostor or spit it out.

Her sister sank down and put both her hands on Vashti's knees, looking up into her face. Their mother had been dead for weeks, and they'd been trying to walk around and eat and live with the gravitational pressure of grief pinning their hearts to their chests. Her death had warped everything, even the natural order that had been their daily lives. They went to bed on time, but Javi woke in the night if she slept at all, speaking through the tongues of her dreams. They sat before the best meals their father could prepare, but Vashti barely ate, then crept outside afterward and filled her mouth with soil from the garden.

Javi licked her thumb and wiped a smudge off Vashti's face as their mother used to do, breaking both their hearts all over again, though they were growing used to the constant cleaving and opening of their hearts breaking multiple times a day now, the muscles developing the seeds of defense that would later grow into Javi's inability to love anything but her work and Vashti's inability to stop loving the boy who would sew her heart back together. "It's just chocolate," she said. "You can at least eat chocolate, can't you?" She reached one of her own fingers into the bucket as if showing her the food was not poison by trying it herself, willing to do that for her sister.

Vashti watched her eat. And as she did, the chocolate made its way down her throat and into her belly, triggering a surge of primal, burning hunger. Vashti filled her palms greedily, the burst of silky, chalky sweetness ricocheting through her mouth, spurting out again with her tears. It was, she was surprised to find, so good. So, so good. Vashti rested her head against her sister's and cried, tears mixed with chocolate choking her until Javi had to pound her on the back and their tears turned to laughter. In the dark and alone but together, they ate.

Remembering, Vashti turned the lever off and stood dripping, wondering if this was the moment she thought it was, the moment when enough was enough, when for some minor reason in the collection of reasons she'd been building over the past several months she found herself willing—if not ready—to take action.

Was it as simple as all that? It wasn't.

But could it be?

Quickly, she dressed. Then changed. Then changed again and, hating what she was wearing, grabbed her still wet coat and a dry umbrella and headed back out into the rain.

Forty minutes that seemed like five later, she was standing outside the doors of the Nob Hill Masonic Center. Not for the first time, she wondered what had brought the Max she'd once known here, into an executive position with an office under the protection of this intimidating three-story glass entry. She knew he'd switched his focus from music to management when they'd found out she was pregnant, going for a business degree while teaching on the side, and then, she gathered, full-bore into the world of work, but she had always assumed that he would go back to music once she left the picture. It was part of the consolation she'd offered herself all these years, and she wasn't quite willing to let it go.

Inside, the grand entry felt monkish, despite the colorful two-story mural ahead; everything hushed and airy and solemn. The marble floor was empty of people, and her shoes echoed on it. The security guard at the front desk didn't look up until she was right in front of him.

Her voice barely came to her in time. "Max Fleurent, please."

The guard looked up, suspicion in his job description. "Do you have an appointment?"

"No."

"So he's not expecting you, then?"

For a split second, she wondered if she could just turn around and run away. But she knew that if she did after getting this far, she would never return, would race back down Nob Hill and across the city and into her bed and never get out. The prospect of no Javi or no Max was bad enough; the idea was unbearable that they might both slip away when she'd barely worked up enough courage to send the barest of smoke signals out to them.

"He knows who I am," she blurted out.

"Your name?"

She told him.

"He's not here," the guard told her after calling up.

She wasn't sure she could find a way to ask if he would be back, but then she did.

"Think so. Pretty sure. He just walked out, probably to lunch."

Was he with anyone? How did he look? How long were his lunches? Did this man know anything that could tether her to that pivotal spot that had taken all her courage to reach?

"OK," she said.

"Do you want me to let him know you were here?"

She shook her head and told him she'd be back later. "Is there a good place nearby to wait, get a cup of coffee?"

"Peet's is across the street," the guard told her. "It's in the basement of Grace."

OK. She could do that. Hide under a church and drink coffee.

As she crossed the street the sun came out, offering a glimpse of the breathtaking sweep of land and ocean to the east, the Bay Bridge bookended between grand hotels, and, farther down California Street, the many-storied, glass-fronted buildings of downtown. She felt suddenly seen. Maybe it was the light, maybe it was the saying of her name and her purpose, maybe it was what she had already done to drag the ongoing affliction of those relentless dreams into the daylight to either burn or clear up.

And then Max was walking up the street.

He had his head bent down to listen to his mother by his side, his hand under her elbow, helping her along. Vashti strained to see his face, but all her view offered was his smooth forehead, the tightly cropped russet curls. Her heart thudded, suddenly remembering his face, his hands, the first time he touched her. The removal of all her clothes, piece by piece, until she stopped him, breathless. *Do you not want me to?* he had asked, one long finger still resting on the crest of her hip, the way someone might hold their place to look up from a treasured book. She shook her head. No, it wasn't that. It was that she hadn't realized how close she was to being without clothes already. She had spent most of her public life covering up her body—to be unpeeled like this and not even notice! It was the first of many new wonders, one of the only times she would ever feel freed by love.

Now there he was, more than fourteen years and how many opportunities to erase all his memories of her later. Her eyes darted to his mother. She had become so old! When had she become so old? Once upon a time, she'd been a petite, ropy woman who was kind but intimidatingly capable. Age had softened her beyond recognition, or was it time? Vashti felt suddenly, dizzyingly disoriented. If his mother had changed this much, would Max have, too? Panic spread across the back of her neck, prickling. *Look up, look up,* she thought, concentrating on Max, his face infuriatingly close but concealed. But then she wondered what would happen if he did look up. The cable car was coming and he was still in a moment with his mother, unknowing. A taxi honked lightly to get her out of the street. Helplessly, she glanced up at Grace Cathedral and its imposing iron windows, each with so much presence that she thought fleetingly that they might just respond to the silent prayer she was offering. As she watched, she could have sworn the glass was startled into a rattle. She was losing her mind. Church windows didn't rattle, or if they did, they certainly didn't for the haphazard prayers of a half-crazed woman, moored to the middle of the street by her own leaden heart.

FEBRUARY 14, AFTERNOON

~~~~~~~~~

Venim h[oc] cupidi, multo magis ire cupimus,
set retinet nostras illa puella pedes

We came here full of longing
now we long to leave
but that girl holds back our feet.

—GRAFFITI ON THE WALLS OF POMPEII

〜〜〜〜〜

7

Max glanced down at his watch: 3:50. A little thrill surged through him as he realized that the workday, which had flown by, was almost over.

He glanced over his quarterly budget update for the Masons one more time. He knew no one was likely ever to read such a thing, but still, he could never quite bring himself to cut corners at work. The Masons had taken him in when he was lost and broken and, perhaps because he was still a little lost and maybe even a lot broken, he had never stopped feeling obligated to them. Still, a rehearsal day was a rehearsal day, and if he kept this up any longer, he'd be late. Stretching his neck and shoulders, Max closed the file and hit Send.

He'd scheduled the first spring meeting of the San Francisco Children's Choir for this afternoon intentionally, as a sort of birthday treat for himself. Sometimes he still couldn't quite believe his luck at having been appointed to the job of directing them. It helped to have a guardian angel, though sometimes he wished the circumstances that led him to need one in the first place had never come to pass.

He straightened the two birthday cards on his desk, smiling affectionately at the formal gilded one: *Every year is a rebirth, every birthday a day to begin anew.* The only two people left in his life who sent him paper cards were his mother and Mrs. Levi-Ward—Mrs. Marilyn "Minnie" Levi-Ward, the widowed socialite responsible for his current position, as well as approximately 60 percent of San Francisco's musical philanthropy (and the woman whose approval or disapproval determined who got to fund the other 40 percent to great acclaim and who had to skulk back to New York or Boston or, *God forbid!*, Portland), had taken a shine to Max when he came to apply for an entry-level administrative position with the Masonic Center. Somehow the shine had never faded, though in recent years it had come with a matchmaking desperation that rivaled his mother's. Well, maybe by this time next year, both women would lay that hatchet to rest. He was pleasantly surprised to find that he was still excited by that morning's surge of optimism. Usually such romantic resolutions faded quickly. Maybe his father's reaching out had been just the kick in the pants he needed to stop nursing old wounds. Mrs. Levi-Ward would certainly agree, that much was sure. She'd wanted him to move on from the moment she met him.

Mrs. Levi-Ward had written a board membership and hiring say into her financial support for the notoriously fraternal Masonic, and they'd agreed to both requests. It was the first time Max had really understood how influential a deep pocketbook could be; until then, he'd only ever been poor, with the blandly unwavering powerlessness that came along with it. But for some reason, that regal-faced, long-necked woman had taken pity on the fresh-faced boy barely in his twenties, equal parts sad and earnest, ready to leave his own ideals—wet though they still were with fresh ink—for the sort of job a young man would take who was stricken by the mistaken belief that a woman who'd left for emotional reasons would return for financial ones.

"But what would you *really* like to do, young man?" Mrs. Levi-Ward smelled of powder and leather and wore pearls that were faintly incandescent even inside, away from direct light. Her eyes, as blue and frank as a child's, despite her wrinkles and puckered lips, held his gaze.

"You're asking about the music."

"I wasn't," she said, unflinching. "I just want the truth, so if music is part of your truth, tell me. If not, I couldn't care less. But don't give me the answer you think I want. I'm bored to tears by insincerity, and I get it all the live long day. Tell me what drives you, Max Fleurent." She adopted a perfect stillness as she waited for an answer. Her face was painted within an inch of its life with expensive cosmetics, but the bones underneath, the jawline and nose, were strong and straightforward.

"I don't want to be a musician, even though I probably could be." Only Vashti and his mother—and his father, for what it was worth—knew that he had become a musician in the first place accidentally, because his grandfather had left a trumpet behind that he picked up one day. He loved that instrument, a Yamaha from the twenties. It wasn't his intention to turn it into a purpose.

"But trumpeters, well, they're lonely," he found himself saying, "all that time on the road." No—being on the road, leaving as his father had, was the last thing he wanted. "I used to think I'd like to teach at a school, maybe conduct."

"*Used* to, my boy?" Her pearls clicked together when she sat up to rifle through his papers. "What are you, twenty-one?"

"Twenty-three," he said, hoping he didn't look as defensive as he sounded.

"Mmm," she said, clearly unimpressed by the additional two years. "So," she said after a tense moment between them, "you go after an MBA and teach privately to fund it and then that's it? No more music for you?"

"No," Max said quickly. The trumpet was as much a part of him as any pet might have been for another boy: a lesser member of the family, but dearer in a sense because of its diminished expectations. And he remembered the way the instrument soothed him when people could not, on those many frustrating afternoons waiting for his father to come home from a cross-country haul that should have taken a week and was taking ten days or more. Max would blow his anger and grief and a little bit of hope into the horn, calling as long and hard and clearly as he wanted because no one was home to stop him. By the time he was nine, his mother had taken a job—teaching home economics at the Learning Annex—because "Well, Max, you never know. It's good for a woman to have a job she can fall back on." So Max was home alone in the afternoons, blowing on his horn like a bugle boy drafted to a war he couldn't understand. The practice was addictive, his own piercing fear and pain eventually transforming into beautiful sounds.

"Someone break your heart?"

He looked away, forgetting Mrs. Levi-Ward for a moment.

When he looked at her again, his face told her she'd guessed correctly. Also that he wished she hadn't.

"Doesn't matter. None of my business. But I will say this: I hope that one day you find your way back to whomever it is you think you can't be right now. I like that boy—pardon me, *young man*—far better than the one you're trying to be, and I wish I were interviewing him for the conservatory. But no matter. Perhaps another day. For now, the job is yours if you still want it."

She'd never really pushed after that day of guessing his true reasons for being there, but she took a shine to him—as if in exposing his heart so incisively, she'd struck a rare note of tenderness in her own—and when Mrs. Levi-Ward took a shine to you, all musical doors swung open. Including the opportunity to direct the San Francisco Children's Choir, one of her pet projects and a way to get "darling Max"—her moniker for him since he'd played at one of her private parties right after meeting her, refusing all subsequent requests to do the same for her friends—back onstage. As much as he protested the favoritism implied in the offer to direct the choir, he did not put up much of a fight. In recent years, it had been hard to make time for practice when other things demanded and music only called.

Unexpectedly, Max found his optimism doubling, fueled by some unforeseen force. *Maybe*, he thought, *this birthday could bring more than one renewal.* Maybe a call to Mrs. Levi-Ward—she expected to be thanked for the card, after all, and she loved it when he called—might be one in which to discuss the potential for the children's choir to become more than a part-time gig. She'd love that, wouldn't she? Her pet young man spearheading the latest thing in her pet field. And it was timely, wasn't it? It was a different world, a different future they were all facing. People wanted, *needed*, more music in their lives, and children who could make such music. He'd be willing to bet that a San Francisco full of people laboring under global warming and liberal guilt would be more than happy to funnel money into a nonprofit that promoted singing children.

He leaned back in his chair, his gaze drifting to his window and the view of Grace Cathedral across the street. A little sun came out, coaxing color back into the stained-glass windows. It was a beautiful church, the sort of church people came from other cities, other countries, to see. You could find everything in San Francisco. You could find love. A good job, then a better one. Looking out at the church, Max felt pretty sure that you could even find God in San Francisco.

But his father hadn't. It was probably for the best that his mother had decided not to bring the letter to their lunch. "It's not going anywhere, Max," she'd cut him off when he'd asked, "so let's just enjoy your birthday."

Staring out into the sunlit rain, Max thought of how disoriented he had been when his father first left, as if his departure had been the mental equivalent of turning someone else around in so many circles that when Max opened his eyes, he would be too dizzy to track another's movements or to move himself.

Even the anticipatory excitement about their new home

had felt strange, like it was something he and his mother and father were holding on to temporarily, or borrowing. There was a lot of strange levity around the packing and planning, a lot of noise. His parents told each other enthusiastic things in other people's voices. Who wouldn't be thrilled by the offer of a full-time clergy position, no matter the pay? Wouldn't it be better than living a trucker's workweek and a small-time pastor's weekend? Wouldn't it mean more time with the family, wouldn't it mean a better life, a more purposeful life, a sunnier life? Everyone they met told them that they would love San Francisco, as though strangers were in on the odd charade. But that never felt right. How could any place be a place that everyone loves?

And then California had been everything home was not. Home—or at least the closest thing to it, a series of small New York towns near the Canadian border—was lush hills and yawning fields; charcoal trees and bare winters followed by pale green rebirth; quiet, heady summer days and bracingly cool Octobers. It was a modest, meditative part of the world, and even though they had never stayed in one place for very long, the area itself held the familiar feel of home.

Nothing seemed familiar in California. To begin with, it didn't even have seasons, it had dramatic scenes: rain so sudden and so hard that the earth ran downhill in places, preferring to collapse under bad weather than absorb it; heat so oppressive that the ground was known to burst into flame beneath it and, he quickly learned, frequently did. Like a jewel rising out of the pressurized earth, the city of San Francisco had all this and more: hulking fog coming in over the mountains like a prehistoric beast; winds so aggressive, they stung; weeks of endlessly sun-filled days, every iota of the light seeming to contribute to great vistas of mountain and sea and rock-studded beauty. How could anyone call a place like that home? It was a movie set, a Brigadoon, a strange, shape-shifting city that was much more interested in cultivating its wild beauty than offering the far more modest and relatable comforts Max associated with home.

Even the food was different. He had never tasted a burrito before leaving New York, and now they were served every Tuesday and Thursday for the school's free hot lunch. Avocado tasted like the inside of something that had been recently alive, cilantro like a punch to the nose. And there were flowers everywhere! The whole city was riddled with blossoms whose colors he had not known could be found in nature: fuchsias and limes and golds.

As the realization of his father's departure set in, it was all Max could do to keep from tearing those flowers out, run screaming and shouting his grief into the unbearable newness, but there was nowhere to run. His mother spent her nights not sleeping in their perpetually fog-chilled and damp apartment deep in the Sunset, her days working two jobs. He couldn't leave her.

Though there were times when the urge to do just that had been almost irresistible. As the months passed endlessly with no sign whatsoever of his father, his mother became as much of a burden as a comfort to him. Both of them were beginning to realize what it meant to be just the two of them for good. It seemed to Max that his father's departure had unmasked her, removing the solid front of motherhood and revealing her fuzzier borders, the softer woman underneath. He did not realize that this happens to most boys when they're about sixteen—or he didn't until much later, when it no longer mattered as much. At the time, he incorporated the changes he saw in her to his growing understanding that you can never lose only one parent.

It was as if she were encouraging him to notice that her seams were showing. She no longer hid the occasional pack of cigarettes or the fact that she'd been crying. She'd taken two jobs so she could support them on her own, but when she got home at night, she sat in front of the television for hours, not even trying to go to bed. When Max asked her if she was all right, sometimes she didn't answer. And even though she vowed to protect him, the fact that she was unprotected herself made him feel just as vulnerable, if not more so.

But then, that summer, he discovered the buses. Thank God for the buses, for the thickets of strangers who would simply surround him, unknowingly meeting that urge to run and scream and hemming it in, the bus soothing them all into miles of circuitous riding, up and through and around, always moving, always something to look at, always a glass window, at least, to press your face against. He felt like he was getting away with something, getting to see and leave so many things in the same instant.

At first he stayed close to their apartment, going up and down the dinosaur-scaled hills of the hushed Outer Sunset, the 66 and 48 buses attached by only their crowns to electric wires overhead that silenced them completely when they came to a stop; no exhaust, no engine, no nothing, just a hovering at the top of the world.

Max left his house day after lonely day and hopped on those buses as other kids might hitch rides to something—anything—better, eventually staying on them until they made their way up and through the maze of busy scrubs-clad doctor-ants scurrying around UCSF; through the kaleidoscopic colors of Haight Street, where the *nouveau* runaways smoked weed on the sidewalks and the sixties had left hippies out in the sun to mummify, limping along in their musty hazes of patchouli and dreadlocks. And still the bus went on, past the Church Street couples too in love with each other to notice a heartsick adolescent staring out at them, past the dog parks with their flirting pups and overcaffeinated owners, past every variety of person using the street as a stage, into the urine-soaked, subterranean tunnels, peaceful and warm beneath Market Street, and then bursting right out of it and into the financial district's throbbing towers of economic preoccupation, stopping on their way to the glittering piers of the Embarcadero to pick up handfuls of freshly minted MBAs on their way to work, most of them too hip to smile.

During the rougher weeks when his mother was working so hard he rarely saw her, he let himself fall apart as he rode, turning his face to the window so no one would see him, though on any given bus in San Francisco, there was usually someone doing something much more alarming than crying. It was comforting to know that, when compared to the average human experience, his misery was unremarkable.

Then, one day, right after junior year began and a new wave of lonesomeness descended on him in the midst of kids who'd been in school together for years, Vashti got on the bus.

The moment he saw the top of her smooth crown of black hair on its way up the stairs, something kicked alive in his heart. Then the rest of her emerged, and it was even better: the mass of liquid black hair framing that huge, slow smile and even huger black-lashed eyes, her too big backpack and coat and the mess she was making dropping things from one or the other as she chatted openheartedly with the bus driver. Clumsy but graceful, enchanting and quirky, these were things he saw in her almost instantly, qualities he would grow to love in her. He reflected now and then on how remarkable it was to know someone who wore her true self on display at all times. Vashti would laugh and say it was just because she'd never had a mother around to teach her how to play by women's rules, and it was true that it made her less popular—she wasn't smartly guarded like the other, more self-conscious girls. Yet that unfiltered openness was what made her so undeniably alluring, in the same way a candid photo captures energy and truth that a posed one cannot.

But, like most boys his age, what Max first noticed was how beautiful she was. And miracle of miracles—she sat beside him. Sat beside him and smiled and looked him in the eye and asked if he was going to Lincoln, too. Which, by some divine providence, he was. She hadn't seen him before, she ventured, had she? Of course she hadn't—or rather, he hadn't seen her. That was probably because he had only gone there for a few months last spring, he said, and she nodded and said her dad was still driving her to school then. Who knows why, he thought, as an invisible line flew from this girl's heart to his and sank deep and true. She was prattling along, seemingly oblivious of the effect her warm-blooded, sweet-smelling, softly curved presence had on him.

Her dad had insisted on driving her the first week, she was saying, but now she'd be taking the bus. They'd be taking the bus together, she said and smiled, introducing him to the first of a million simple pleasures that could delight her. Was he a junior, too? She'd just turned sixteen that summer, she confessed shyly, and was a little on the young side for their class; but she was sure they could still be friends! She smiled again, leaving him tongue-tied. Was that his trumpet? How long had he been playing? Where did he live? Her laugh was silvery and soft; when he closed his eyes, he imagined ice melting after a relentlessly cold winter. She only ever took her eyes off his to laugh.

Thinking of her, he'd forgotten again that he promised himself he wouldn't.

It was a bad habit, recently rekindled. It would die down again soon enough. It was only those e-mails she'd sent last September—could it have been six months already?—the ones that said she was back in town and hoped he was well. Static and chaste, as miserable as fake food after a lengthy starvation. "Hi, how are you, I hope you're well" e-mails should have secured the seal on the grave that was their relationship, but instead they had him thinking of her anew. Struggling, if he was going to be honest with himself. For the life of him, he still couldn't figure out why he'd never found a way to neatly write her off, as any normal man would do when a woman left him abruptly right in the middle of love. And with so much at stake. But then, to be left in the middle of something means it's perpetually unfinished.

Max snapped out of it, powering off his computer and racing down the hall to catch the elevator. As he crossed the quiet corridor, the sun shining once again through the windows to the west, he reveled in the satisfaction of knowing the best part of the day was finally here. A few hours of music and children on one of those thrilling winter afternoons that hinted at spring, the kids' voices enchanting in their unfocused way of stretching toward something beautiful, the sound of it soothing something deep inside him that he sometimes forgot was there. He caught the elevator just in time and opened the door at one minute past four, the music drifting in from below.

Rafael at the security desk rolled his eyes in solidarity, sure to have withstood more than his share of bellyaching in the fifteen minutes since he'd buzzed Max with the announcement of the accompanist's (some very distant relation by marriage of Mrs. Levi-Ward's who managed to be both disinterested and judgmental) early arrival and the passing along of the message that Max was running late. "Sorry," Max said as the harmonies kicked in. Rafael shrugged. "It's nothing." He rifled through his notes. "You got a few more interesting visitors in the meantime. They're waiting inside, too, get this." He lifted a piece of paper, squinting at it beneath a narrow desk light. "Friar Schmuck and Sister

Cock-a-Doo-del-Doo," he said, raising a conspiratorial eyebrow toward Max. "Said you were expecting them? Tried to buzz you, but you didn't pick up."

"Sister who?

Rafael narrowed his eyes. "They said you were expecting them. Nun? About six feet tall, bright pink hair, a wig? Ring any bells?"

"The Sisters of Perpetual Indulgence? But they were supposed to be here tomorrow." How had he messed that up?

"Here," Rafael said, turning the paper toward Max, "they signed." Max peered at the names: Friar Schmuck and Sister Coco. One in tight print, the other in flaring cursive, the acronym SPI and the date beside their names.

"Shit," he muttered, "I had them down for tomorrow," he told the waiting Rafael, whose last name he could never remember but who reminded him vividly of a tiny, squawk-prone bird, voluminous in his fierceness. "I must have double-booked." He grimaced his regret. Rafael took a beat before nodding skeptically in return, still waiting for an explanation for what had seemed like an unacceptable entry into his world, one he didn't quite feel like waiving for Max.

Max couldn't resist. "Never heard of the order?" Rafael returned his gaze blankly. "They're a San Francisco original, Rafael!" he scolded mockingly. He was fond of this pair, an old gay priest and a transgender nun, and was more than ready to go up against the conservatives on his board to make the Masonic their permanent home for Play Fair. Raised as he was with a father whose religion separated him from those he loved, he found an order devoted to safe sex and universal inclusion nothing short of miraculous. "You must have heard of them!"

"I'm a Catholic." Rafael frowned, sitting down and turning back to his notes.

Inside the auditorium, Max checked his watch again. Six minutes past four. Shit. She already had the kids in formation and warming up. And now he was going to have to manage two clients as well as her. Oh well. The kids sounded great, and no one had seen him yet.

Max took a seat in the back, using the low light to remain anonymous for a few more minutes and take a breather. The only person near him a small girl slumped into her jacket, as if she were hiding in the dark. *Good idea*, he thought, leaning back and closing his eyes to listen.

When his seat leapt beneath him, he had just begun to drift off.

8

"He must really be something. Or is it a she?"

Vashti looked up at the waitress squinting down at her. She had small, dark eyes. Her skin was leathery from too much sun and smoke, but her mouth was kind.

"Excuse me?"

She poured more coffee into Vashti's mug. "You've been sitting here all afternoon, hon, nursing that coffee like whiskey. Where I come from, we'd say you're wound up tighter than an eight-day clock."

"I'm finishing up."

"Of course you are." The waitress looked over her shoulder before leaning in. "You want to know something?"

Vashti wasn't sure she did.

"I loved someone like that once." They regarded each other. "He's dead now."

"I'm sorry."

"Doesn't matter." Her earlobes were empty circles lined with silver. *Did it hurt?* Vashti wondered. Maybe once, but certainly not as much now.

"I loved him the whole time he was alive, when all our friends were having one fling after another and getting married and then getting unmarried. *Why bother*, we used to say to each other"—she shook out a damp cloth and ran it across the empty table near the window—"*falling in love if you don't like what comes after?* Crazy, huh?" She looked up at Vashti, wanting a response.

"I guess."

"You *know*, I'd say"—she went back to rubbing the dirt and crumbs off the table and onto the floor—"a romantic streak ain't nothing to be ashamed of, hon. I'd say it's a bigger shame to just go with the flow, you know—go for the up-grade the minute the older model starts to break down."

Vashti felt her cheeks grow warm, then hot. She scrounged around in her bag for a cash tip and scurried out with a botched thanks. She had been there most of the afternoon, hadn't she, but she was still not ready to leave. She ducked into the Grace gift shop across the hallway, idly drawn to the beautiful crystalline figures in the cases filled with hushed light. She reached out to touch one of them, a sheep or a lamb. Yes, a lamb. She picked it up off the shelf and held it gently in her hand.

If only she hadn't *seen* him before she'd seen him. If only he hadn't looked so familiar. If only seeing him hadn't imme-diately resurrected the sharp, thrilling kick of anticipation in her gut, brought the feel of him to her hands so that she clenched them now, brought the very smell of him back so that she felt almost stifled by a sense of rightness and desire. She had never been very successful at hiding love, though it seemed so simple to hide an invisible thing.

Before February fourteenth was Max's birthday, it was just another day on which she and Max had a friendship she re-fused to recognize as love. It had been going on like that for the better part of the six months they'd known each other, but she had stockpiled reasons like swords to fend off love: she was not ready to date; Max was confusing friendship for a different kind of affection; her father would never allow her to date anyway, much less a boy with no roots. Maybe if Max had been a wealthy Iranian traditionalist who could take her off her father's hands as soon as possible, he might have conceded to Max's attentions. But to date simply because she wanted to? He'd never allow it. What she wanted was rarely a factor in what her father wanted for her.

She was thinking about these things while standing in her kitchen and cracking eggs over a bowl as Max sat across from her on a stool, reading. His hair had grown longer, and he kept pushing it back off his forehead with his long fingers absentmindedly, making it stand on end. The eggs were warm in her hands, as was the butter—she'd left them out overnight, and by the time she and Max got home from school, they were perfect for the soft melding of fat and liquid and sweetness that could be baked into the miracle of cake. No matter how many times she did it, pulling confections from the oven always felt at least a little like drawing rabbits from the empty hole of a hat.

"Are you sure your mom won't miss you?" she asked again.

Max shrugged, not looking up, the sharp bone of his shoulder showing through his T-shirt. "She has to work this afternoon. She's glad I'm not alone, at least."

She'd been planning the cake for weeks but only worked up the courage to actually ask him over that day. Even though her father left to open Edible Apothecary at 8:15

every morning, he liked to show up unannounced to check on his younger daughter. Yousef Shirah was proprietary about both his daughters, and Vashti suspected that although necessity took Javi into the store at an early age, her father found it to be the only remotely positive result of his wife's death—having his older daughter under his watchful eye whenever she wasn't at school or sleeping. As for Vashti, she was monitored until she was in high school by a hostile great-aunt when her sister or father wasn't around. Then she was trusted to be alone, but only as far as they understood "alone" to mean that her father would drive her to school, have Javi pick her up, and drop by regularly and without warning in the afternoon. Other kid's parents texted; their father appeared.

It was true that even if her mother hadn't died, Vashti might have always made her careful father nervous. But it was so much worse once Nasrin was gone. Yousef found his wife's death to be a punishment, his flourishing daughters a thin salve against the intolerable insult of raising them without a mother. No matter how well they were doing, he firmly believed they would be doing better had she lived. There was more than a little anger in his grief. In their father's worldview, their mother had been penalized for a life in which regular mammograms were forgone for afternoons too beautiful to sacrifice to the doctor, mornings with her daughters in the kitchen, or any of the many other spontaneous joys that called to her, despite the fact that both Vashti's grandmother and great-grandmother had died of breast cancer. Yousef believed that the way his daughters' mother had chosen to lead her life had resulted directly in her premature death. Vashti supposed he must have tolerated or even loved that spontaneity about her once, but after he lost her to it, his grief was such that he had to shift some of it into blame. Sometimes, when she caught him frowning at something when others were laughing, Vashti thought her father might have blamed her mother simply because she had allowed herself to be so loved. Of course, Javi had been a great comfort—she was dutiful and responsible, like her father—but the daughter most like his dead wife disturbed him so profoundly that Vashti sometimes wondered if he thought she had conjured up the resemblance herself.

For weeks, she had warned herself repeatedly against having Max over, citing the potential of her father's anger if he found out; she tried to talk herself out of it, but she knew that Yousef would use Valentine's Day to have a sale on exotic spices and herbs, and he would stay at the store until the last possible customer had come through. Anyway, she told herself, nothing would happen between her and Max; they were close friends, and nothing more; did everything between a boy and a girl have to be about love?

A breeze came through the window she'd cracked open, carrying the fragrance of any number of newly growing things, February in California after the rains. It was warm, and her nostrils were suddenly full of nothing but flowers and food. And Max. Sitting right there, in the close, quiet space of her kitchen. Every time she neared him, she was sure she smelled the faint, dark sweetness of his flannel shirt; the brassy trumpet smells always on his hands, bitter but not unpleasant. Earlier she'd smelled it in his hair, too, when he'd leaned over to look at the recipe she'd chosen. She found herself fumbling, suddenly nervous. As he usually did, Max sensed her discomfort and looked up, smiling to make her feel a little less self-conscious, a little more at home. All at once she felt sick and dizzy, unsure of what was coming or if she could stop it.

"What?" Max asked.

She shook her head. "Nothing," she said, "nothing." She began cleaning up the shells of the eggs she'd already cracked, crushing the small, fragile nettles in her hands. Suddenly, she remembered a story her mother had told her once, or maybe Javi, about a girl who had to crush nettles into flax to make woven wings for the ones she loved.

"Do you need help?"

"No," she said, avoiding his eye. And then he told her about something that happened in school that opened his heart to her and made her laugh and forget she shouldn't walk in. On any given day, for over a year, Max had been there with a million tiny ways of making her want to forget that she was supposed to put up boundaries between herself and him, to keep her own heart's doors locked, even though they threatened to swing on their hinges whenever he came around. His tenderness seemed reckless to her, frequently terrifying in its ease and generosity; he asked Javi questions about her day when she was around, befriending her because he somehow understood that the two sisters came as a pair. He told Vashti that she was beautiful whenever she let her guard down enough to allow him to, and that he loved her in bright colors and hated the oversize brown puffer jacket that was two sizes two big, the one she wore even when it wasn't all that cold. The only other time she'd had him over, when she was sure he would be just a friend, she'd come in from the bathroom to find him holding up a small, framed picture of her mother that had been hidden behind the huge ones of her father's relatives in Iran, squinting at it as if he could see her even better if he just looked hard enough. He tried her terrible attempts at grapefruit and ginger and salted agave muffins and told her they were terrible; he told her about New York and the forests and about his dad without actually telling her about his dad. *Why?* she often wondered. She needed reasons, it seemed. Because how else could she accept that a lonely, independent boy who'd only ever been loved by his mother was falling for a motherless girl reluctantly chained to her father?

He turned a page, pushing his hair back again, this time leaving a faint ink smudge on his forehead. His skin was pale in winter, with only a few freckles remaining on his cheekbones, and his lips were pale, too. She turned back to her recipe, but she couldn't understand what she read, because amid all the aromatics coming from the magical elixirs of spring and sugar, the scent memory of Max was the one she'd latched on to unwittingly, wanting to inhale it as deeply as she possibly could, sneak even closer to him so it would be stronger, so it would be the only thing she smelled. She reached clumsily for a measuring cup, knocking an egg to the floor. "Oh no," she cried softly, looking down on it as Max came around to see. "I needed that," she said, looking into his face.

There was a long silence between them.

Just as it became almost unbearable, he stepped closer to her than he had ever been, and there was that scent. Max.

"It's OK," he said softly. "I don't need a cake."

She watched herself reach for his fingers as if from a distance, but the moment she pressed her palm to his she was instantly, acutely aware that something she hadn't known she'd wanted was finally there. His lips on hers made short work of sealing the thing between them that had been awkward lately, smoothing it over, bringing her home, closer to him. Love, Vashti found herself realizing, wasn't some kind of mysterious merging of forbidden, adult desires amid the negotiation of locked cages. It was innocent, breakable, and essential.

The lamb in her palm fell onto its side. She righted it. It was a nice little thing. She could buy it for him. Buy it for him and give it to him for his birthday. It was, she figured, as good a place to start as any.

The clerk was eyeing her. She nodded, assuring him she was ready to buy. But as she took a step forward, she stumbled.

The second it happened, she knew what was coming. The clerk did, too, jerking his head up, instantly on full alert. They locked eyes with an urgency that had nothing to do with anything that had come before, but there was nothing to be done, nothing to do or say or think or feel but pure, undiluted fear. Then, with another sickening lurch, the ground beneath them began to convulse violently, and the rows upon rows of Marys and Jesuses and saints in their glass cases came crashing down over their heads.

〰〰〰〰

9

The car behind Gene beeped to get him to move into the six inches that had cleared between his Fiat and the Yukon XL in front of him.

He turned off the radio. Another pledge drive had interrupted the Ahmad Jamal marathon he'd been enjoying on KCSM. He forced himself to take a long, deep breath, realizing that he'd been holding it again. He hadn't factored in Valentine's Day traffic when he told Franklin he'd be home in forty-five minutes. That was ninety minutes ago.

He probably shouldn't have tested his luck and swung by the Stanford Shopping Center on the way. But in his rush to get home, he'd scrapped the idea of flowers from Nigghl's and chocolates from TCHO and just grabbed the iNfinity Franklin would be expecting for his birthday next month. Two birds with one stone, he'd figured, a minor detour and an unexpectedly luxurious surprise to smooth both their ruffled feathers. A lot of good the gifts would do, though, if stopping for them made him lose their reservation. Not that Franklin was all that pleased by eating at the geriatric hour of 5 p.m. But it was all Gene could swing last-minute on Valentine's Day. He cracked his neck, easing the tension there before reaching for the glove compartment to see if he had any aspirin. The driver behind him leaned on his horn.

Gene gripped the wheel, his stomach in knots. He should have taken 280 and wound his way around the city. It would have taken just as long, but at least he'd be moving. Instead, he'd been stuck in this narrow valley between the gorgeous relief of bay behind him and the familiar city in front of him for more than thirty minutes. Where *was* he, exactly? he wondered, looking at the tall green hills on either side of him. Suburbia? No. South San Francisco.

More horns. Whoever designed the city so Bay Bridge traffic from the peninsula had to go through downtown had clearly never had to do just that. And it was only getting worse and worse, the traffic piling up earlier and earlier. When was the last time he'd left Stanford in time to avoid it? It used to be that if you hit this section before rush hour, it wasn't so bad. But now it was always bad. Gene looked at his neighbors, frowning. What had happened to all those good old-fashioned worker bees, chained to their desks until five o'clock? Didn't anyone have a normal job anymore? He took in all the Volts and Teslas; the Google self-driving car he'd tried to race up to and study several miles back, before the traffic hit, hoping it really wouldn't have a driver—but it did, he saw now, a grungy twentysomething with a rabbinical beard and a white T-shirt. Plus there was always the ubiquitous parade of BMW sedans and shiny Escalades, broken up every now and then by an ancient, boxy Buick with bass so loud that you could feel it vibrating your inner ear; or one of those long, whalelike Pontiacs older than Gene, waving its fishtail in the slow line or the occasional VW van soldiering cheerfully on into its indefinite old age, faded rainbow curtains in its rear window. One thing was for sure: there was no such thing as a normal car in California anymore.

He switched the radio back on, changing the channel to KFOG. He treated himself to their lineup of retro love songs from the '70s and '80s—Donna Summer followed by Foreigner and Carly Simon! When was the last time he sang along to Carly Simon in the middle of the afternoon? Thank God *he* didn't have a normal job. He found himself smiling. *Tenure track, Gene—tenure track!* He grinned and turned up the volume. He hummed along when he couldn't remember the words, his fingers tapping the steering wheel. It could have been worse, he told himself. It was probably less than a mile to the last exit by now, and he could have hit traffic much earlier—even if he had to sit in this mess for the next thirty minutes, he'd still be home in time. He'd better be. He doubted they could even get on a waiting list if they missed their window. Maybe he should give Franklin a heads-up, see if he could call and work his magic with the maître d'. Gene glanced down at his phone, wondering if he could risk a call. He needed to get a Bluetooth headset.

They'd fought about it, Franklin insisting that any talking while driving was dangerous, Gene insisting that emergency calls on the road were less risky than Franklin's not being able to reach him at all. Gene frowned.

KFOG went to commercials, and Gene opted for some quiet, turning the radio off. He eased his foot off the brake and checked his phone low on his lap, glancing around for the CHP as he did. He started when the man in the car behind him honked his horn again. He glared into his rearview mirror, then back down at his phone. Damn! He couldn't text in this stop-and-go nightmare. Would Franklin guess that Gene was in traffic, or would he think he got caught up in work and left too late? Would he be upset? Any little thing could set him off these days; it was like he was trying to pick a fight with the world.

Gene sometimes felt the same way. Even before they had a diagnosis, the invisible foe of Franklin's illness struck fear and anger into both of them without warning. But the whole situation was probably far easier for Gene to live with than it was for Franklin, and not just because he wasn't the one who was sick. Gene's Midwestern, Germanic upbringing had made him adept at bottling up emotions of all shapes and sizes. Franklin, on the other hand—who was also technically Midwestern, but had been raised outside Chicago by a Jewish father and an even more Jewish mother—refused to hide even his darkest thoughts. In his worldview, anguish wasn't just something to be expressed—it needed exorcising.

But honestly, even Franklin knew better than to drink and pick fights at one of Rico and Jon's white-tie-optional dinner parties. Jon was a city planner, Rico a real estate agent, and together they loved to host small, if a little precious, gatherings at their gleaming Pacific Heights apartment. Rico was responsible for the invite list, and it was a well-known fact within their circle of friends that the guests were chosen for such an evening as carefully as the wine, which was always presented at the perfect temperature and accompanied by a hand-lettered card describing its provenance. Yet somehow Franklin's inebriated alter ego decided that after the game hen and before the cheese was the perfect time to interrupt a civil discussion of city politics to declare, at a volume indicating he was well beyond paying attention to other voices, that *the San Francisco I've known and loved* was *in its death throes*. As if Rico's visible mortification at such indelicate behavior wasn't bad enough, he and his partner's professional identities and financial abundance depended on the very city Gene's lover was announcing so glibly to be on its last legs. Everyone had tried to underreact politely as Gene tried to shut Franklin up, but he kept going. *You can't silence me, Genie. I'm your elder. Show a little respect, dammit!* It usually wasn't a sore point, their age difference, but everything had become a sore point these days. Eventually, Gene had to excuse them both and leave the party early.

Franklin would never have pulled that kind of stunt if he were well. Which made Gene more tolerant, but also more resentful of how tolerant he had to be.

"You're all just a bunch of Pollyannas, you know, you and your friends," Franklin persisted as Gene put him to bed, still upset, but Franklin looked too tired in the soft lights of their apartment to be upbraided. Deflated, Gene was glad to be home, ready to forgive. "Where are your pigtails, Pollyanna?" Franklin asked, tugging on Gene's ears. "Always thinking the best of people. Always so sure everything's going to turn out just fine." Gene pulled his lover's shirt over his head, leaving him red-faced and mussed, like a petulant toddler.

But Franklin was unwilling to be soothed into submission. He grabbed Gene's collar, the way he might have to make love: desperate, passionate. His lips, as he spoke, were moist and paler than they should have been.

"This used to be a real *place*, Gene," he whined, turning his head to the side in despair. "It used to have a soul. People came here because there was nowhere else for them to go, and it took them in, and then the place and the people made something beautiful out of what everyone else gave up on. Now it's all about who's making the most commercial toy or who's going public or who's got a reservation at International Orange. It's a tragedy, Genie," Franklin said, pounding his fist into the mattress, "a tragedy! And no one is doing a god-damn thing about it. Then you and your fancy friends"— they were always Gene's friends when Franklin was angry with them—"stand around telling me it'll all work out, it'll all be for the good. Well, it won't, Gene. Our city is dying. The soul's sucked out of her. And I don't care if speaking the truth makes me unpopular. It's a hell of a lot better than that crap you were dishing up. I mean, a twenty-first-century Gold Rush? Millennial prospectors? You kids are nothing but starry-eyed naïfs with overworked vocabularies," he muttered affectionately.

"Isn't that funny?" Gene asked, drawing the covers over Franklin as his tipsy partner lifted his arms. "That the very idealism you're mourning is sitting right in front of you?"

Franklin rolled his eyes. "Stop blowing smoke up my ass," he huffed miserably. "Those *kids* are ruining the best city America ever had the accidental luck to create. A city of art-ists and free thinkers and people willing to stick their necks out for what they care about and who they love." Franklin sat up again, the veins in his arms standing out against the pale skin. "A city for people who actually had the courage to live on the edge of the world. Where are *those* people, I ask you? You want to know where they are?" Gene waited patiently, sure he'd run out of steam sooner rather than later. "Oregon." Franklin sat back, letting his coup de grace sink in. "They're in fucking Oregon."

"It's time for bed." But as Gene reached up to turn out the light, Franklin grabbed his hand.

"You don't get it, do you? These kids don't care if the city is *reinvigorated*," he snarled meanly, "they just want it refurbished. And don't act all cool and academic. It's your city, too. You have something to lose if they take over. Don't pretend you don't."

"I wasn't pretending," Gene sighed, wondering if he should just turn in for the night also. "I'm just not sure I'd say it's as bad as all that."

"Well, that's because you're from Wichita," Franklin explained. "They're Gold Rushers, all right. Kicking out all the artists and runaways with their ridiculous paychecks and ridiculous pants, developing pie-in-the-sky apps they think are going to save the world. Well, what about our world, Gene? What about us?"

What *would* happen to them? Gene wondered, no longer thinking about the city. How bad would Franklin get? Things were going to get worse, they both knew that. But they could get a little worse slowly, or a lot worse fast. And what if something worse than getting worse happened?

Gene looked his lover in the eye. "The gold was all gone within a few years, Franklin. And the dot-com bubble burst." Leaving a city full of shell-shocked twentysomethings, but at least rents plateaued, and a fresh-faced Gene got his first apartment at Parnassus and Stanyan, a tiny space in a cream-colored Victorian where, on the second floor, the fog was at window level, visiting him in lovely swirls every afternoon. Everyone was in recovery mode, which in San Francisco always came with an inordinate and exhilarating amount of honesty and hope. He pulled the blanket over Franklin's thin chest, tucking him in. "It's just scary because we're in the middle of it."

"Nothing ever lasts, does it?" Franklin murmured. "Especially youth. The young are always the first to leave when the going gets tough, aren't they?" He was teary-eyed now, his lids drooping.

"I'm not going anywhere." Gene kissed him on the forehead.

Franklin grumbled his response.

"Yes," Gene said, turning out the light, "I know."

They needed a vacation. To go somewhere warm for a weekend. Palm Springs. Or Arizona. Sedona would be beautiful in February. In fact, that was a great idea! He'd bring it up tonight. Wasn't that new resort down near Joshua Tree having an innkeepers' weekend soon? He closed his eyes, trying to visualize the brochure that had come in the mail. The Red Rock? Red Roof? Maybe he'd have more news on the job by then, something more solid, something more they could celebrate.

As Gene finally rounded the corner before the Vermont Street exit, the rain abated a little and the cityscape came into view. It used to be that a night together staying up and talking until morning was all he and Franklin needed to repair anything weak or broken between them. Toward dawn, they'd go up to the roof deck with blankets, watching the sun rise over Washington Square Park, as the bums and the regulars started the day shouting and teasing each other, opening for the larger act that would be that day's motley crew of tourists and locals and drifters swarming into the grassy oasis, one of several San Francisco spots where an urbanite's poorly repressed desire to connect to the earth concentrated and flourished.

The man behind him leaned on his horn again, bumping into the back of Gene's car. *What the hell*, Gene swore, cursing his neighbor as he glanced up into the mirror.

But the mirror wasn't where it had been.

And then it was. His gut twisted viciously, his eyes locked on the stuttering mirror. But it wasn't the mirror stuttering, he realized, fighting through the sudden and all-consuming haze of shock. It was the car, and all the other cars, and the ground beneath them all. He grabbed at the leaping steering wheel, the entire vehicle bucking under his hands, rattling and jerking as if in the jaws of some great cosmic dog determined to shake it to death. He held the wheel as tightly as he might a lifeline, his palms burning with the effort. All around him, vehicles slid and crashed into each other like bumper cars in an amusement park, the confused sounds of horns going off unwillingly and alarms shrieking and metal crunching metal and glass exploding piercing his ears, his arms now in front of his face, over his head, his mind a ter-rified blank as the car jumped and jittered and finally bolted, smashing into a Range Rover driven by a small, white-haired woman whose mouth was open in a wide, inaudible *O*.

Then, as if someone shot the dog dead, everything stopped.

Gene was frozen to his seat, trying to understand. But only fragments of sense wafted through his consciousness, untethered. *Moment magnitude*, his mind said. *Strong motion*, his brain said, *strike-slip*, relevant words puncturing his awareness as if someone had released the entire lexicon of his professional career out of its neat storage box and the pieces were dropping and slipping into irretrievable domains, plinking and twanging like an infestation of dissonance in an orchestra.

A Camry that had been rolling slowly toward Gene's car struck his passenger door. The sight of its senseless driver frightened him into action. Quickly, he fumbled off his seat belt and shoved the door open and then slammed it behind him, all the while pulling and pulling at the air, trying to get it into his chest. But outside it was worse, with strange smells and sounds, a mixture of smoke and gas shot through with sounds primitive and wordless.

People who could were emerging from their cars like pas-sengers from rough seas, unsure of their balance on land, their bodies shivering in the wake of a mind-boggling assault. Many were hushed or otherwise tongue-tied, trying to hold themselves up against the crushing pressures of pain and fear and disbelief. *This wasn't supposed to happen*, their faces begged, right in the middle of afternoon traffic, a day lived almost to its close with the thoughtless assumption that it would be no different from the countless days that had come before it, a day promising no interruption in the patterns of life until the moment they were no longer. Armored in rainboots and jackets and corrective lenses, ready for a quick dash from car to apartment or hotel or plush dining room filled with wine and waiters, they stood still, disoriented and defenseless.

Gene's heart was ricocheting in his chest. He pressed his hand to his ribs, trying to keep it in. His throat was constricting, growing tighter, try as he might to keep it open. As he watched, a collection of people began to limp and walk and jog toward the freeway exit, as if by keeping order and following the exit signs—holding up their end of the pact they'd made with a certain reality—the sort of reliable truth they were expecting might be waiting for them just around the corner. And even though Gene knew better than most that it wasn't, he suddenly found himself straightening up and breathing a little more easily as, lemminglike, he followed the crowd. He knew the signs of shock in himself and others, but how much good does it do a man to know he's drowning if he has no chance of overcoming the water?

All he could do was put one foot in front of the other like everyone else, heading toward the city streets as if in a nightmare. He was already sweating with fear, cold under his clothes and soon to be wet on the outside, too, as a silent drizzle was blanketing everything, sealing them all in with the glue of misery. A bottleneck formed at the top of the exit, forcing him to stop momentarily, then inch forward, keeping his eyes on his shoes, scuffed with something dark green and something white. He fought the urge to examine them closely, find out what that *was*, just as he was trying desperately not to look up and take in the scenes unfolding around him. The cursory glances he'd taken had suggested there was more to see than he could bear to know.

His hand went to his lip and came away bloody. He examined it, stars and spots swimming before him, a velvety blackness coming in from the periphery of his vision. But someone was tapping him on his left shoulder and holding out a Starbucks napkin, which he took, meekly thankful, to press against the gash. The woman who had handed it to him was saying something, but Gene's ears were unable to make sense of what she was trying to tell him. Frantically, he remembered his phone, hunting for it in his pocket, knowing it would be dead as he pulled it out, hoping against hope that he would be wrong. It flickered on: no reception. He stared at it anyway, until the screen shot of Franklin popped up.

Franklin.

Oh God.

A wave of fear wormed its way into and through him like a toxin.

North Beach—he calculated quickly, his mind stumbling as it raced—a few miles away by foot? More? He broke into a trot, trying not to push people over as he wove between them. Images of Franklin swam through his heart and mind, clouding everything else around him: Franklin and his sprained wrist, Franklin stuck somewhere, Franklin unable to find his way out. All at once Gene was irrationally furious that every single scenario he could imagine was terrifying. How had he managed to finally find a person to love, only to have him become so weak, so susceptible? What if there was no way to get to him? He shook his head vigorously, as if he could physically rid himself of worry. No. There would be. There had to be. He grabbed onto the thought and allowed it to propel him through the crowd.

~~~~~~~~~

10

After the first wave of shaking stopped, Max found himself wedged between the seat he'd fallen off and the one in front of it, gripping the chair legs that had been bolted to the ground at his feet. He looked up, amazed to see the overhead lighting, the thirty-foot extensions of metal and glass and wiring that had been swinging enthusiastically for the past interminable minute, slow down and then stop, seeming to decide at the very last second not to drop to the floor. He took a deep breath, his chest hurting from the effort to unclench itself. Then he stood up quickly, taking in his surroundings, trying to make sense of what he saw. But the room was drawn in shards and upended angles, and the distorted view only encouraged a creeping hysteria to draw closer.

Near and on the stage, the children were getting to their feet on unsteady legs. Like newborn foals, they were determined to stand, undeterred by their own clumsiness as they struggled to right themselves. Better to be on their feet than vulnerable to the great predator that had just roared through the room. Everyone was strangely hushed, adults included, as though what had hit them was indeed alive and still out there, ready to pounce.

The first cry came from a small girl; Max knew her face, but what was her name? He felt the blood rush to his face.

How could he not know her name? He did not know the children well enough. It was too early in the season! But still, he felt terrible. A child under his care, even if that care was only temporary and musical, should be remembered. Something with an *A*. Anna? Allison? Allegra! Yes, that was it! A girl who could sing named Allegra, how oddly surprising that had seemed.

Now her left leg was crumpled under her, and her face was a river of pain. Recovering his senses, Max bolted out of his row and down the aisle, his mind directing him toward the injured girl without thought of what he could do for her. The others were now trying to help one another, too, but their movements were stiff and uneven, like grasses suddenly released from a prison of frost. A door at the entrance slammed open. Rafael stood there, calling out to him. Max had to focus to hear, to listen. Rafael was waving his hands. Of course! Max suddenly understood, looking up at the light fixture. As he watched, its swinging took on momentum. They had to get out. He glanced down again at the girl.

At any other time, he would see the odd angle of the leg beneath the knee and know she should not be moved. But, dumb with desperation, he tried to slip his arms under her so he could carry her out of there, even though he knew as he did that to move her would be to risk even more pain or damage or both. She did, too, her face pleading with him for another way, both of them listening intently to the silence, pregnant with the knowledge that it would be worse to move, far worse even than this. Incongruously, Max remembered her audition song: *a star, a star, dancing in the night with a tail as big as a kite.* Such an odd choice for a young girl! But it was Christmastime, her sister had explained, defensive, and all they had at home was a radio. Her sister! Of course. That was the girl he'd sat down beside, who'd run down with him, who was with her now, hysterical to the point of being furious, wild with helplessness. The younger girl locked eyes with him, her face as pinched and frantic as her body.

"Stay," Max said. "I'll go get help, I'll be right back."

He called out to Rafael, scooping the next nearest small child into his arms before he ran up the stairs with her, shouting at the other children to follow him as he did, all of them soon racing away, their minds and bodies jointly hopeful that danger was simply something that could be fled.

~~~~~~

11

Vashti unclenched her fists and opened her eyes, afraid to believe the shaking was over. She sat up cautiously, a smattering of debris dropping off her neck and shoulders. The lights in the basement gift shop were out, which meant she had to feel around carefully with her trembling hands. She could just make out the form of the clerk, curled up against the wall beside the cash register. She told herself he might be resting or unconscious, her observations hasty and thin, the desire to mask the truth more powerful than the desire to see it. Her eyes adjusted to the dark as she crawled toward him tentatively, trying to make sense of the state he was in. It was only when she was a few mystified feet away that she realized she had been both drawn in and repulsed by him because his head was bent awkwardly back from his body, as though he had been craning his neck to see something far overhead when he died. A gash still bleeding from his forehead made him seem more alive than dead, and she fought the urge to find something to wipe up the blood. She tried to stand but couldn't yet, her legs and mind weak with shock. There was glass everywhere. Crawling toward him, she'd had to make fists inside her sweater to protect her hands. Everywhere she looked were empty shelves and a carpet littered with the shards of glass relics.

A brief aftershock made her curl in on herself like a tortoise and toppled the clerk onto his side. Vashti's heart stopped, then started again violently. She'd seen a dead body before, she told herself. Worse than that—she'd seen her mother, daughter, and husband dead. But still, she shuddered, none of those three deaths was as gruesome as this stranger's, whose sudden, violent end triggered some primal fear of contagion. She scuttled back to where she'd been and searched frantically for her purse, pulling it to her and somehow managing to get her phone out and into her hands, its comforting light responding as soon as she touched it.

Her fingers shook so hard, she couldn't pull up what she wanted. Finally, she managed to stab at the call-back button, but even as she lifted the phone to her ear, her hands were shaking. Outside, the sounds of sirens and anguish began to drift in. *No.* She found herself chanting to herself, shaking her head, *no no no*. She fumbled her way back to the phone's keyboard, dialing 911. Still nothing. Three more times, three more nothings. Javi would know to call before long to find her, wouldn't she? And oh God, their father, in his one-story Sonoma retirement rancher, would be fine, wouldn't he? She felt sickened, thinking of how he'd be reacting, how he was probably already dialing her number on a loop, his anxiety ratcheting up with every ring.

As suddenly as if she'd been slapped, she was desperate to get out. She eased herself up and—slowly, squinting—made her first few steps toward the door. Once mobilized, her legs ached underneath her with the anxious desire to flee, to lead her back outside into the world. Before she knew what she was doing, she'd stumbled past the empty wreckage of the Peet's kiosk—barely able to peek in to confirm that no one was still there—and through the doors and up the steps to street level where, *oh God, oh no,* her consciousness began working its way out of the muck of shock, knocked into awareness by a wall of a thousand more hapless souls stretching up and down and across California Street, each one announcing anew confusion and chaos and fear and wonder. When she'd entered the cathedral earlier that day, California had been a solid, long street in the middle of this solid, packed city, the block she was on one of her favorites for many reasons, not least because it was flanked by the intricate Gothic majesty of Grace's glass windows and stone heights to the north and the midcentury modernism of the grand Masonic structure to the south—landmarks so central to the street's identity that they seemed to have generated a spiritual corridor, like a great stone mother and a somber marble father standing witness to the millions passing back and forth on the cable car between them. But now people swarmed at their foundations like panicked ants, gaping and picking their way among the broken detritus of trauma. Vashti tried to make as much sense of it as she could, but the run of glass doorways that marked the sobering entrance to the Nob Hill Masonic Center had shattered at its feet, its storied height nothing more than a space that was letting the wind blow through; and the Grace spire had overturned and plummeted to street level, as if someone had shot a majestic, mythical bird out of the sky.

But what she heard coming from people and their alarms was far worse—wordless anguish and confusion, a Babelesque blathering puncturing the sky—and what she smelled was worse even than that: the unmistakable nose tickle of wood smoke. As a child in school, she had been taught about the great earthquake and fires of 1906 as if they were points of pride, myths on which the city was founded, not an inheritance they were doomed to receive. History never actually repeated itself, everyone knew that. Everyone knew that San Francisco might dip into economic turmoil or political chaos—but no one, really, she was sure of it now, now that she was standing right in it, no one ever imagined it could be lost to earthquakes—or *fire*. This was the new age; old-age horrors were nothing but stories now, weren't they? She blinked at the bright horror of her surroundings, confused momentarily about where she was and why and how she had come there.

Then, her mind woken fully, she looked up at the still standing Masonic Center and raced across the street and up its steps and through its doors, where she nearly collided with Max, who was racing through the lobby with a young girl in his arms.

~~~~~~~

12

At the top of the exit and Vermont Street, Gene found himself on a block he'd never known was there: a residential stretch backing up to the freeway, dirty and dusty with old Victorians like aging geishas he'd rather not see without their paint on. He tried to place what he was looking at within his catalog of San Francisco: Potrero Hill? Or at least the Inner Mission side of it, shadowed by overpasses and empty streets with old shopping carts embedded in their shoulders. He tried desperately to orient himself, to see what was before him as familiar, but even if there hadn't been an earthquake, he was on foreign ground. The downside of living in a city that meant so many things to so many people was that every one of its dense blocks changed according to its own peculiar pulse, almost deliberately hiding its beat from infrequent visitors.

To his right, an entire wall of a grand two-story building had dropped open like a dollhouse, its moniker—Slovenian Hall—undisturbed on a sign stuck in its front lawn. Gene stared, the destruction visually mystifying. Three sides remained stately and upright, the panes of their elaborate windows still intact; the fourth's absence was so incongruous and neat, its disappearance might have been the work of a magician. The neighborhood was similarly upended, the aftermath of such inhuman violence hard to comprehend. A tree with a shredded torso lay across a car, its exposed parts pale blond and wet with life. A big dog limped heavily across the street, the hunted look in its eyes making it seem more wild than domestic. Everywhere people wove and drifted, similarly unhinged, many of them openmouthed and silent. And just as Gene realized he was even more afraid to look up and out at the city than he was to look into yet another stranger's devastated, questioning eyes, his eyes lifted skyward.

The drizzle and twilight didn't do enough to obstruct the view. Like any good city, San Francisco presented a jagged line of architectural prowess to the distant eye. But now, like the city in a bad movie or other distortion, it presented a handful of tall buildings looking back or tilted in unfathomable disrepair. Gene wanted to look away. The cityscape seemed larger than life, too close—had it always been so close from up here?—certainly it had never seemed so easily consumed.

Columns of smoke had sprung into the sky like sinister, living things, rising up through the mist and haze in black and billowing defiance. Gene felt the hair on the skin of his arms rise, as if he had come into contact with a predatory animal. Looking around him, he saw the shadows of photographs he'd pored over a thousand times in the archives of Berkeley or Stanford libraries: photographs of stupefied, well-dressed people facing vistas of fire, walls of smoke on the morning of April 18, 1906. The similarities were so acute that he felt a new wave of disassembling, as if the passage of time were nothing more than a falsely soothing construct, a frame through which his vision had been warped into seeing a first-world metropolis's vulnerability to naked tragedy as a thing of the past.

He tore his eyes away from the gathering smoke. The desire to see nothing clearly was overpowering, even as he was acutely aware that of all the people right then and there, he was one of the only ones who could make sense of what he saw. In truth, there were few people who knew as well as Gene exactly what sorts of disasters lurked in the aftermath of an earthquake.

Broken gas lines and downed power lines. Fire. The volatile San Andreas running directly beneath an already severely depleted water supply. Wooden buildings packed side by side, and soft stories over garages. Crowds and debris. Panic and liquefaction. Each possibility surmountable on its own, but when they worked as a collective, small armies advancing from all directions on a surprised and handicapped target—well, the stone that sets off an avalanche does not speak to what it will trigger.

A flush began creeping up Gene's neck and into his face. He had read about all of these contingencies and probabilities and likelihoods so many times. Read and studied and analyzed and lectured and spoke. And here it was. Here he was. Dazed and dumbstruck. His knees threatened to buckle, even as he shouted silently to himself to keep going, to run toward Franklin, away from here, but suddenly he couldn't. He stumbled to the sidewalk, heavy with the knowledge he dragged along with him like an anchor too large for the ship it was supposed to steady, pulling it under instead. What use was it now? What he knew. What he had known.

If the Big One hits in the next six months, Sam, then we all owe you an apology. It had been warm. A rare warm day in the midst of an overcast winter, after lunch. They had taken their fill of the smorgasbord of salads and sandwiches provided by Bon Appétit, followed by fresh polvorones, courtesy of a colleague who lived by a Mexican bakery. The windows were cracked open in January, lending a robustness to their faculty meeting that usually wasn't there. Gene's promise brought chummy laughter all around.

Sam had smiled, but his eyes had narrowed. Unlike everyone else, he sat as if at any minute he might stand up. *As charming as your patronization* always *is, Dr. Strauss,* Sam said—then, stopping himself, *Gene* (he always reverted to Oxford customs when riled, isolating himself further from the informal first-name basis at the heart of Stanford culture)—*it doesn't change the fact that we're staring down the barrel of a massive seismic event, the effects of which could yield unprecedented urban catastrophes. How long are we expected to sit on that before it jumps up and bites us in the ass?*

Gene hesitated for a moment, frowning. *Six months?*

Everyone had laughed.

Sam stiffened even more, suddenly looking too thin, drained. He'd been putting in ridiculous hours, and now Gene almost felt bad, even though he really couldn't hold himself responsible for a colleague willing to kill himself just to score an academic win. He smiled generously at Sam from his seat, leaning back ever so slightly to milk the contrast between his relaxed confidence and Sam's uptight proselytizing. He dropped the smile just as generously before speaking, replacing it with a look of sympathetic concern.

Sam, you're right, the data is concerning, and I don't think any of us is suggesting we ignore it. Quite the contrary: we need to take it seriously. And to do that, we need to take the work that produced it seriously. And right now, it's just too new to be reliable! God, Sam, if we run off to the media with unproven results, it'll be academic suicide. You know that. We'll look like fools.

Sam sat down, the fight gone out of him. *As always, you make some excellent points, Dr. Strauss,* he muttered. *Of course, the work, our careers, must come first. If lives are unnecessarily lost, well, I guess that's just bad luck.*

Our work and its impact are one and the same, Gene had rejoined, rising above Sam's emotional barbs to adopt the sober tone and expression of measured reason. *The peninsula section of the San Andreas has been threatening to go for decades. Centuries! A few more months won't make a difference, and we'll be glad we waited in the long run. You know as well as I do, Sam, that earthquake prediction is just too new a science to risk premature exposure! Let's let it mature, hold our horses, and it will save many more lives than either you or I could imagine.*

He had really believed that, too. When he said it, and for the past twelve years of homing in on a technology so enthralling, he almost dreaded the moment it would be perfected.

Gene leaned against a broken railing, listening to nothing and everything in the chaos around him. If only he didn't have to look up. Like a lifting veil, his life's work seemed suddenly to disappear before him, or to be metamorphosing into a nightmarish version of itself: a poorly defended city taking blows from the enemy he'd built a career on promising to foresee. Just as the full weight of regret and humiliation began to settle on him, the earth began to stutter anew, a rollicking that increased in volume and intensity. The railing he'd been leaning against came loose under his palms and he fell, beginning to slide downhill. Scraping his palms and shins, he regained his balance in time to grab onto a street sign—NO PARKING, 9–11, MONDAYS, STREET CLEANING—holding desperately on to the only solid thing he could find, a man dangling over the edge of the world.

〜〜〜〜〜

13

Maybe, Max thought dumbly, none of this is real. The earth-quake, the overturned lobby, the chorus of untraceable, unrelieved despair, both human and non, drifting in from outside. Maybe it was all a figment of an imagination that had already begun to take over earlier in the day, when he thought he had glimpsed Vashti.

Because now, standing over the kaleidoscopic litter made by the lobby's second-story glass and felt and linen and silk and feathered and shelled mural when it shattered, amid the panicked children running by him and out the door, Vashti was there. Standing right in front of him.

Still so beautiful. A little older and softer, though just as luminous as ever. More luminous. More beautiful.

She was close enough that if he lifted his hand, he could touch her. The idea was like an overwhelming pain, un-bearable and hypnotic. How quickly everything surged for-ward from the past, his heart swelling so rapidly he felt like it might drown.

Where could she possibly have come from? What was she doing here, still in the body and face he had once memorized with his hands, standing right in front of him? He *had* seen her, after all. And his mother hadn't believed him. Oh God. His heart began to shut a series of quick locks, knowing that if he conceded one inch of territory to terror or panic, he would lose the whole battle. He forced himself to speak.

"Vashti," he said slowly, as if pronouncing an unfamiliar name.

For her part, as many times as she had imagined the possibility of seeing Max again, Vashti would never have guessed that she would have, in the end, run right into him, nor that she would find him with a child in his arms, and that the sight of that would make her lose control of the kind of tears she'd promised herself she'd hold back. But one look at Max, and there they were. As if she hadn't only run into him bodily but also figuratively, the sight of the man she'd loved and left instantly bruising her heart, exposing tenderness that was still raw to the touch.

"Vashti?" He sounded so stricken, her name itself might have been a question.

"Max. I—"

"Is that everyone? Are we clear?" A huge, blue-black fireman in full regalia had materialized beside them, gesturing toward the child in Max's arms, who was wriggling to be let go. He put her on her feet and let her scamper toward the door, vaguely aware that he should be monitoring a child that young more closely, but she was already gone. The fireman was waiting for an answer. Then the delayed panic set in that he couldn't have stomached until help appeared: his mother!

"My mother," he told the fireman. "She's older, elderly." His head was swimming.

"Is she in the building?"

"No, no," Max said, "she's over at Buena Vista." He

glanced again at Vashti, still trying to piece together her presence, the complete reversal of what he normally understood to be constant truths: his mother present, Vashti gone, a stable earth.

"Are there any more children in the building?" the fireman asked sternly.

"Yes!" Max exclaimed, startled into comprehension. "A girl. Her name is Allegra. I mean Ally, I think they call her Ally. She's down there. Hurt her leg, maybe more. I didn't think she should be moved."

"Show me," the fireman said, striding away so quickly Max had to jog to catch up, then he stopped short. He turned around, still not knowing what to say to Vashti but desperate to keep her there until he did. "Please," he implored. "Don't go. Wait."

He was strangely grateful to find Ally and her sister where he'd left them, even more grateful that the two representatives from the Sisters of Perpetual Indulgence—who'd slipped his mind yet again—had stayed behind to watch over her. How could anyone forget a six-and-a-half-foot-tall transgender nun and her sidekick, who looked for all the world like your average priest, were it not for the *Make love, not war* tattoo across the back of his neck. "Hello!" he called out cheerily. The heavy wrinkles at the corners of his eyes, cultivated by sun and tragedy, squinted in on themselves when he smiled. "She's doing just fine," he reassured Max as he approached.

The fireman knelt by the child while her sister hovered

beside him. "I think it's her ankle," she said, her young voice high with tension, "or her leg, or something."

The leg was clearly broken near the shin, just above her ankle; Max could see that now, standing over her, his head clearing as he watched. The fireman grabbed a seat back from a broken chair to wedge underneath the leg and stabilize it, but the girl cried out when he touched her. Max heard the mannish, pink-wigged nun suck in air through her teeth, and a wave of sympathetic repulsion passed through him. When he'd found his mother after she'd broken her hip, he remembered thinking that the break had seemed to puncture her spirit, too, the cries she made small and shrill. His mind wandered to her room at Buena Vista, with her knick-knack shelves and books, the heavy painting over her bed. If only he hadn't passed her off to a retirement community, had taken on the job of looking after her. He forced himself to imagine her with a blanket around her shoulders, someone bringing her a drink of water. Just then, the eight doors from the anteroom to the auditorium rattled en masse. Everyone froze, but it was only the wind, blustering as greedily through the new rents and tears of the building as a new lover might explore his beloved's body.

Left alone in the lobby, Vashti had drifted through the anteroom and through the auditorium doors. She stopped near the back of the orchestra section, watching Max. He was thinner and a little taller than she remembered, and his face, his whole expression, was much more guarded. It used to be that she could look at him and know what he was thinking. Now he was a man with a set jaw, his curls cropped close to his head. For some reason, that sight above all filled her with a measure of regret so deep, she wished she could look away.

Curiously, as if he could hear her thoughts, Max suddenly looked up. He was wondering what he might say to her, wanting suddenly to reach out to her. That had always been the way to get to her essence, and he could not fault himself for having only the old ways to fall back on; for wanting, above all, to touch her. She took a few more steps forward, her eyes locked on his, when the ground beneath them heaved, wrenching loose a section of the balcony over her head.

Vashti ducked and Max ran, reaching her just in time for the second earthquake to begin in earnest, a pregnant rumbling that gathered in volume as ominously as a stampede of beasts devouring the earth. The loosened balcony dipped and swayed, threatening to fall. Max grabbed a stunned Vashti by the hand and yanked her into the nearest row, where they half fell, half stumbled to the floor between the lifted seats. Max hunkered down as the rigging began to moan, but Vashti looked up, peering toward where the children were. Below, the lighting over the stage began to swing again. And seconds later, as if it had been holding on by just a thread, the rigging dropped from the ceiling, crashing to the floor seventy feet below, right on top of the priest and the nun, the girls and the fireman. Vashti screamed, a sound that hadn't ended when an earsplitting pop came from overhead.

The balcony's right side came down first, tilting in and then crashing onto the seats and floor below, bringing the center section with it seconds later, all fifty rows and nine hundred seats collapsing in an avalanche of thwarted stability. And then, just after the earth had finally stuttered to a stop, the remaining overhead section of the balcony moaned out its death rattles and dropped. For a long moment, there was nothing but absolute silence.

~~~~~~~~~~~~~

Then came the season of the awful silence, the hush of awe, when mankind held its breath and things stood still and humanity gazed on havoc and hideous horror and then, out of the silence, out of toppled buildings, ruined palaces, and dismal hovels, came the besom of flame. With a hideous roar it advanced, this terrible thing, this red and yellow monster, and, its fiery arms outstretched, it reached the seven hills and it hissed and roared and with infernal intensity, it consumed, ate, and devoured.

—PIERRE N. BERINGER, 1906

We had passed some engines on their way to extinguish a fire at North Beach, where a huge gas tank had exploded, and we had noted a smaller fire nearby, but the possibility of a general conflagration seemed too remote to be considered. "Why, what nonsense," I said. "The whole city can't burn." As we reached the crest of the hill, [a] man pointed. "See," he said, and from the northern shore of the city to the extreme south, from North Beach to the far end of Mission, fires were blazing aloft.

—MARY ASHE MILLER, 1906

We tried to make the fallen Brunswick Hotel at Sixth and Folsom Streets. We could not make it. The scarlet steeplechaser beat us to it, and when we arrived the crushed structure was only the base of one great flame that rose to heaven with a single twist. By that time we knew that the earthquake had been but a prologue, and that the tragedy was to be written in fire.

—JAMES HOPPER, 1906

14

Gene slid halfway down Vermont Street with the dislodged parking sign in his hands, its jagged concrete base the only defense he could put up between himself and the bucking earth. The violence with which it shook seemed almost jubilant, wild in its thoughtlessness.

Then, just as suddenly as it had all begun, everyone and everything came to a stop.

Like figures in a fun house, Gene and everyone else around him rose on unsteady legs. Gene found himself staring at the face of a woman with an afro as symmetrical as the moon, one hand clamped across her mouth, the other pointing out, toward downtown San Francisco. In the distance, a collapse of buildings distorted the familiar skyline to the east, the tip of the Transamerica Pyramid neatly upended into a high-rise beside it. Gene swallowed back the hot, acidic liquid that raced into his throat. Frantically, he fished for his phone in his pocket, thinking it would be dead. The battery was almost gone and there was no signal, but a text from Franklin, sent while he'd been in traffic, greeted him: *Where RU? Smelsmerelda won't go until you get back. I'm in olfactory hell.* Thank God. Thank God! He almost laughed his relief. Esmerelda would carry Franklin out on her back before she'd leave him in danger. He tried to drape himself in the comfort of that, thin as it was.

One block north, a fire truck broke through a crooked garage door and dove into the street, sirens and lights blazing. Despite all its urgency, it wasn't long before it was choked by a distended mass of people and cars and trees and the bricks and woods and steel and the unnamable, hidden parts of buildings. The machine honked desperately, its alarm insisting that access was either a matter of negotiation or battle. But its outrage was a sound swallowed into the air, already thick with an indecipherable jumble of noise.

Gene's first instinct was to get to flatter ground in case another tremor set in, and he found himself nearly tripping over his own feet to get the rest of the way down the hill. He stopped short when he did, dizzy again, unsure of how to make sense of where he was and how he had found himself there. He took a deep breath. He couldn't panic. He could be, must be, helpful, couldn't he? But how?

Like a doctor faced with his own fatal injury, he tried to make objective sense of what was happening, what had just happened. A 7.0 or higher on the peninsula when he was on the freeway, followed by a significant aftershock or another event farther up the San Andreas just as he walked off the exit? But he wasn't even exactly sure where he was. He looked around. His hand went to his pocket to check his phone before remembering; helplessly, he checked it again anyway. He forced himself to put it away, steeling himself to find his bearings by what he could see in front of him. The street signs told him he was at the intersection of Vermont and Seventeenth. Gene could feel the speed of his heart in his chest, but his mind was hesitant, his thoughts clumsy and disconnected. He looked down at his wrist, remembering that he was wearing a watch. It was 4:26. He had to stare down at it to make sense. Had he left Stanford only an hour and a half ago?

He made his way haltingly down Seventeenth on stiff legs, his entire being a divining rod for further hazards; he wanted to look nowhere but couldn't look away. There was no narrative to guide him in the aftermath of upheaval, only pieces of stories: a car sideways in the middle of the street, a tiny, elderly woman sitting in the driver's seat, unseeing, the doors locked around her; an uprooted trio of topiaries, cement still clinging to their roots; a girl running with a small dog in her arms, its leash dragging loose and threatening to trip her; a bicyclist crashed into an art gallery's display windows; a downed power line and a river of water emerging from no obvious origin about to converge.

He started to see stars again, pinpoints of light.

Surely it was only this bad in this particular area of the city, he tried to tell himself, all the brick buildings packed in so close together. It was the design district's own fault, wanting to preserve the beauty of old buildings. Even the newest building didn't stand a chance if it was sandwiched between brick high-rises, as many were, or bookended by blocks of wooden Victorians in the path of a thirsty fire. Mentally he ran through the catalog of disaster prevention and preparedness that every good geologist in the area would have ready on the tip of his tongue, but his lips were chapped and dry with fear. He was walking unevenly over ground still wet with rain and now covered in every manner of liquid and he slipped, catching himself at the last minute, though his chest tightened and his forehead broke out in a sweat. *Think, Gene!* he told himself. *Pull yourself together!*

But his ability to think things through, to make sense when nothing made sense, the ability he believed in more than any other he had, was gone. Or it was there, but it had undergone dissolution, his thoughts suddenly airy and impossible to direct. Every building that he could bring to mind seemed sickeningly vulnerable. He tried to look up, away, out, to latch on to a sight, a person, anything that would steady him, bring him back to himself. He tried to remind himself that it wasn't he who had sustained the injury. It was the earth. The earth had been—was—was always?—yes—had always been—fractured. Fractious.

He had the strange sensation that, if he could just find his way to some hidden alley, the right knob to turn on some door he'd failed to notice, he would find himself back where he should be. Maybe he could find himself back even further, so that he could correct what he'd done several weeks ago, a mistake sure to haunt him for the duration of whatever was left of his career.

In the days leading up to that fateful faculty meeting, Sam Smythe had been pestering Gene nonstop about a cluster of correlated seismic and electromagnetic activity registering on their joint baby—CERISY (Correlative Energies Interpretive System), the new darling of NCEPT—along the peninsula section of the San Andreas Fault. CERISY's ticket to fame was its unprecedented ability to measure correlative energies around seismic events to a level of unheard-of refinement. After playing with their creation incessantly, Sam identified what he believed to be her first prodigal work: a previously unidentified correlation between seismic and electromagnetic activity in the weeks leading up to Loma Prieta in 1989, Northridge in 1994, and Tōhoku in 2011. And—far more controversially and controvertibly—Sam claimed that the same correlative patterns were showing up in data he was beginning to collect on current activity around the peninsula section of the San Andreas, and that the similarities should not—could not—be ignored.

Gene had been quick to concede that Sam's observations were interesting, but—arrogantly, foolishly, probably jealously, at least a little meanly—he told himself and others that Sam's desire to broadcast them was just a premature attempt to draw attention to their work. Didn't others think, Gene said around the department, that it was a little odd that Sam wanted the results published right before his teaching contract was up for renewal? Of course the data was exciting, very promising, but the name of the research game was provable, replicable findings, and all they had were a few tests they'd conducted themselves. It would be at least several more months before they could get them reproduced, if they were reproducible; several more after that to get their articles peer-reviewed.

Sam hadn't relented, though, using every opportunity to convince Gene that the exact same correlation that preceded the two most damaging Bay Area earthquakes in recent history was coming together right beneath their feet. He was sleep deprived, Gene told himself, overblown and grandiose, generally out of touch. And both of them knew that without Gene's support, Sam wouldn't have the social capital to breathe a word of his concerns to senior faculty. At best, they'd laugh him off; at worst, he'd be accused of crying wolf: an occupational hazard for geologists in the nascent and, some even argued, soft science of earthquake prediction— and a potentially fatal blow to the career of any junior faculty member. But still, Sam could talk of nothing else when anyone stopped to listen. And unfortunately, the person who usually did was Gene.

He realized that his gaze had suddenly settled on something quiet, something several blocks away to the east with less activity, fewer people. He had to think: What was in that direction? It couldn't be more than a dozen blocks from the bay. If he remembered correctly, Third Street wound along the coast out here. He closed his eyes, trying to jog his memory. His heart jerked violently.

Of course.

Oh God. Of course.

Everyone knew that the edges of the city were built on landfill—a friendly term for what was really packed sand and dirt and houses and old ships and probably hundreds of luckless materials easily forgotten and paved over. "Made" ground, as hastily erected and collapsible as straw houses made by pigs in a fairy tale.

How many thousands of videos on liquefaction had he watched, he and his colleagues soberly analyzing the mistakes people made all over the world, building and living on surface area that turned to liquid once the undulating began, the earth's stability in such places nothing more than a sleight of hand.

Of course, though—it was never said, but it contextualized every scrupulously somber conversation they had, every discussion that dutifully spoke to possibility but never edged into any real sense of fear—San Francisco was different. San Francisco had modern building codes and retrofitting. Stanford and Berkeley geologists as insurance against the worst. Money and significance. Culture and history. Simply too many important people and places to be instantly struck down by anything as impersonal and random as a geological event. But they knew—deep down they had known, hadn't they—that people could prepare themselves for seismic activity of this proximity and magnitude exactly as well as ants can protect their nests from backhoes.

Gene's face prickled with shame and fear. What a fool's errand to be a geologist in San Francisco, of all places. An entirely impractical, egocentric exercise. The earth was an organism of its own design, mostly insensible to the creatures swarming over its surfaces. Creatures who believed in the protection of governments and kings. And among them, Gene was nothing but a jester.

He turned away from the sinking coastline and walked quickly back from where he'd come, veering sharply right onto Kansas when he came to it again, the first right that looked halfway passable, keeping to the center of the street, avoiding the sidewalks shadowed now by partial brick buildings, heading north. North. Yes. That was it: he needed to get out of his head and onto a path. To North Beach and their home and Franklin. It was only a few miles away, after all, and closer to stable ground. In fact, the inn was on a rise, which was just as good as a bedrock foundation—maybe even better. Maybe, just maybe, it would be OK.

Gene broke into a stiff trot, forcing himself to focus now on an image of Fin de Siècle: its charmingly neat white stucco exterior draped with scads of brilliant pink bougainvillea; Franklin's rooms on the top floor with their perfectly preserved midcentury modern furnishings and Gump's sinks, the windows with their views of the water. If Gene kept up this pace, he might be there in a matter of hours, even though darkness was descending everywhere, the city already beginning to resemble a wilderness of extinguishing light.

〰〰〰〰

15

The summer before Max and his parents moved to San Francisco, a young girl drowned in the Altona town lake. She had been playing near a long, wide dock, practicing somersaults, and wound up underneath it, unable to find her way out. The newspapers said her sister tried to save her, calling out and reaching underneath, but the girl panicked and became disoriented, struggling to find her way out. By the time her sister got help, it was too late.

It was the first time Max had heard of something that he couldn't forget or make bearable. He'd be fine during the day, but then at night, the thought of the drowned girl loomed like something that must be swallowed but can't be chewed. One night, after he had lain in bed staring at the ceiling until well past his bedtime, his father came in and sat at the foot of the bed. It was clear that he somehow knew Max was still awake, despite the dark between them, but he didn't speak for several minutes. Just before his father stood to go, he squeezed Max's ankle. "Never panic or struggle if you're stuck," he said into the opaque dark. There was a long moment during which Max wondered if his father would say anything else. He did, though he heaved a long sigh before offering his parting advice, "If she hadn't struggled, she might have lived." His father's voice sounded as sad as Max felt, and Max stiffened under the unexpected softness. All at once, he wanted his father and his awkward comforts to leave so he could sleep. When he did, Max closed his eyes, relieved.

Trapped and barely conscious, Max felt the familiar, desperate pull of a waking nightmare. Suddenly he was looking over his father's shoulder, watching him try to write a letter, but the ink wouldn't form itself into words. What did he want to say? *What?* he demanded, tearing the paper out from under his father's hands. His father looked up, sad again. *Don't struggle, Max. If she hadn't struggled, she might have lived.*

Vashti opened her eyes to a dark garden full of bluish-white flowers, each petal smooth and luminous as marble. She wasn't quite sure where she was, but it seemed familiar. She squinted, trying desperately to see better, to remember.

Once upon a time, before her mother died and her grandfather moved back to Iran, he would visit them and tell her stories. Usually he came to her parents' spacious but perpetually fogged-in home at Twenty-Third and Vicente on an afternoon when Vashti's father wasn't there, but sometimes Vashti's mother would take her daughters to visit him at his apartment in Cupertino. Her grandfather would sit over a steaming cup of tea on his sunny patio, sipping from it though the water was still so hot, it burned her finger to touch it. He'd laugh and squeeze the juice from a slice of lemon into the golden liquid, sucking on the rind while he told Vashti about things she wasn't sure were real.

In Tehran, he told her once, there were gardens with flowers so beautiful that they shone even at night, the light itself unwilling to part company with them. Her mother scolded him for his romanticism, but she was smiling when she did, and later, sometimes very late at night, her mother would tell such stories, too. *Maybe this is such a garden*, Vashti thought, touching a petal experimentally. Her grandfather's garden? Her own? Had either one of them ever had a garden? Vashti squinted even harder. Who was that in the distance? Were there other people there, too? Yes, there were!

She moved forward cautiously, approaching a bench where two figures were seated, a man and a woman.

Vashti, the man said, smiling warmly.

It was Dale, still pale but looking better, sitting beside a woman in shadow. Dale! She was glad to see him, relieved, wanting to explain where she was and why she'd come there. But as she rushed over, he stood to block her way. As he did, his color returned and the smile disappeared.

Wake up, Vashti, he said sternly. *Wake up.*

The woman stood, too. Vashti peered at her, her heart fluttering dangerously, equal parts joy and disorientation. Vashti suddenly felt as desperate to see that face as she had once wished for the woman herself, as if this vision of her mother could be a conduit to the lost parts of her own life. But as soon as her mother stepped toward her, Vashti's mouth filled with dirt.

No, her mother cried softly, reaching out to wipe Vashti's lips, but her mouth was still filling and then her mother was cupping Vashti's jaw and, in one decisive and intimate stroke, used her other hand to deftly scoop the dirt from her daughter's mouth.

It was a movement so gentle and quick, as natural and strange as what Vashti often found herself doing to clear her infant daughter's mouth, using her fingers to open her throat or her fist to press into her rib cage because there wasn't time to reach for anything else when she aspirated or otherwise choked on something sudden and simple and life-threatening, or simply stopped breathing yet again. It was strange how, in such moments, the bodies of mothers and daughters no longer recognized separation, as if the physical self could lose track of its own boundaries.

Near the stage, in a lucky space that hadn't been the direct victim of the mechanical avalanche, everything and everyone—no more than a priest, a sort of priestess, the two girls, and a stray boy—were covered in a fine, snowlike dust of plaster. The five of them were corralled between the fallen lighting and the collapsed balcony to the west, walls of debris all around them. On the floor where the stage and an aisle and the fireman had been, a monstrous chunk of wire and ceiling and black curtains and glass and casings had settled into a treacherous pile more than thirty feet high.

The girls stared out into the new dark, the whites of their wide-open eyes seeming to glow. The questions poured from their mouths, whipping by so fast that the priest could barely speak quickly enough to catch them. The debris had blocked the exits, and in the dim light of the draining generator, there was no clear way out.

"Oh my God." The nun began weeping into her hands.

Watching her, Ally's face crumpled.

"Don't cry," the priest said, addressing the girl.

"We're stuck here, aren't we?" Her sister's expression was pinched and insistent, falsely collected. Terror looked different on children, distorting their smooth features grotesquely. This one's face seemed to have gone dry with fear, as if it might crack if she moved it. "He's dead, isn't he," she said, gesturing to where the fireman had been.

The priest glanced toward the fallen balcony, his gaze traveling up and out toward the heaps of debris blocking the doors. The fireman hadn't stood a chance. And what of that young director, Max? The priest tried to look toward where he might have been, at least a hundred feet away and thirty feet down. Why had the poor man run up there? *Ah yes*, he remembered the woman. The priest shook his head in wonder and dismay, though he was not without understanding. Still. If they had survived, he guessed, it would only be because the auditorium seats had created some kind of cushion from the blow, some kind of cramped cave for them. He shuddered. That was probably the best-case scenario—and the least likely. "We'll let the experts decide that when they come," the priest said after scrambling for an answer that wasn't exactly a lie but wasn't exactly the more horrible and likely truth. "Don't worry," he said.

"What about Max?" Ally asked, newly anxious. "Did he get out in time? He got out, didn't he?" she asked her sister, who shrugged, staring.

"It's going to be OK," the priest told her as cheerfully as

he could. He guessed, correctly, that if he could comfort the younger one, the older would follow. "Don't cry," he said again to her. "Tell me your name."

"I'm Tia," the older girl blurted out. "Concertina Velasquez. But no one calls me anything but Tia. She's Ally. What's yours?"

"Father Jon," he said.

She narrowed her eyes to slits. "We're not going to call you father anything." There was the briefest of pauses while she regarded him. "Our father is dead," she declared, as if challenging him to defy her tragedy.

"Jon then, if you'd like," the priest replied, trying to sound nonchalant. He was not an old man, but he was old enough to have been a young and impressionable social welfare counselor when AIDS hit the city like a battering ram. Those years exposed him to every manner of cruel and lingering pain, made him more fluent in reading the expressions of grieving than he honestly cared to be. Within the year, he guessed. Better to back off. Grief that new was still charged, ready to go off at any moment, and they had enough on their hands without having to crowd in further sadness.

"Her real name's Allegra," Tia interrupted his thoughts. "But everyone calls her Ally."

"Your parents must have loved music."

"My dad did," Tia said, pinning him with her eyes.

"This is Willie." He gestured to the nun, whose heavily made-up face was streaked with tears. "Sister Coco. Honey," he addressed her, "did you bring anything for your nerves?"

He remembered who was listening, their ears as wide as their eyes. "Just a little medicinal clonazepam," he explained to them. "It's something adults take for sleeping."

"How are we going to get out of here?" Tia demanded.

"We'll figure something out," the priest said soothingly. "It'll just take some thinking."

"You don't need to lie to her, and you don't need to lie to me." He studied her momentarily, wondering if there was an approach to her that wouldn't result in disdain. She was thin and narrow-chinned, and she would have had the strangely appealing good looks of a wild colt—all dark hair and wide eyes and sinewy power—had her expression not so easily collapsed into the sour. But his own exhaustion was weighing him down, and he didn't have the energy to imagine another way in.

"OK," he agreed wearily. "Let's just settle down. Make your sister as comfortable as we can."

"I will not settle down, and we can't make her comfortable." She looked as miserably compromised as her sister while watching the other girl in pain. "What about food? Water?"

"It will come," the priest said. "Listen . . ."

"I might have some food." A boy everyone had forgotten about and no one had noticed emerged from the shadows, tall and lanky. "Sorry," he said, seeing the priest startle. "I'm Phil," he added, fishing his backpack out from under the rubble. He had the giraffelike limbs and acne-scarred skin of someone in the final throes of adolescence. All this made him pitiable and strange, but also endearing. He wasn't handsome or particularly charismatic; he wasn't there because he'd been trying to save or help anyone; he'd just stuck around because the sister he'd escorted to rehearsal—Anna Louise, age thirteen—had made fun of him thirty minutes earlier in the lobby, when he'd said they should go back into the auditorium to see if the girl Ally who couldn't walk out on her own was OK. Anny Lou guessed aloud—and loudly—that his concern was driven by his *pathetic* lust for Tia, a girl who, his sister had heatedly and mercilessly pointed out, didn't even know he existed. Phil—who was as lovesick as they come and, like so many seventeen-year-olds before him, had actually convinced himself he could march blithely into and out of the front lines unscathed—denied his sister's truths and insisted that they needed help and he couldn't just walk away and that he'd be fine and that Anny Lou should just go home. It was only an earthquake, he told his disdainful and incredulous sister, and the building would have already fallen if it was going to.

So Anna Louise, sure the earth had shaken loose her brother's sanity, left in tears while Phil worked up the courage to race back into the auditorium, hoping to find some way to win the attention of a girl who had no desire to be noticed. Still, youth lent a disproportionate eagerness to his actions, and there was a certain charm in how he fished out half a package of gummy worms and two PowerBars and held them up over his head as triumphantly as a more reasonable person might a cache of jewels.

Tia remained studiously unimpressed, though the boy

kept his eyes on her face as hopefully as a stray dog looking for any hint of promise from the food source it had fixated upon. *Poor thing*, the priest thought, thanking his lucky stars that, despite his generally poor luck in life, at least he'd had the good sense never to have loved a woman.

~~~~~~~

16

As Gene made his way deeper into the city, he saw that those not also on the move had collected dutifully in clusters of need. Here, a man on the sidewalk with his wife and some concerned strangers standing around him; there, some dirty teenagers huddled outside an apartment where they had been squatting or toking or both, watching smoke pour from one of its windows as they might watch a movie screen. Waiting, no doubt, for help, for rescue—not quite sure why it hadn't already come. This is how people live in cities, emergency services their first thoughts in an emergency. Passing them, Gene battled a wave of hysteria worse than any so far. He was beginning to guess at a truth most of them would never have imagined: that there might not be any help coming.

There was only so much a state-of-the-art hospital or an underfunded fire department could do when the city's narrow, hilly streets were blocked by all manner of debris. And earthquakes weakened bridges, potentially limiting or even preventing access into the city from two of its three entry points. That third point—which was accessed primarily by the 101 and 280 freeways to the south—was in the area where Gene suspected the epicenter had been. Thinking of the spot on the 101 where he'd left his car, he knew no one would be able to pass through there. And with the wind and rain and cloud cover typical of such a bad winter, air and sea arrivals would be nearly impossible.

The terror was squeezing his throat, the full impact of what was coming dawning on him with brutal clarity. Because it wasn't even the seismic events themselves that truly frightened Gene. It was what the damage had no doubt ignited and the wind was spreading and the water would never reach that brought scenarios to mind Gene could hardly bear to imagine. The moment the earth began moving beneath them, he knew that gas lines and power cords would have snapped and sparked, igniting anything from the complicated tangles in multistory office buildings to faulty kitchen toasters and in-wall wiring not up to code. All this and more would have started fires in many of the thousands of buildings sandwiched in next to each other citywide, ready to share flames like whispered secrets between lovers. And the city's only defenses included a severely limited firefighting population, a statewide drought, and major water sources over the San Andreas Fault itself: early city planners had found "lakes" there and assumed they were the result of good fortune long before they were understood to be "sag ponds" created by the fault's earlier shifts. As far as fire was concerned, San Francisco was nothing more than an overpopulated tinderbox, a feast that took moments to prepare and could go on for hours or days. Possibly even weeks.

Fresh pinpricks of light pierced his vision, making Gene nearly stumble as he walked. How had he ever been able to bear this information clinically? How had any of his colleagues, or anyone else? Had everyone within shouting distance simply been laboring under a collective, contagious insanity? As the self-doubt swelled, Gene's deeper fears began climbing steadily to the surface. God, was this going to be the moment when he realized his father had been right? Was he nothing more than a talking head? But it was even worse than that. He hadn't just built his career on this house of cards; he'd built a home here, too.

Home. *Franklin. Oh God.* Again. Those words in his heart and on his lips were half-prayer, half-plea.

Every block revealed a new terrain of blown-out windows, streets as wet and shiny with glass as they would normally be with rain, crumbling buildings and disarray of every kind. Gene broke into a trot and then took the mess at a run, eager to be on the other side of it. Passing by the brick warehouses of the design district, Gene found himself in the midst of a shouldering, shoving crowd. He pushed through, desperate to escape. But pushing only got him jostled to the left toward a building that had crumbled, a cloud of dust still filling the air all around it. Gene was just steps away from the rubble when, like a circus performer with a gruesome act, a bald man with a copper-colored handlebar mustache emerged from the building's remains carrying a small, silver-haired man in a torn security uniform with an open gash on his left thigh. The cut was almost obscene, blood pouring from a part of the body too intimate to be exposed. Gene locked eyes with the rescuer, and as the space closed between them he heard the victim muttering incoherently in a language Gene didn't recognize. Then the old man was looking up and reaching out to him, reaching toward Gene as if he knew him, or expected him, or both. There was nothing Gene could do but receive his injured body and lower him to the ground.

The rescuer spoke only a few words to Gene, most of which he did not comprehend. He stared up at his moving mouth, noticing he had wax on the corners of his mustache. When the rescuer turned and went back into the collapsing building, Gene saw a star tattoo on the nape of his neck. What made a man do that? Take ink into his own skin and offer himself to strangers, just walk into a building that was more likely to fall on top of him and walk out with someone who was almost dead?

The older man was tugging at his pants. Gene bent down, trying to understand the man's hands as they gesticulated wildly, describing light circles in the air like two hysterical birds. He was speaking, too, a stream of words in a dialect of Chinese it wouldn't have done Gene any good to name. Still, the words spilled from his flat-lipped mouth. He had liver spots on his cheeks, the stubble on his jawline as coarse as the silver hair on his head was thin. *The man must be in his seventies*, Gene thought. *Maybe even eighties.* Gene couldn't blame the man for growing more and more frustrated, bleeding out in the care of a stranger who could only stare, dumbstruck, as the unmistakable urgency of your last words streamed out of you.

"Please," Gene begged. "I can't understand." But the man went on.

He must know some English, Gene thought, listening, *to work in security.* Though in San Francisco, with international investors of every kind in every kind of industry, maybe English wasn't much of a necessity. The man was slowing down, muttering. His hand now on Gene's wrist was delicately soft and defined, the bones protruding like sticks under the surface of mud.

What was he supposed to do? Franklin would know. While Gene's academic accomplishments might be impressive to some, when it came to people, Franklin was the real genius. Gene looked desperately around him, searching for someone to give him guidance, realizing as he did how much he lived every moment of his life with Franklin by his side, either in spirit or in mind; and at this, one of the worst moments of his life, certainly the worst since he'd known Franklin, Franklin was not there. Was this what life would be like if Franklin died? Or worse, when his illness progressed? While he was still alive, but no longer living the life he'd created for himself.

"Your best bet is a hospital." The mustached man was suddenly there again, another anonymous life in his arms. "Though he's pretty far gone." As he met Gene's gaze, his expression shifted into something darker and more truthful. "I could use the space," he added plainly, though Gene could see that it pained him to say so. The block was already choked with the dead and dying.

The man on the ground between them had closed his eyes. Gene pressed his fingers cautiously to the pale skin at his wrist, startled when the man lifted his hand and slapped

Gene's distractedly. Was this hope? Tentatively, Gene slid his arms beneath the man, collecting him, expecting him to cry out in objection or pain, but instead he seemed to relax in Gene's arms, as if he had been waiting to be carried.

"Where?" Gene asked as the mustache set a still body near them, wrapped neatly in a blanket, the clinical cocoon of it a horror all its own.

The man indicated with his chin the direction from which Gene had come. "SF General. Corner of Twenty-Second and Vermont."

Gene tried to thank him, but the man had turned around, wholly reabsorbed in his nightmare, quick to be rid of its minor characters.

SF General, Gene thought, turning back around dutifully. Twenty-Second and Vermont was south of there, on the border of Potrero Hill and the Mission. Which meant he had to turn away from home, away from Franklin. The man was bleeding heavily; a hospital was his only hope. Maybe Gene could find someone else to take him. Just go in that general direction for a few blocks, find someone, then run back to make up for lost time. He began to walk toward the hospital on stiff legs, even as his heart pleaded with him like a dog to follow the path home.

"No, no, no," the older man rasped furiously, squirming in Gene's arms. He reached out and grabbed Gene by the collar as he opened his eyes and locked a desperate gaze on him, his lids collapsed with wrinkles. He was older than Gene had first realized, perhaps even older than anyone he had ever held before.

"Stockton," the man insisted.

His face seemed to be losing more color as Gene looked into it, the amount of blood coming from the wound dumbfounding. Gene was already soaked in it, the lines between them quickly blurring, not only in blood, but in thought. Although Gene was the engine of their movement, he did not feel he was directing their path. He took a few more hesitant steps south, toward the hospital.

The man released his hold momentarily, stabbing the air over Gene's shoulder.

"Stockton. Sacramento."

Which one was it? "You need a hospital," Gene said, his voice swallowed by the multitude of indefinable, inescapable noises around them. They stared at each other with the intensity of love, though they were attached to each other by fear, a much more unforgiving bond.

"Please," the man begged him. "Go! Stockton!" He shook Gene's collar as he might a stubborn mule's lead. "Quick, quick!"

You need a hospital, Gene wanted to cry out. But the man was now clawing at him, trying to clasp his hand around his throat or chin or neck, his desperation escalating as quickly as the blood was draining out of him. "Go!"

Stockton. Sacramento. Stockton at Sacramento? Was there a hospital there he didn't know about? If there was, it was miles away, practically in Chinatown—no, definitely in Chinatown.

"Chinatown?" Gene wondered aloud.

The man released his hold, nodding or deflating or

sinking deeper toward death, but quiet again in Gene's arms. Maybe there was a hospital there. There must be, right in the middle of the city. Gene was tall and fairly strong, but he certainly couldn't keep walking if his load wrestled with him every step of the way. He stared down at the stilled form in his arms. The man's skin was growing waxy, his lips dry.

Gene turned around and quickly began heading north again, toward Chinatown and North Beach and Franklin, heading deeper into a city on the verge of falling to its knees, a half-dead man in his arms. As he did, a small pinprick of elation ignited inside him and his pace took on a new rhythm. There was nowhere safe to go, so they might as well go home. It was a relief to recognize at least one truth, and to head directly into it. He ducked his head and set his jaw and surged forward, as compelled and terrified as a man staring down new love.

〰〰〰〰

17

Ellen Santiago was already in hair and makeup when her boss, Silas Demetrious, KSRO station head and chief pot stirrer, stormed in, scattering interns and assistants as he walked.

"Where the hell have you been?" he barked. "I've been calling your cell for ten minutes."

"Right here," she replied evenly.

He grabbed an apple from a basket on a nearby table and bit into it viciously. "I'm putting you on anchor," he said, watching for her reaction.

She nodded professionally. Though they both knew this was the story she'd been praying for, the once-in-a-lifetime news event that would reach all the way to Sacramento and pluck her up and onto the national scene. All of a sudden, four years of reporting on small-town car thieves and local dog shows didn't seem quite so bad. "Where's Natalie?"

"MIA, apparently," he said brusquely. "You realize, don't you," he said, staring her down, "that we're closer than anyone on this thing, the first station with power between here and San Francisco, which means we've got a worldwide exclusive for the next few hours, maybe more." He narrowed his eyes, watching her closely to see if she'd betray the excitement he knew she must be feeling. Satisfied, he went on, "But we don't have much yet. You're going to have to be prepared to do some fluffing at first. No, no, no." He grabbed the makeup artist's hand as she reached for a lipstick. "This isn't *Entertainment Tonight*. Jesus, do I have to spell out *everything* around here?" He glanced at his watch. "You ready?"

"Of course." It was her job to be unflappable.

"Great. We're live in five."

〰〰〰

18

Max opened his eyes to blackness. Unseeing, he wondered if he was still alive. Could a person be dead without knowing it? Maybe. But he must be alive, because death couldn't possibly bring so much pain.

He moved his neck first, trying to turn it. The pain ripped up his ear and down his collarbone. He lay still. Without moving, he could tell that his right leg was in the worst shape; it was painful in a way everything else wasn't, a searing so acute it verged on numbness. He guessed that it was pinned above the kneecap by something that—his fingers stretched to feel—might be wood, dense, but with some give. His right arm was twisted under him and he itched to wrench it free, but wasn't sure he could move without injuring himself more or toppling whatever had fallen just short of crushing him. He could breathe, but the air felt thin, contaminated. As far as he could tell, which was very little—but every detail he could glean felt essential—a large section of balcony had fallen over them. The rows they'd ducked between must have stopped it from crushing them.

Them.

Had Vashti really been there? Was she there now?

Surely she had been; surely she was. But maybe he had hit his head, been hurt worse than he realized. He worried suddenly that he was in the midst of a cruel psychotic distortion, one he was too far gone to recognize. Perhaps he was already dead; perhaps this was not his birthday, but the day of his death. First there was his father, then Vashti, a cluster of unexpected visits from ghosts whose voices he had never expected to hear again.

"Vashti?" He barely heard his own voice. He swallowed the panic brimming in him, the urge to shout so powerful that it was a physical thing he had to battle, a wild creature thrashing against a foreign enclosure.

But if he screamed, no one would hear him. Anyone who could have helped had cleared out long before he'd come back inside the auditorium. His head began throbbing and he felt a new wave of panic as he recognized the agonizing wait that was before him. If only he could make everything just come crashing down and finish him at once. *If she hadn't struggled, she would have lived.* Typical. His father giving great advice for once, but at the worst possible moment. Max's anger flashed incongruously, forcing out fear. Typical of his father's timing to reach out to his mother now, unsettling her just before she headed into catastrophe.

His mother. He froze. *Please God*, he begged silently, knowing he had never been a religious man, but also knowing there was no one else to call, *protect her from at least some of this, shield her somehow. Please.* He closed his eyes again, trying to picture her safe and tended to up on that beautiful hill, an oasis in the middle of this hellish nightmare, sure to be surrounded by competent caretakers. She would be so disappointed his birthday was ruined.

But he could only hold on to the hope for an instant before it wriggled free. Panic spread through him again, even as he continued to fight it. Heat flew into his cheeks and head, drying his mouth and closing his throat.

There must be plenty of places in the city that were just fine. *After all*, he told himself, *it couldn't have been that bad, could it?* If there was any city to be in during an earthquake, it was San Francisco, without a doubt. Surely citywide preparations for just such an event were kicking into gear at that very moment. Of course there would be a way to get out. Rescuers. Holes. Possibilities. He closed his eyes, trying hard to imagine these things, as if imagining them could conjure them up. But he found an ocean of negative possibility lurking in the back of his mind, threatening to draw him in. He touched his toe to it. He had never thought of his own death, not really, and he wasn't sure he could bring himself to entertain the possibility of it now. Or rather, he did not think he could manage to think of dying there without going right ahead and stopping his own heart with the terror of it.

"Vashti?" he tried again.

He heard something stirring. *Oh God, please*, he prayed anew, but he couldn't land on the words that might soothe him. Words that would convince him she had survived. If she had been there in the first place.

Vashti wanted to answer, but she was still drifting in and out, trying to grab the line of his voice though it kept slipping away from her. It was shock or pain or both that had submerged her, and she did not want to crawl out from under the weighty blanket. But her hands didn't want her to go back to sleep; they were fidgeting or trembling so hard, they made her shoulders ache. She closed her eyes.

"Vashti?"

The panic began to climb again, and Max was seized by the frantic desire to know if she was there or not, alive or not. He felt around with everything he had available to him, using his free hand to snatch at the dark as if hunting for his last bit of food, the overwhelming fixation drowning out the jolt of pain in his neck and the shriek of warning reverberating through his head about shifting the rubble. But then, after an excruciating few minutes, his hand found its mark—his longer fingers could just reach her ankle. Gratefully, he rested them there, the pulse steady, the skin warm. He sobbed in relief and astonishment. He was about to speak to her again when he heard his name—whispered, but definitely there. "Max."

His stomach sank with delayed joy. Why had she come? On that day, of all days? Were people actually as unlucky as this?

"Max," she said again, as if about to say something else. But if she did, his straining ears didn't hear it. Still, a moment later, she stirred, a movement he felt only indirectly, but the thrill of it was electric. Suddenly, the urgency to find a way out caught up with him like a frightened beast, impossible to hold back. "Vashti," he said insistently, still working through the circuitous, illogical problem involving why she had come in the first place, "we have to . . . do you think . . . there must be a way . . ."

"How?"

Her voice was a memory in itself. He struggled against its pull, the urge to go back in time, even if that meant being haunted by memories he thought he'd put to rest. Even those who didn't love her thought it a lovely voice, he remembered noticing that, the way people turned toward it—bright but warm, melodic, the sort of voice that didn't need to be raised to draw attention. He closed his eyes, allowing himself to savor a few of his favorite memories of it: the way it sounded building to a laugh; the hundreds of times she'd lulled him to sleep with it, even when the prospect of dreaming was much less alluring than staying awake. The endless number of times he'd tried to get it to say his name again, the endless number of times it mocked him with a recording. *You have to stop calling her, Max*, a Vancouver-based Javi finally told him, taking pity on him when Vashti wouldn't return any of his messages. *I'll call her until she answers*, a belligerent Max had answered, speaking in a new voice of his own, one informed by the yawning ache of being without her for months. *Max*, Javi had said gently, so gently that the similarities between how she and her sister spoke pierced him, *she's not going to answer*. He raised his voice, beginning to take his anger out on her. *Max*, she'd interrupted him calmly, so calmly it froze his heart a split second before what she said did. *She doesn't want to hear from you. She's started a new life. She's married now, Max*. He thought he hadn't heard her correctly. He told her as much. She spoke to him as simply and plainly as she would to a child. *She married another man, Max. You have to let it go. You have to let her go.*

"Max?" Vashti brought him back to where they were. "How? How will we get out?"

"I don't know," he said, "but there's got to be a way. There must be a way." His mind sparked with renewed energy, leaping to sure thoughts of repair, revision, rescue. They wouldn't just lie there until they starved; they were in the middle of San Francisco, for God's sake—surely they would be found, even down here. Good shifts could be made. Someone might look for them. Someone *would* look for them, would look in a collapsed auditorium for survivors. Of course they would. And in the meantime, they might find a way out. Maybe in the morning. Yes! That was it. "Maybe in the morning, the light will get through. We'll be able to see more, see a way out. We can call or dig ourselves out or both."

She didn't answer. Then, "OK." But he could hear that she didn't believe him.

"Vashti," he said after a moment's painful hesitation, "why did you come here? And why today?" He was suddenly as confused and irritable as he was afraid. Why did she have to choose this day, of all days, to come, whatever the reasons might be?

Her voice, when it came, was very thin and soft, like old fabric. "I don't know, Max."

He tried to make sense of this. "You don't know." The sudden racing in his heart felt like anger again, though surely it wasn't. He had not been angry about Vashti in years. Surely his blood boiled as a way to make it flow, an excuse his mind was using to keep its body alive, a trick of survival. He was just afraid. And surprised. She was here, even though it was clear she should never have come.

If only he'd been more of a man, in the way people spoke of men. Strong, resilient. The sort of man who would have known what to do in an emergency, who wouldn't have had to run up and down stairs to take care of the simple problem of a little girl who was hurt—*God, please let* her *be out already, of all my broken prayers, please allow at least that one through*—the sort of man who didn't have to go looking for help when help was needed and run into the woman he'd once loved so much that he never quite wanted to love another woman again.

"You have to know. Why did you come? Why today?"

She was grateful to him for his insistence on this particular question. There were so many others he could ask. Still, she had no answer ready. She had come without an answer to *why*, the simplest of questions! Javi would have known why. If only she were there to explain to her sister, once again, why she'd done such a foolish thing. To explain why she'd ever done anything.

"It's your birthday," she tried.

"Yes. I have a birthday every year."

"I know. I'm sorry," she began. She was sorry. She heard her own voice as an echo. For what, exactly? The list of reasons for why she might be sorry was longer than either of them cared to recite. "I should never have come," she whispered. How had she been so clearheaded before? Was it only Javi's influence, her borrowed courage? She wondered when her sister would hear about the earthquake. Would she check the news? Would she call when she landed, then call again, worrying when no one picked up?

"I promised Javi," she tried again.

Max didn't trust himself to speak.

After all this time, she had come to see him on his birthday because she'd promised her sister. Was this nothing more than a joke? A memory of a similar outrage engulfed him, even though, had he been asked even the day before, he would have said it was long behind him. The heart was a pathetic muscle, never able to return to its original shape after a wound. Max shook himself back to the present. "You make it sound like it was some kind of dare. Your sister made you come."

She did. But a dare between sisters almost always flirts with a pact. Vashti could taste dirt in her mouth. She could hear her sister's voice. She suddenly remembered, the relief cooling, easing the confession.

"I came because of the dreams," she said, though that suddenly sounded hollow, too. Why? It was the truth, wasn't it? She closed her eyes and plunged further into it.

"I've been dreaming about you, Max. After Dale died, I started dreaming about you. Constantly. And the dreams won't stop." She hesitated, her voice breaking. "It's been six months, actually, almost exactly six months. Every night, another dream."

Max was silent. If he could have said what was in his heart, he would have said that he was wrong to have ever believed that people could just walk away from love, that they don't have to rip themselves away, taking the torn edges of the other person along with them.

"You came because of a dream?"

"No," she said, because he was only glimpsing the truth. "Many dreams."

She could hear him listening to her. Waiting for more.

"I know," she said, her words flailing, "it sounds crazy. It is crazy. I thought I shouldn't come, but then I couldn't stop the dreams, and then Javi started hounding me, but I wanted to come anyway, even if you—"

"No," he said quickly, the tone of her voice telling him what he wanted to hear. "I'm glad you came."

The unsaid things between them crept in from the edges, bloating the space into which they might have spoken. For several long minutes, they were both silent, not knowing if those unsaid things needed to be stated and expelled or brought along stoically, like so many limping soldiers.

For her part, Vashti understood that a love so deeply entrenched defied explanation, maybe even reason, but she was not immune to being frustrated by the way it left her dumb and baffled. She wanted desperately to speak but felt herself growing more and more untethered from words, grasping about for footholds that weren't there.

For his part, Max wanted to ask about the dreams. He wanted to know the details of them: what he had done and what she had done and why they had made her want to see him. And why she hadn't come before. If this was the first time she had wanted to see him, or if she had wanted that all along. He wanted to know why she hadn't just come the moment she returned to the city, instead of sending him those deadeningly polite e-mails. In a buried corner of his mind, he still wanted to know why she'd left at all, in the first place, midlove.

"There's no way we can care for her, Vashti, even if we both take on several jobs." He had knelt in front of her and taken her hands, which were resting as if in prayer on her knees, in his own. "We'd barely have any idea what to do with a child to begin with." He wiped the tears from her face, his thumbs like flat moons on her cheeks.

"No one ever knows what to do with a baby to begin with," she sobbed.

He waited, guilt and hope consuming his face. He let her cry, holding her hands still and looking into her face, and spoke again only after she showed signs of stopping, "We'll have another baby, Vash. Lots of other babies. This one was just never meant to be."

She nodded so he would look away, but instead he kissed her, because he thought that nod meant she understood or, at the very least, agreed.

Out in the rest of the auditorium, the air was thickly quiet, particles of dust floating around and vying for a place to rest, as if every atom of the world were holding its breath.

"Well," the priest said, "let's have another look at that leg."

He flicked on a miniature flashlight that Phil had found in his backpack. The light it spread was eerily bright, focusing in such a way as to emphasize the dark. The priest didn't have to see much, though, to confirm what he'd feared. The break needed to be set immediately, if they weren't already too late. He looked into the girl's anxious face, wondering how she'd found her way in there with only a testy older sister and no mother. How brave could he ask her to be?

"I don't want to go to the hospital," Ally said, feeling his stare.

But it was her sister who reached out and grabbed him by the shoulder, stopping him just short of touching the injury. Phil moved in as if caught in a gravitational orbit, watching Tia, his hands at his sides, palms open, ready to receive whatever fell his way. Tia took a moment, visibly reconsidering the priest who had approached her sister.

He was dressed as normally as the nun—obviously the sort of person who dressed in such a way that made it clear she was not interested in the opinions of children—was not: a navy sweater with a white collar, pleated gray trousers, and black shoes with black socks. He wore glasses, and the bald part of his skull shone in the gathering dark. Tia had never quite understood that expression before—gathering dark— but that was exactly what the dark was doing, creeping up and around them, maybe on its way to creeping through them.

"What's your name?" she asked suddenly. "Your real name. None of this father stuff." If he was going to hurt and help her sister, she wanted, at least, to be sure she could remember how to find him. After this, they all might scatter. It could be over very soon, like he said, people could come and lift all this up and away from them, like the top of a dollhouse coming free, and then this would just be a story, a bad memory.

"Jonathan," he said.

"And what kind of priest are you?"

"We are both fully professed members of the order of the Sisters of Perpetual Indulgence," he replied solemnly. "Friar Schmuck and Sister Cock-a-Doo-del-Doo, at your service."

"The what? Who?"

"Just call me Jon."

Tia frowned. She didn't understand, but it was only one of many things she didn't understand, and she couldn't find a way to begin to ask.

"I have to go to the bathroom," Ally looked up at her sister, too nervous to listen to anything but her own needs. "And I'm hungry. Am I wet?" she whispered.

"No," her sister said softly, kneeling down, "just cold."

Ally bit her lower lip, her jaw tight with fear. Her sister placed both her hands on her arm, as if in benediction.

"May I?" the priest asked, deflecting, his hands hovering over the leg.

Ally nodded.

Starting at the ankle, he pulled back the thin left pant leg from the horrible, sparkly pants she kept pulling out of the dirty laundry and trying to wear every day. Her favorite pants. Tia wondered what time it was. Late. Probably about the time when she was yelling at her sister to change into her pajamas already, or trying to help her clean up her funky-smelling room, find that stupid doll she was always losing. She stared openmouthed at what the priest had revealed: the long bone above the ankle jutting out where it should have been straight. How could that be? Her eyes were showing her too many things she just couldn't accept. How could she trust them?

"Ally," the priest said quietly. "I think we might have to set this. Do you know what that means?"

Ally shook her head.

"I do," her sister said, swallowing the bile that rose in her throat. "It means," she started brusquely, then faltered. "It means . . ."

"It means," said Phil, stepping in, "that he can fix it, but it will hurt first." He looked up at the priest, ignoring Tia's glare. "Right?"

Tia wanted to scream and push him away, close her eyes and open them again, confirm that this was all a nightmare. But instead she watched in horror as her sister nodded dutifully and the priest began to examine her leg as if it were a piece of meat, his small stranger's hands moving gently, quickly, over her sister's body, which was also her body—the rare sort of curiosity, another's body she knew as well as her own, the fact that it did not obviously belong to her just a technicality. Ally was watching, too, looking stunned.

"Are you also a doctor or something?" Tia spluttered, desperate to redirect his attention. What kind of training did they give a priest?

The priest looked up and smiled at her. "Actually, once upon a time, I used to be a nurse."

Good Lord, Tia thought. *Once upon a time?* "I think we should just wait for a doctor."

The priest didn't answer. He was focused on Ally, checking her eyes and pulse with fixed hands before moving to her leg, asking her the right questions as he rolled up her pant leg farther, checking her knee and foot and the surrounding areas for further damage.

"Are you going to need any help?" Phil asked, summoning his courage.

"Yes." The priest spoke gently, watching Tia stare down the boy. He tried to keep his voice as even as possible. "I might need your help steadying her."

"No," Tia said quickly, startling forward. "I don't think that's a good idea. You don't know what you're doing. You're not strong enough." Tia bit her lip even harder, tasting blood.

"I don't have to set it," he said, watching her. "We can wait for help."

She nodded, knowing he was just being kind. It had to be done. But everything in her did not want it to have to be done. Didn't that count for something?

The priest eased into her thoughts as gently as he could. "I'm afraid that if we wait much longer, it will need to be rebroken and reset, most likely involving a surgery of some kind. She's young, but it's a bad break."

"Rebreak it?" Ally said, her voice lifting.

"Yes," the priest answered, turning back to her, trying to balance both girls on his trust as evenly as he could.

"Won't it hurt?" Ally squeaked.

"Maybe," the priest said. He looked from one small face to the other, the resemblance between the sisters striking. The older one was much taller and clearly filling out, but they had the same narrow ovals for faces, the same triangular chins, the same wavy hair and black eyes rimmed with long, black lashes. "But it will also hurt more the longer we have to wait."

"How bad?" Ally asked.

"It'll be quick," he replied.

"OK, priest," Ally said. Tia took her hand with a steely grip, and Ally squeezed back, sensing that her sister needed comfort, too. Tia held on tight, trying to keep her frightened mind from flying up into the rafters and hurting itself.

"Good," he said. "It'll be over before you know it. And as soon as the phones work, we'll call the hospital and your mother, and we'll have you in a warm bed eating ice cream before you can say boo. Now here's what we'll need to do. You, boy. Phil. I'm sorry. Of course, Phil." He hadn't forgotten his name, but Phil lurked as only a boy will. "You'll need to hold her leg firmly here," he said, indicating an area over Ally's thigh, just above her knee.

Tia balked at the thought. "I can hold her leg." She steeled herself. "I can hold it," she said again, her voice coming out too loud.

"It's OK," Phil said. "Let me."

The priest put out a hand, holding it just in front of Tia's chest. "He's bigger," he explained. *And less likely to implode,* he thought, watching the older girl's eyes grow wider by the second. "The more weight to steady her, the better."

"It'll be quick," he said again to Ally. She looked him in the eye and nodded. Just like that, she handed over her trust. And just like that, Tia's began to waver again, tilting like a top about to go over.

She sucked in her lower lip as hard as she could to keep

her mouth shut. The boy Phil stepped delicately in front of her, forcing her to cede her spot. She moved quickly to Ally's other side and took her hand there. "You squeeze when it hurts," she demanded. Ally nodded, her eyes unblinking. Tia's bladder clenched right along with her stomach, the rising sting of anticipation unbearable.

The priest said a few more words to Phil that Tia couldn't hear and then, with one horrible, impressive effort, they yanked on her sister's leg like sailors pulling a rope, snapping the bone back into place. It was done before Ally could draw enough breath to scream, but still she did, so loudly she almost tore Tia's ear off and knocked her sister hard onto her back. Tia lay there, the wind flown out of her, her chest turning to iron. Staring up at the ceiling so far overhead and broken that even the loudest voice would get lost in it, she tried to inhale. Nothing.

Phil was suddenly at her side.

"Breathe," he demanded in a voice she hadn't heard before.

Tia gasped, staring at him uncomprehendingly, the air in her chest gone. Just gone. Her ribs closed in on themselves painfully. She couldn't even cry.

In one swift move, Phil grabbed her under the armpits and stood her up like a doll, shaking her until she pushed him out and away, gasping. But then her breathing came too quickly, like hiccups, and her head started to feel dizzy.

"No," Phil was saying, close by again, "slow down. Deep breaths. You're hyperventilating." He put his hand on his own chest to show her. "Like this. In and out."

She tried to do as he said.

Phil reached out and took her hand, putting it over his so she could feel him breathing. Instead she felt his heart beating, the thicket of movement under his rib cage. She left her hand there and didn't blink.

"Everything OK over there?" the priest asked loudly.

Phil broke abruptly away and stood back, his arms limp at his sides. "I was getting her to," he said, hesitating, "she wasn't . . . "

"I wasn't breathing," Tia stuttered, her lungs and mind releasing the last of their rigid grip on each other. *He saved me*, she told herself. A moment later, after Ally started to talk again and Phil peered down at the leg proprietarily, she said it to herself again, experimentally, as if she wasn't quite sure what it meant. *That boy, Phil, saved me.*

~~~~~~~

19

The man was dying in his arms. Gene knew it, even though he was still fighting for him, walking as fast as he could. He had only ever held someone for love or its approximations, and the feeling of lightness, the loss of density, like a balloon filling toward flight, was unmistakable. It seemed to seep into him, as though toying with him, a force that could easily sweep him off his feet if it chose to. He tried to focus away from the aches in his shoulders and wrists that were building past pain and on to something else: a path, a plan. He forced himself to pick up his pace, even as his feet threatened to go out from under him.

The quickest way north would have been to take Eighth to Market, where he could head through the Tenderloin toward Chinatown. But the entrance to Eighth was blocked by the runoff of people and bricks and glass from the Zynga building, and Seventh was crisscrossed with downed power lines, so that Gene was two blocks down Townsend before he could make a left on Sixth, two blocks down the street that had been named for the town's end, back before the city had spread like an inkblot all around itself. Before now, he had never looked at a tall building as anything but a fixture; with so many of them tilting in the softened earth like gravestones in a muddy cemetery, he wondered how they had ever come to be solid in the first place. All around him, the city was shifting before his eyes. Part of him still wished that this unfamiliar version of his world could shift again, this time in his favor, the way it might in a story—a portal opening up that he could walk through and find himself home. For the first time since he'd moved to the city almost a decade ago, he felt the sickening certainty of true loss settling in his belly.

"You live in an inn?"

"I own it."

"But you live here, too?"

"Upstairs. I can show you if you'd like."

Gene would like that, though he hesitated on the door-step. Where he came from, an inn was a concrete block in "downtown" Stilwell with its name in neon lights on a post in the parking lot, a place for those unfortunate folks who passed through the rural suburbs of Wichita without any family to stay with.

Gene caressed the beautiful door in the entryway, glossy chestnut with the kind of heavy brass knocker he'd seen only in pictures. This one also had three diamond-paned windows, the cut glass in them blue and purple and green, cobalt and violet and jade. Gene was saturated with color, standing inside a doorway while a beautiful older man he'd just met invited him to step farther inside. He'd never seen anything so lovely, much less touched it. And he did not know if it would all fall apart if he got any closer, if disappointment would take him out of this pool where he was splashing around in wave after wave of unfamiliar beauty.

"Is the whole city this beautiful?" he asked Franklin,

standing on the other side of the threshold Gene wasn't quite sure was real enough to cross. The past month, his first in California, had been so full of wonders that he couldn't decide if he'd arrived in paradise or was beginning to lose his mind. He and his fellow graduate students had left Berkeley for San Francisco every weekend since their first, a new party or parties seemingly awaiting them as soon as they arrived. He wondered if life really could be like this, and part of him didn't think it could. The part that was waiting on the doorstep, afraid to take another step for fear the illusion would be broken.

"Fresh off the boat, are we?" Franklin murmured, reaching out to cup Gene's chin, a move so gently intimate, Gene felt it to his core. He blushed. Or so Franklin said he had. He liked to tell the story as if he were the wolf, Gene the lamb who came walking innocently into his path. For the longest time, Gene had been defensive about Franklin's side of their story. It had been important for him to think that, as the only Kansan in Berkeley's famed geology program, he wasn't as green as people suspected he was.

The man in his arms stirred, muttering. Gene had slowed without realizing it, the rhythm of the man's diminishing pulse creeping in on him unaware. He glanced down again into the man's fading face, each peek harder to take than the last. But why was he so anxious to see what he knew was coming? He would have thought that death's certainty would have been at least a little comforting the closer it got, that resignation would ease the fear of the unknown. The weight of the man in his arms was the only thing solid about him. Gene thought of his mother, how many people she'd shepherded toward death. She would know what to do. If there was a chance at saving this man, she would have already recognized and taken it.

Had he missed something he should have taken from her? Had he never learned something he was supposed to know? Now that he loved someone who would need a level of care he'd never given, he feared he had. How sick Franklin was, really, was anyone's guess, but they both knew that the last stages of his illness, when they inevitably came, would be debilitating. The doctors reassured them both, but on the fringes of their lucky lives, Gene and Franklin had seen the untucked edges of friends whose partners were dying or had died of AIDS or cancer or old age—the things that, toward the end, they didn't have the energy or desire to hide from polite company. Franklin's doctors had mentioned none of that, though that didn't mean it wasn't coming. Gene hated modern doctors with their ability to diagnose so smugly, even when they knew they couldn't heal. As if knowing were the entire battle.

Was a geologist any better, though? Even now, he wanted so desperately to be able to offer something of himself for sure, to call this battle as a general might instead of limping through it like an injured foot soldier.

He readjusted the weight of the man to take some of the pressure off his back. Maybe he should ask for help. But help with what, exactly? And from whom? The others out and about in the black, broken night looked just as vulnerable and animalistic, as if the earthquake had shaken the civility out of them, leaving their unguarded selves exposed. None of them walked or strolled; they'd devolved into a hodgepodge of skittering and plowing and limping, avoiding or obsessing over one another, many with a desperate, open-eyed stare that suggested their rational minds had driven them to project their thoughts elsewhere. He wanted to run, to race toward Franklin, but he couldn't release his load.

He looked up at the nearest street sign, surprised that he'd made it only to Howard. Usually he knew where he was and how fast he was going, and when he would get there and why. But being somewhere was suddenly unraveling into being everywhere, as if someone had shaken up the familiar parts of San Francisco in Gene's mind like a kaleidoscope, so they landed in upended fragments. And not knowing *where* he was felt too much like not knowing *what* he was. He knew that his work had been like the earth itself, stable and life-affirming, something he could stand on. But without the mantle of professionalism, he felt thinned, transparent, all too easily brushed aside. He had allowed his work to define him and, like any good devotee, he was spectacular when cast in its light, lost once he stepped away.

Franklin used to chastise him. "You're too pretty to have so much self-doubt," he'd scold. Gene couldn't explain to him why such a statement was exactly the sort of thing that made him feel even more dispensable. In Franklin's world, beauty trumped all. Gene so wanted to believe in that world, to inhabit it. But he had been raised differently.

"It's so yesterday's news, though," Franklin once complained, "to be a homosexual riddled with self-doubt! Especially in San Francisco. Gene," he scolded, "it's simply déclassé."

It was. And it wasn't that Gene doubted himself, really—it was just that he was unaccustomed to hoping he had anything more than usefulness to offer. He met Franklin when he was still so young, barely in his twenties, that he confessed on one of their early dates that San Francisco felt to him for all the world like Pleasure Island in *Pinocchio*, the place where mischievous boys went blindly to indulge their bliss, only to be turned into donkeys after an afternoon of candy and ribaldry. Franklin, comfortably into his forties and well into his third decade as a San Franciscan, had laughed aloud, his ridicule both stinging and comforting Gene, like the laugh of an older brother who's already discovered that the monsters under the bed are stuffed toys.

The man in his arms groaned again, straining against him, babbling nonsensically. Gene's arm slipped and he had to set the man down, not bothering to check more than his pulse. He appeared senseless to the fact that he was no longer being carried, no longer going in the direction he'd so eagerly demanded.

It was cold and dark now, the streets emptying. Those who remained were scuttling or running or calling out for cover. Gene shivered, a primal need to be inside raising the hair on his arms. Would it matter if he left the man where he'd laid him? Gene studied him, acutely aware that he was waiting for him to die even as he couldn't shake the sensation that the man still deserved someone to hope for him. Gene placed a protective hand on the man's side, surprised by the comfort it lent him in return. He didn't even know this person. Who had he been, and did it matter now? Gene wasn't sure. He wasn't even sure if who he had been was gone yet. He was surprised that he had to watch so carefully for the end; he would have expected that a man's final breath would be as obvious as his first. But there wasn't a clear definition between the body's last moments of life and the early hours of death.

He wondered if his own family would hear about what was going on and think of him. His mother's aunt was the only one who'd bothered to keep in touch with him, but her e-mails were nothing but chatter about her dogs or doctors' visits; nothing she ever mentioned represented an attempt to truly attach herself to him. He heard sirens again in the distance, nothing close. Shivering, he tucked his arms in at his sides, and he wondered how long it would be until he was warm again.

A dusty memory shook itself off and rose to the occasion.

"I'm doing this for your own good."

His father stood like a reed in water, their kitchen looking like it always did on any other day, right down to the usual accessories: his mother's dish towels and a box of Wheaties on the counter. It was messier than usual, maybe, but still bizarrely familiar, given that fear—that leaking, odorless gas—was seeping into the room and making it difficult to breathe.

It was the end of his third-grade year. A lot of boys he knew were still doing childish things, though he couldn't tell his father this. He couldn't speak at all, his tongue as thick and clumsy as his heartbeat was fast. But he knew for a fact that Edwin still slept with a stuffed bear, and that Sam's bedroom still had one of those blue blankets with red trains on it and a matching rug: the sort of things Gene wouldn't have been caught dead with if someone came over. But all he could do was stand in the doorway and watch as his father wiped down the kitchen counters, setting his jaw and fighting against the tears Gene knew would only strengthen his father's resolve.

"It's for your own good," his father repeated, his expression grim but determined, the expression of a good father delivering a tough punishment. Even then, Gene was confused as to whether or not his father believed that what he was saying and doing was good. Gene was too young to know the difference himself, yes. But he also sensed that his father's rigidity meant there was something absent somewhere, in judgment or love.

The day before, his mother's bed—for that was how he thought of it—released her scent when he leaned into it, watching her pack. He toyed with the embroidered bumps on the bedspread, the worn spaces in between so thin and soft, he was sure they might wear away completely one day under his touch.

"It's only for a few days, Gene," his mother said, frowning into her suitcase, tucking things in that hadn't anything to do with him. She gestured for him to pass her the belt that lay by his hand, then a sweater and slacks that she refolded and packed after he passed them to her, all the while watching the deep downward lines near her mouth and hoping desperately for something to happen that would make her stay. She put a hand on his head, kissing him. She wasn't a cupcake mother, he reminded himself. She was an emergency fund-raising mother, a task no other mother wanted that everyone was grateful she took on; an emergency nurse mother, even if it meant working the night shift at Comanche General, or taking double or triple shifts when the staff didn't show or were otherwise light, which was often. Sometimes he imagined his mother at work as the captain of a ship on a lonely ocean, standing at the helm come any weather or mutiny, probably able to steer the entire vessel herself should it come to that. He loved her for it, but he also wished she spent a little more of her life on land.

A few hours after she left, when Gene thought he was busy in the garage, his father had walked in on him again. It had been months, and the sting from his father's rage the last time he'd caught Gene had healed and faded. Or maybe the seduction of joy had muted the likelihood of threat, like music played during wartime.

But his father had not forgotten, and he felt disobeyed. Maybe even betrayed. Maybe he truly thought that by shouting enough insults and grabbing Gene by his collar and growling hateful words into his face—every physical intimidation short of actually hitting him—he could shake Gene's undeniable instincts out of him. He didn't understand that Gene's fascination with his mother's clothes came from a place that anger couldn't access, from a deep, private euphoria his father couldn't touch or even try to understand. Or maybe he did. Maybe he also wanted to be close to Gene's mother when she was gone, felt lost without her. Maybe his father had joys, too, that he couldn't bear.

After a dinner heavy with suppressed rage, Gene hadn't slept much. He woke to his father's rifling through his drawers and closet, the muscles on his forearms taut. After he threw all of Gene's clothes onto the floor, he checked under his mattress, lifting it and Gene together so the boy had to hold on to its sides like someone on a capsizing rowboat. Gene was desperate for air, not knowing where his voice had gone or even what to say, sure that this horrible thing between them was nothing he could make better, and that one or both of them would have to be sacrificed to appease it. All of a sudden, dropping the mattress and turning on his heel, his father strode down the hallway toward his own room. After a while he was quiet in there, and Gene hoped it was over. But when he came out a few minutes later, he had a small blue dress balled up in his knobby-fingered hands, a dress from a hand-me-down collection his mother had kept of her own things when she was a girl. Gene trotted out to him like a boy on a fishing line, not wanting the hook to tear his mouth but unable to pull away. His father thrust the dress between them, staring down at it until Gene did, too, his final punishment sinking in.

His father broke his gaze and scrubbed at the stove with a paper towel that was tearing into pieces under his hand.

"You'll miss your bus."

Gene didn't move. He was waiting. To be brought back, to be drawn back into the realm of fairness and safety. To be forgiven. For what, exactly, he still didn't know, but he didn't care.

"If I have to drive you, I'll be late."

Gene didn't move.

"It's for your own good, Eugene."

There it was again, that refrain that meant anything else said would be insignificant.

Gene clenched his fists so his nails hurt the insides of his hands. If it was so good for him, why did he know his father would never do this if his mother were home? If it was so good for him, why were his father's eyes avoiding his? Gene put a hand on his stomach as it clenched in protest. But the fabric under his palm reminded him: soft and smooth, draping over his narrow chest and long legs like a habit or a robe.

He creaked open the screen door and ventured out, keeping his eyes down, the tears streaming without sound. Maybe he'd be out of them before he got to the bus. Maybe he just wouldn't be able to cry, sooner or later.

Later, when the fifth graders stopped laughing and pulled him aside and administered the requisite beating for the twin crimes of being different and homosexual—a beating he had been honestly grateful for, after all that tension of waiting for it—he came home with the bruises his father had wanted to see, the ones he probably didn't have the courage to give Gene himself. Only then did his father pull the dress gently over his son's head and blink into his face as he surveyed the dirty work of others, satisfied and relaxed again as he bandaged the cut over Gene's eye and pulled a bag of frozen peas out of the refrigerator for Gene to put over the swelling on his cheek. As he did, the ice like salve on Gene's skin, his father turned around, wadded up the dress, and threw it into the garbage.

"Enough of that, then," he declared, his hand on Gene's shoulder, squeezing it firmly in the way you might clench a heart long enough to make sure it was done beating. Then he made them a dinner of eggs and toast and set up two TV trays in front of *Wheel of Fortune*, and together they watched the primary colors spin and spin and the people clap and clap, and before long it was time for bed. Gene crawled under his blankets and stared up at the forever dusty and dancing circus of animals along the border of his walls, wondering why he was surrounded by images of places that didn't exist.

~~~~~~

20

Max stared unblinking into the dark, wondering if he was beginning to see shapes in the things surrounding him or if his mind were already playing tricks on him. He shifted to relieve the spine-tingling ache of being in one place, but it only lit the pain in his leg on fire. He wanted to call out to Vashti, to say anything and everything to her, but if she was sleeping he didn't want to wake her. He tried to refocus, but what was there to focus on? He thought of his mother, the touchstone he'd depended on for years. Would she wonder if he was alive, or would she think he'd died and left her? The silence was so absolute, it choked him. Even if no one could possibly hear them, it suddenly occurred to him, shouldn't they scream for help anyway? He began to fill his lungs, then stopped himself. No, better to save air, wait until they heard something. As hard as he strained his ears, he could hear nothing but the sound of his own breathing.

He tried again to tell himself that it couldn't possibly be all that bad outside. The possibility of San Francisco's being unable to overcome a natural disaster quickly and expediently seemed as unlikely as an alien invasion. Surely they would be rescued; surely most of the city had fared well. After all, twenty-first-century American cities didn't just go down overnight. This total silence spoke to plans in the making, plenty of foresight about this exact situation. He read about it all the time in the paper, all the retrofitting and seismic technologies and emergency protocols. Heck, every water heater installed in the city came with elaborate instructions in case of an earthquake. People would be turning off the gas and pulling out their earthquake kits and waiting in safe areas for help.

But lying there and listening closely to the relentless silence, he felt a kick to the stomach.

What had been in his own earthquake kit? A few flashlights, some emergency water and food, bandages and gauze. Standard supplies sold as a package at Walgreens. Sold and then tucked away in the back of storage closets, forgotten in overcrowded garages.

"Max?" Vashti finally spoke out into the silence. She was awake! It struck him that even after all that had passed between them, even in the horror of their current situation, it thrilled him that she was nearby. He wondered if couples who'd never lost each other felt the same way. He waited for her to continue, but she was quiet again. He had almost started to drift off when she murmured something so softly he had to strain to hear her. "You do know why I'm here, don't you."

It was less a question than a statement. A statement of affection and longing, the music in her voice sad and true, the very essence of a beautiful sound. Slowly, ignoring the searing protests of his collarbone, Max crept his hand a little farther so he could wrap his palm around her ankle, his thumb fitting perfectly into the hollow beneath the bone, transporting him instantly to another place and time when she used to undress in front of him.

She was shy at first—they were both so young—but then they discovered sex, and the exquisite details of its rituals. She'd always begin with her shirt and end with her hair. In between, she unzipped her skirt and slipped it off, or wriggled out of her jeans—he hated to see her stuff herself into them. Some women's bodies, like hers, even when she was newly a woman, were not meant for jeans. After her top and pants were off, she'd look at him and draw the things closest to her skin away from it, folding them as carefully as she did all her other clothes, and then her eyes would lock on his as she pulled out whatever she'd wound or clipped or knotted her hair into. She'd just be reaching up to push the hair that fell in her face back when he'd close the nominal distance between them.

"You must know," she insisted, her voice so hushed it came to him as tenderly as a kiss.

He didn't answer right away. "Tell me about her," he said after a moment, closing his eyes. "Tell me what Anita was like." He had never said her name aloud, and the feel of his daughter's name in his mouth was like the opposite of a trumpet's blare; a taking in of air, a collapsing of sound so essential, it could only resonate internally.

"I didn't want to come." The tears choked her as she tried to speak through them. "I tried not to. I thought that if I tried hard enough, I could just . . ."

"Please," he whispered. He could not have said for sure what day or time it was, wondering about tricks of the heart and death. "I want to know."

"Sick," Vashti said after she'd collected herself, unspooling information as carefully as she might dismantle a bomb, letting each utterance settle in before she tested the volatility of the next, because truth has a volatility all its own, especially when it is spoken aloud for the first time. "She was sick all the time, right from the start. I had no idea what sickness was before her. I mean, my mom was sick, but I was so young. I didn't see her, they kept me away when"—here Vashti hesitated—"when they knew she was dying, I guess.

"Anyway, I had no idea what being sick like that would be like, what dying would be like. I thought it would be like in a movie or a story, where the mother gives up everything to care for her daughter and it's rough but it ends eventually, and everyone's better for it. I really did think that, Max. Because I only knew about the kind of sickness that has *life* on the other side of it, you know? And she wasn't that kind of sick. She was the kind of sick that, even when she was alive, she was always closer to death than life. Before her, I would never have imagined that babies can suffer like that. At first I thought that maybe if she at least recognized me or smiled, it would be enough. But then she started to do those things, and it just made everything else worse, because she spent most of her life not recognizing me and not smiling. The nurses said I was a good mother. Maybe they believed that. But I was the reason we kept trying, and the longer she lived, the worse it got. More surgeries and stents and medications than anyone should have to deal with, much less an infant, or a toddler. But those surgeries were like a drug to us! *Just one more*, we'd say. *This will be the last one. The one that turns it all around.* I started to wonder, after I learned to love her a little better, if I'd just been selfish. She'd never asked for life, not really. I don't know why it was so important to me that she have one." Vashti's voice threatened to drift into nothingness. "I used to wish that a mother could bring about the end of her child's life with as much love as she began it."

As quick as relief, a sudden image came to Max's mind of a baby with a head covered in black curls, though Vashti was thinking of a girl with pale eyelashes and light brown eyes that shone amber in the light.

"She reminded me of you," Vashti said. He could hear the tears she was holding back as she continued. "All the time. It felt like all I had to do to bring you close to me was touch her face, but it never worked. She had the most beautiful face. Like one of those babies you see painted on the ceilings of churches: round, with that thin, pale skin and freckles. I always had to cover her from head to foot whenever we went outside."

He closed his eyes to remember Vashti's face as he'd just seen it, to remember that her hair had come undone and her eyes were older. It seemed important that he see her as she was now. Wasn't that what remembering was for? A revision of someone or something that once belonged to you, a portion of your life reconceived?

He heard sirens as if they were coming from another world, traveling faraway roads that would never reach them. The bomb had been dismantled, but it proved itself to have been laid in a field of great vulnerability and was now openly exposed, the parts that might create a blessedly quick oblivion now rendered ineffectual. There was peace, but there was also powerlessness.

"It was a terrible thing you did," Max said after an indeterminable amount of time.

"I know."

"It was cruel," he added.

"Yes."

He waited for her to understand that he had more to say and not to interrupt, to hand the story over to him instead, to stop clenching it with such propriety. He imagined her staring up into the dark, trying to control her breathing as well, and he wanted to know how badly she was hurt; though he also didn't want to know, he just wanted to be with her, to focus on the conversation between them, even if it was fraught with old pain and neglected possibilities.

"I might have understood better if you hadn't run away. But you left me with all these extremes, Vashti. Terrible love and terrible anger. Nothing soft to just wash you away with. I've wondered sometimes," he said, "if it was your way of forcing me to keep you. When you wouldn't let yourself stay."

"No," she said. "I wanted you to let me go."

"Not something I do well," he said. "You know that. You knew that." He was no longer angry. He did not know if he was supposed to forgive her, but he did know now that she'd come to him because he was still in her heart, and that meant as much as he'd suspected it would.

"I don't know what to tell you, Max," she'd said the day before she left. They were standing on the smaller bridge over Stow Lake, a place they'd once loved because it allowed them to be outside and mostly alone. In the early autumn light,

Max stood apart from her, watching her weep. By that point, she'd had nothing to give to him but sadness, and it was of small comfort that he felt bitterly glad about that.

"How is that possible? How can you go without knowing why?"

"It's not that I don't know." She just couldn't tell him in a way that could make him understand. She wasn't even sure she understood herself. Nothing that had happened recently made the kind of sense she could form into an understanding. It was month after month of indigestible news—first the pregnancy, then her father's reaction (unmitigated shame) and Max's mother's (mitigated shame), then the terrible news about the baby, then Max's trying suddenly to become the man his mother and her father insisted he couldn't be, and Vashti's becoming in the process a person who doubted the boy she loved. It was as if time itself were warped, looping in and over itself, refusing to resolve into any kind of bearable vision of the future. She felt beaten by it.

Eventually, her thinking and heart became bruised beyond recognition, unable to repair themselves properly. After a while, all she could do was bring her hands to her belly and know that time was indeed passing, despite the nightmarish evidence to the contrary; that time would bring them and their baby out of this. And all she knew, after a while, was that Max did not want to believe what she needed him to believe, what she needed to believe herself—which was that the baby, their baby, the one growing in her despite all the chaos and upheaval around them, could astonish them even further by living. Not just for a few hours, as the doctors grimly predicted, but live and grow up and become a real person, live to convince more than only her mother that she wasn't merely a narrow probability. This belief began to separate Vashti from those surrounding her, singling her out as a zealot because everyone else had lost faith. But Vashti didn't just believe; she was angry. They'd named Anita's defect before they named her: *spina bifida myelomeningocele*, an unpronounceable horror. Even as she grew inside her mother, all anyone wanted to talk about was what would keep her from surviving.

"If the doctors say she won't live," her father had said with his usual weighted resignation, "she won't live. Do you not understand this?"

"Doctors aren't always right."

"Neither are mothers, believe it or not." He rubbed his palm over his face. "You will be left with nothing but a broken heart." Vashti had kept her mouth closed and her head down, silence the most powerful tool in their household of broken communications and deep ties. She could feel him studying her face. "You can forgive me for wanting to make a plan for you?" *Us*, she thought, *make a plan for us*, but she only nodded.

They were sitting at her father's small kitchen table, the same one on which she'd served countless meals to him, all of them eaten in her father's manner: methodically, attentively, with a quiet pleasure in his daughter's work that bordered on mournful, an inexplicable emotion that never failed to make her want the next meal to be even better, as if it might edge out that tiny kernel of pain in both of them that interrupted the natural flow of their love. He watched over Javi in the store the same way, more so when she was too young to work there but did anyway, and then again just before she left, bookends of affection though he'd been unable to read much in between.

"And this boy, this Max." Her father always hesitated over Max's name, as if its very pronunciation mystified him. He had a similar reaction the few times no one could stop their paths from crossing: cordially stupefied, as if baffled to find that the boy was truly real, a boy he seemed to be expecting to disappear. Not because he disliked him, but because he saw no place for him in the daughter he saw as Jewish first, Persian second, and his above all. It did not matter to him that his religious loyalty was ingrained rather than expressed, and that he no longer had anyone in Iran he kept in touch with; his heritage was as much of a fact of life as life itself. No one—especially not Vashti or Javi—had the heart to break it to him that his daughters' lives of curiosity and humor and ambition were nothing like the quiet, similarly sorrowful, duty-bound daughters he felt he was parenting, if only by example. Still, he'd taken the news of Vashti's pregnancy surprisingly well, albeit unsurprised that his life's terrible luck could only get worse.

"This boy will have to go, yes?" He locked eyes with her as the full impact of what he was saying dawned deep within her, his gaze never wavering, reminding her that they had ridden through heartbreak together before, that he could witness hers and would not look away, that if she allowed him to care for her, she would have to accept his way of caring, too. "I have an idea." He put his hand over hers. "I have someone in mind." Vashti bit her lip, afraid that if she spoke she would lose her grasp on the first, timely answer to her prayers, unsettling as it was.

Dale was a longtime customer whom she probably wouldn't recognize outside her father's store, but who had been talking emptily about things like "sharing his wealth" and the "loneliness of overabundance" for far too long, and had found it hard to keep from noticing her. The marriage had, for all intents and purposes, been arranged. "Perhaps a practical marriage is the best marriage of all," her father said, the sadness he felt over his own ill-fated choice sinking deep within her like a swallowed hook.

Indeed, Dale had offered to do everything he could—which was far more than most people could even imagine doing—with such warm generosity that she believed she might eventually begin to appreciate the marriage, not just the man who was offering it. He'd been careful to say that he did not believe the baby would live long, but at the same time he'd serenaded her with talk of doctors and developments and technologies, of science's triumphs over probability, of man stepping in to take over where God seemed to have left off.

And in all the despair and confusion, Dale was astute enough to recognize that one note continued to rise clearly above all the others, which was that Vashti believed there was a way to help her unborn and imperfect baby live, despite the fact that almost everyone did not think she would, and she would not—could not—listen to anyone who believed differently. Especially not Max, who thought that it would be best to move forward as if the baby had never existed in the first place, to follow the doctor's implied advice and abort. That conviction was horrible enough, Vashti contended, without it coming from the very person whose support she most craved. Their separate arguments didn't really matter, though, toward the end. After a while, they were no longer discussing anything of substance. They were just hurting each other enough so she could walk away.

The younger girl was crying again. Her sister watched her, as actively distressed as a dog witnessing another's injury, unable to do anything but bark or whine in response. "What?" Tia demanded. "Is it hurting? Are you hurting again? You said it wouldn't hurt after." She glared at the priest, her chest a vise.

As if he could control grief. As if the girl might be crying only about her pain. Oh, to be young and willfully in denial, to have that work for him again.

"It's not my leg," Ally said between sobs. "It's Max. We forgot about Max! He's been up there all this time!"

Max. Max? Her sister tried to place the name she knew. "Oh my God," she said aloud. "She's right. We forgot about Max." She said the words slowly, as though she couldn't quite believe them.

The priest sighed. He hadn't forgotten the man and woman under the debris, he'd just chosen not to remind himself of them.

"He's dead, isn't he?" Tia asked, not as softly as she thought. Her sister gasped, ready to sob again.

"No," the priest said quickly, desperate to avoid another breakdown. How to deflect from certainty to possibility? "We don't know that."

Tia studied him as if trying to decide whether she was going to believe him. Though the priest sensed that what he had said was almost irrelevant. It was his character that was on the line; Tia looked like she was trying to decide if she was going to believe in him, too. Pulling her lower lip in with her teeth, she grimaced and squatted beside her sister. "He's right," she added with surprising gentleness. "He might have gotten out."

"He didn't," Ally insisted, not so easily swayed, "he couldn't have. He's dead. He has to be."

"No," the priest said, unexpectedly buoyed by the older girl's confidence. He went to her sister's other side, "he doesn't have to be dead, does he?" He smiled sadly. "Who knows what a person can survive? Now take a deep breath and relax," he said, placing his hand gently on the uneasy rib cage, "or we'll need Phil to save you, too." But he, too, couldn't help but listen to the terrible stillness above them.

~~~~~

21

The first interview was going even better than Ellen had hoped. On a whim, the ever-resourceful Silas had snagged a city-planning expert who'd worked in San Francisco—drier than toast on any other day, but Si had a hunch he'd work an angle none of the other networks would have thought of, and that his plain, all-American looks would bring it home. And so far, Si had been spot on, not that Ellen couldn't take credit for steering the man away from too much technical speak and into the good stuff, the stuff people could understand.

Then he suddenly veered too close to being reassuring, to skirting the real picture. She understood why, of course: he was used to smoothing things over—it was an occupational hazard, just as hers was to rile things up. She'd have to nudge him in the direction of the story they needed.

"But seismic building codes are really quite sophisticated in the San Francisco Bay Area," he was saying. "Anything that went up in the last few decades has an excellent chance of weathering even temblors of this size."

"But what about all the other buildings?"

"You're right to ask, Ellen." His hair had been parted on the side and combed smooth. *What a nerd*, she thought, not unsympathetically. "Unfortunately, the majority of buildings in San Francisco were built before these technological advances were available."

Bingo. "Was any retrofitting done on those structures?"

The poor guy had been made up to look brighter than he felt, but the lights and conversation were wearing on him, a fine sheen of sweat beginning to stand out on his forehead. "Well, that would be up to the owners. Retrofitting is quite expensive, and many of the buildings that need it most, what we call 'soft story' buildings, especially those on landfill, are owned by landlords or homeowners who don't have the financial means or inclination to make improvements."

"Soft story on landfill?"

He thought for a minute, knowing he didn't have much time to explain a pet topic. "Imagine, if you will, a sandbox. If you fill it with water, smooth the wet sand, and leave it to dry, you can probably place a board across it and—temporarily—place any manner of objects on top of that board. But the sand still remains underneath, no matter how much that board might look like solid ground.

"Now imagine you put two boxes stacked on top of each other on top of that board. That's our two-story house. But in many areas of San Francisco, the bottom level of that house is poorly supported, usually because it's a garage with only three walls, really. When the soil moves underneath, and the structure moves accordingly, the chances are unfortunately excellent that that first, 'soft' story will buckle under."

Ellen paused. Line upon line of houses in the entire western half of the city came to mind, their colorful garage doors facing out under homes. *Chance of a lifetime*, she reminded herself. If she had to fill her veins with ice water to get the best story, she would. "It boggles the mind," she said quietly.

"Yes. What most people don't realize is that the very things we prize about the Bay Area landscape—the mountains, the coastline, the canyons—are the result of a very unstable area of the earth's crust. All over the globe, impressive topographical features are really nothing more than road maps of catastrophic shifting."

"I'm going to have to stop you, Peter. My producer is telling me that we've got some footage of the city, thanks to the ability of aerial cameras to get in a lot closer than we can from the ground."

"Excellent." Ellen would remember later the relief she saw on his face, the relief she herself felt, reluctant as she was to admit it, to at least be out from under the baking lights for a moment, to have some more information.

The first image was of AT&T Park, the closest helicopters could get to the heart of the city without crashing in its winds. Despite all the warnings, it spoke of a desolation no one there was prepared to witness. Information was one thing, the sight of it another. The landmark stadium tilted like a keeling boat into the bay, its overhead lights looming down into its rafters, its seats askew, the perfectly groomed grass not yet underwater marred with rivers of mud.

"Damn," Si said through her earpiece. "Goddamn."

The only other sound in the room came from the steady whip of the helicopter struggling to hover in the wind.

An hour after the shock, in the district between the Bay and Sansome Street, with rolling smoke above, and roaring, furious flames breathing hotly on our faces, I came upon a fire engine . . . about which firemen stood with idle hands. . . . "No water," said the chief. "Mains all broken by the shock; can't do a thing."

—HENRY ANDERSON LAFLER, 1906

I climbed to the top of Potrero Hill to view the conflagration. . . . A fierce and awful fire ate at the heart of the city and breathed up a suffocating black smoke. From eight-, ten-, and twelve-story buildings, supposedly fireproof, flames issued at every window, and gushed from the tops like the blast from a rolling mill. . . . It was too clearly apparent that San Francisco was doomed. That stupendous fire, and not a drop of water! Already the desert had followed the drought far in, where a great city stood.

—F. O. POPENOE, 1906

The fire, which had swept the wholesale district below Sansome, jumped Kearny Street and with a rattle of eagerness fastened upon Chinatown, with its carved balconies, its multicolored signs, its painted and gilded flimsiness. At the same time, doubling back, it came down Montgomery, San Francisco's Wall Street, and Kearny, fairly whistling down the deep, narrow corridors. By eight o'clock the Kohl and Mills Building and the Merchants' Exchange flamed like torches, and the destruction of the business blocks of the city was complete.

—JAMES HOPPER, 1906

〜〜〜〜

22

"Max," Vashti said, the way a person speaks in a dream, "Are you there?" She didn't wait for him to answer. "Are you sleeping?"

"No," he said, though he had been, in a way, thinking of her.

Vashti began meditatively, still deep in thought. "Maybe it was foolish to get so attached to someone else the way we did. Maybe that's just a doomed way to try to go through the world. Sooner or later, one of you is going to lose their balance, don't you think? Maybe a love like that just isn't meant to last."

He didn't answer. He didn't know how to. Who decided how long love was supposed to last? "But we didn't. We didn't drown, and the love lasted, even when we both wished it wouldn't. I used to think that something horrible had gone wrong with one or both of us because you could only think of how you wanted her so much, and I could only think of how I wanted you, and we couldn't find our way around those things—like the pregnancy was a pill we both swallowed that should have given us the same result, but instead it grew strange in me, became something I didn't know what to do with or how to manage, while you developed this strength around it that I couldn't touch." Another thought of his mother bubbled to the surface, but he caught it just in time, reciting what had already become a litany at that point: that she would be surrounded by caretakers, that she was stronger, now that she lived at Buena, that she'd always been resilient, at least in spirit. Was there any other kind of resiliency? Certainly a body couldn't survive if its spirit refused to cooperate, could it?

"Also," he went on, "I was afraid I wouldn't really love a child who wasn't totally wanted. I thought maybe it was better not to be there at all, rather than be there only because I felt I had to be, or leave her feeling lonely."

How could he think such a thing? Max had been left to feel lonely, and he had still found his way to her. But, Vashti reminded herself, he had never carried anyone so closely that her very presence became as vital to him as he was to himself. Also, she was surprised to realize, he might not remember being carried that way.

"Did your parents ever carry you, Max? To bed, when you were sleeping?"

"I don't know," he said, trying to imagine how they might be carried out of there now. "But how would I? How can you remember someone carrying you if you were sleeping?"

I guess you can't, she thought, a foggy memory of Javi's trying to wake her after she'd fallen asleep in the car, jarring her out of slumber so that she could walk on her own into the house. She supposed he was right, that it was better to be abandoned before birth rather than midstream, or in spirit. "I always thought it would be a good sign in a parent, to be able to carry a child in such a way that he doesn't even wake up." She thought for a minute. "I bet your mom did that, Max." He had been thinking the same thing. "I bet you would have, too."

He thought the sound of her voice was like being held and taken somewhere, though to where he couldn't begin to guess. He should have been preoccupied with railing against this terrible thing that had trapped them, leaving them most likely to die. He could not imagine a worse fate, and yet here he was, wandering into a reawakening he would have thought was impossible to find.

"I know it sounds ridiculous, but when you were gone," he said, closing his eyes, remembering the blinding confusion, "all the things that usually made sense to me didn't for a while. Some days nothing made sense, then on some other days everything did. It got easier to make things up. All these unreasonable ideas—of your coming back, of how things could change back or be close to what they had been—didn't get shoved aside like they should have. It was so strange! To be separated from you physically but not emotionally, to have so much to say to you that couldn't be said, like turning to talk to a ghost half the time."

Max knew he still had all those things to say, that they were threatening to let loose. Was it his imagination, or did he hear a change in her breathing? Was there enough space between them to carry such a delicate sound from her to him? He wanted to reach out and touch the jagged materials that formed the prison around him, but he could not move well enough to do even that. He listened again, but no new sounds introduced themselves. Still, it suddenly occurred to him, if he was not sure he heard her, they might not hear rescuers making their way to them from far overhead. The thought made him feel hopeful. Though it was a giddy hope, like a drug. He wondered if it was just better to imagine the worst, though that, too, had never been his strong suit. And so he let his words go free, feeling them unravel from within him even as he spoke.

"After a while, I realized I had been asking questions you'd never answer. Still, I didn't want to stop asking, because if I did, it would mean I had accepted the way things were. I don't think I ever managed to do just that. I know. We were only nineteen. God, you'd just turned nineteen that summer! I knew even then that we were young and inexperienced. I knew that your father had good reason to step in. His reasoning made sense to me. It was yours I couldn't swallow.

"So I started asking myself the questions I could answer on my own. I started to try to understand your life as you'd chosen it, tried to imagine where you were and what you were doing. That's when I knew the anger was fading, because, to be honest, the anger got boring. I still wanted to know you. I had gotten so used to knowing you. I loved you. I wanted details. It wasn't enough just to know generally where you were and why. I wanted to know if you ever got to plant that garden you wanted and what you ate for breakfast. Then, after I got up the courage to track down Javi and she told me the baby had lived and died, I was bewildered for a while. The hurt of your having married someone else came back, but what could I do with my grief except wonder if you'd ever leave him, and if I could reach out to you, and if you'd cut your hair because I'd heard that babies grabbed their mothers' hair and

I wondered if you'd just chopped it off or pulled it back, and I wondered how you could live with someone you didn't love. I should have been angrier with you, but I missed you too much. Then I knew the curiosity would never end, because there were questions I could never find the answers to until I could stop imagining the person I loved. Still living. Still loved. Just a few hours away. It made me sad, knowing that distance wasn't keeping us apart, or love. If I hadn't loved you quite so much, maybe I could have forgotten you. Though I don't know how that's done. I don't know how people can forget each other."

Long after he stopped talking, Vashti hoped he would continue, but he didn't, and she didn't know what she could say. She wanted to say she was sorry. From the moment she agreed to marry Dale, through her pregnancy with Anita, her daughter's birth, her exploding star of a childhood, her death, for countless moments after. How many times had she fantasized about finding her way to the kind of apology that would get them back to where they had been before she left, negating both time and injury? Or for the kind of wholesome regret she had ached to develop, to be able to come to him and say that she had been wrong about everything that hurt him. If only she could be so selfless, find a way to relieve him completely of pain. If only she regretted everything she'd done to hurt him as completely as she loved him.

But she had been compelled to choose a different battle than he had, and the hope and desperation that made her want to fight it were not things she could regret. They had been important. It was important to live a life you could become desperate about. It was also important to know that no one can be completely sorry, protected from having to carry into the future the self that made old choices.

"I did love him, Max. He took us in. He allowed me my broken heart and stood by me when it broke all over again. How could I not—for that, at least?"

He took a while to absorb this information. It didn't hurt as much as he thought it would to know this, to touch it with his heart the way one might run a finger over a cut, gently, to see how deep it is.

"Is that why you stayed with him?"

"Yes," she answered truthfully. "But I mostly stayed because I promised him I would. Sometimes it felt like a sort of backward fairy tale, you know? Like the one where a magical creature promises the girl something she needs if she promises him her firstborn. Except I promised myself in exchange for Anita. We never spoke about it like that, but there wasn't much we spoke about. It made stories too easy to invent, anything to fill in the blanks."

"How did he die?" Max asked, thinking of his own heart failing.

She had known Dale was about to die a few days before he did. It wasn't just his waxy skin or the fiery blush coming into his cheeks and igniting something in his eyes; she had seen these things before, and they'd only been signs of fever or his weakened heart's overtly desperate attempt to get through a few bad days—which it had done until then. She couldn't have said why this new light in his eyes made her believe that his spirit was rising to the surface before making its final exit—though she'd never believed anything like that before—or why the waxiness of his skin was something she suddenly wanted to touch, felt suddenly compelled to memorize. We cannot speak to the unsystematic, the knowing older than science that creeps in surely and soundlessly at times of birth and death. Vashti had felt it just before her mother died, and her mother had guided her through it with the tone of her voice and the way she ran her palms over the crown of her younger daughter's hair; the way she smiled wryly at the secret they shared; how she told Vashti, for the first and last time, that some of the strangest stories she'd told her daughters had also been some of the truest.

"Let's talk about something else. Let's talk about getting out."

"Why?"

Because it felt too close in there. There wasn't enough air to stir up all those old demons that were crowding them. The past was running into the future, which made the present impossible to understand. Her head felt odd and light, her heart leaden.

"I can't. Let's just, let's just talk about something else, Max. Anything else." He heard a noise, as if she might have tried to move.

"Don't move," Max said. "It'll make things worse."

"How do you know?" she asked. He thought he heard tears in her voice.

"Vashti. Just talk to me. It's the only way through."

He could hear the tears in her voice. "I can't, Max. I can't. It's too much."

"You can," he said. "Think of what you have to tell me! Just tell me everything I don't know. Tell me about taking care of him toward the end," he said after a moment, knowing he'd never stood by and watched anyone die, that there were probably countless brave things she had done that he would never even know to ask about.

When she and Dale were married, and Vashti was still daydreaming about the possibility of falling in love with him, she used to fantasize about how they might have met. At a grape-stomping party, the kind everyone thinks Californians are beyond, but they're not—so a grape-stomping party, one that started in an afternoon that fell into an early evening with lavender skies threaded by orange-gold strips of cloud, one where a quietly elegant man came to talk to her, she with her purple-stained feet, the whole thing as colorful as a painting no one has any business inhabiting. Or maybe they'd have run into each other week after week at the farmers' market, he selling his wines, she wandering among the goods, the two of them noticing each other, coming to a natural affection.

Instead, Dale had approached every problem in life as he did his business. So finding a spouse, when it didn't happen right away, had been shaped into an exercise in expediency and efficiency. He waited until he was old enough to no longer be expected to father a large family or form any romantically naive attachments to his wife, then he put out feelers among his business contacts. A man of like mind, her father had reached out to him almost immediately, as Dale had hoped he would because he'd noticed Vashti already. He was, after all, not above beauty. The deal was almost done before Vashti agreed to it, her father and Dale having convinced each other that it would be hard for her to refuse such a satisfactory offer.

"I'm not a cow to be sold," Vashti had spat out, suddenly regretful and as angry at herself as she was at her father. "This isn't the nineteenth century."

"I don't care what century it is. You think you're above old solutions to old problems? And who's selling anything? You have as much to gain as he does. Many people would say even more!" A telltale vein stood out in her father's neck, his face almost purple with frustration. He'd have a heart attack before all this was done, she was sure of it.

"So why bother with me?" she'd challenged him, unable to keep the terrible bitterness inside.

"A man needs a wife!" he shouted. Vashti suddenly felt paralyzed, irretrievably tangled up in multiple unhappinesses, and she saw her father struggling right alongside her. It constricted her throat. And ultimately, it silenced her.

The next morning, she agreed to meet with Dale, and while she told herself she could still walk away easily, she was growing more pregnant and entranced by impending motherhood every day, more tormented by Max's persistent belief that the baby wouldn't live, more guilty knowing that if she told him she intended to have the baby, he'd stay with her anyway, limp along until they all inevitably crashed. That would mean none of them—not she, not Max, not the baby—would have a chance. Almost overnight, she felt desperate to escape it all, to be focused exclusively on her daughter's well-being. If her own life was falling to pieces, at least there was another, more precious one on its way. She grabbed it by its slippery tail and held on to it like the lifeline it was.

By the time she and Dale met, Vashti was relieved and grateful to find him easy enough to be around, not least because he took to the idea of helping the baby try to survive. It was something good to do with his money, he'd said, which wasn't the most romantic statement ever, but it turned out it was exactly what she needed to hear at the time. A cynic might say that Vashti offered him the ideal child, unlikely to be a burden into his old age. But Vashti saw things differently. She saw the practical grace and hardness of a man who makes his living off the land and knows that, in an instant, life is gone, no matter what your attachment to it may or may not be. She had liked that. Eventually, it was what taught her how she'd be able to love him—matter-of-factly, the way you love a home or the land beneath it—not because of a spark of kinship, but because of how you can coexist peacefully with so much unsaid.

"It was peaceful," she said finally, the word releasing from her. "He had heart troubles, then he was horribly sick, and then, all of a sudden, he wasn't sick anymore. He was dying. It's hard to explain the transition, other than to say that his pain took on a different purpose. Like it wanted him to stop fighting, told him to stop fighting, to just ride it out until it was over."

Max wondered aloud if she missed Dale. She didn't, not really. Especially not there with Max, in the midst of a reunion that felt so complete, it washed other losses away, as if she could be cleansed of them. She closed her eyes and imagined bringing Max back to where she'd been, walking the places of her life with him until he knew them, too. The hills that turned gold in the heat, looking for all the world like the pelts of great animals, their larger humps like those of bone, the smaller ripples like tendons and muscles, all of it covered with grass that was light at the top and dark at its base, so when the wind blew through, its undercarriage shifted with the light. Or the walls of hushed trees in the forests to the north, the corridors of looming stillness, Anita asleep in the backseat as she stopped the car deep among them to get out and fill her lungs with that peppery, nutty aroma, the smell of dirt condensing for centuries in shafts of sunlight. If only she could make such things in her kitchen, spread them out on a plate and feed them to Max spoonful by spoonful, filling him up with what he had missed, never doubting what could be recovered.

23

The first public service announcement flew out into the air after Gene crossed Market Street—an activity that usually made him feel he was crossing from one side of the city to the other, but which just then made him feel he was walking over the jagged seam that held the city together—and found himself at the outskirts of the Tenderloin. A disembodied, canned voice ringing out as dully and ominously as a foghorn warning ships of unseen rocks:

This is the City and County of San Francisco's Emergency Outdoor Public Warning System. We ask for your continued cooperation as we work to restore power and water to the area as quickly as possible. Residents and visitors alike are advised that a twelve-block section of Chinatown, at Powell from California to Jackson, at Jackson from Powell to Kearny, and at Kearny from Powell back down to California, has been blocked to pedestrian and vehicular traffic as a safety precaution that will enable our firefighters to direct all their attention toward the work at hand. We ask that you please refrain from using your cell phone or other phone services once they are back up and running, as we expect a larger than normal call volume at that time. Further public service announcements regarding temporary emergency shelter,

*food, and medical care will begin shortly. Thank you for your
cooperation.*

A man shouted into the silence that came after the message and another answered, a tussle beginning over the last dregs of an already looted store, its insides out on the street. Gene watched, mesmerized by the endless carousel the men played at, the unexpected ways in which the world couldn't be slowed, even if it continued to spin unheeded.

Then it hit him: cell phone services! Gene almost dropped the man right there, but he spied a grimy doorstep and ducked under its awning, setting the man down hesitantly on one of two long, filthy stairs, promising them both it was only so he could check his phone. After lifting him back into his arms earlier, Gene had resolved to carry him only until he was sure he was dead, but the closer the man got to dying, the more anxiously Gene checked him for signs of life.

He fished in his pocket for his phone, but when he pulled it out and wiped off the grimy screen, the battery icon glowed red. Still, he couldn't help but dial and dial again until it blinked and went dark. Gene closed his eyes, trying to convince the anxiety rising in his chest that Esmerelda was there, that the neighbors would help, too. Gene knew for sure that they'd had a few gallons of water and some energy bars and a flashlight stashed away at one point, but he was pretty sure it had all been replaced with bottles of '08 cab from their last trip to Sonoma. Franklin had figured he'd rather be drunk when the Big One hit, anyway, that a happy drunk would be more likely to relax and wait it out than someone more sober and responsible. Gene's chest tightened with thwarted impulses, with guilt he wasn't sure was misplaced. He couldn't even have supplied his lover with a decent earthquake kit? When had he stopped believing in his own inevitabilities? He stared down into the man's waxy face, wanting to stroke it with kindness. He couldn't help feeling partially responsible for his dying, and that reaching out to him in tenderness would be no better than the wolf nuzzling the lamb for comfort.

As he heaved him back into his arms, the ache in his shoulders and back shot through and into his legs, and he could only stumble a few blocks up Taylor. Sensing defeat, Gene tripped and nearly fell into the alcove of a grimy building, weeping now with grief and frustration. His arms were slippery with blood and sweat as he tried again to lift the man, but he was too weak. The ground was so cold, dirty, and damp. It was a terrible place to lay someone to rest, but he no longer had much of a choice.

The skin on the man's face had slackened and gone gray. It was unexpectedly beautiful. Smooth like a statue's. Was that how art came to be, as a way for people to remember their dead before life could be recorded so easily? He slid a hand under one of the man's rough palms. The fingers were thick and soft with life, but they did not bend to Gene's touch. Lately, when Franklin was sleeping and Gene couldn't, he would slide his palm under his lover's, waiting until Franklin's fingers wrapped around his hand. When they finally did, Gene would close his eyes, amazed that he could be loved even in sleep. Gene wiped at his eyes like a child before checking for a pulse. Nothing. Gene held his breath, perhaps in solidarity, more likely in grief.

Surely others in his position, like Sam, would have done the right thing despite the haziness of the data. Because a finding was a finding, and he'd held Sam back not because he thought the work was faulty, but because it needed "road testing," as he'd put it, a way to replicate the kind of solid results that would bring in funding. It didn't matter that the smaller, riskier sample data pointed toward something of real life-or-death significance, as it turned out. Instead Gene had banked on his career.

Polite company. An image of his father waxing and buffing their wooden kitchen floors before anyone came over, even if they weren't eating together, came to mind. Scrubbing toilets, vacuuming the upstairs rooms where no one but the family went, as if to say, *Our dirt is not for others to see, for others to even suspect.* Then Gene went and immersed himself in rocks, sure that a world of actual dirt and disaster could bury the tendencies he shared with his father, the tendency to overwork and overclean, to worry about what others might say, to shun the intolerable. No, he was going to save the world by getting his feet dirty and shedding light on its darkest fears.

But when all was said and done, his desire for legitimacy had gotten the better of him. The pleasurable taste of acceptance slowly eased his hunger for rebellion, though now there was only the metallic tinge of smoke on his tongue. Because once he began to fully appreciate the mask and title of professor, the ability to walk into almost any room and be addressed as Dr. Strauss before he was known as anything else, his conversion from meaning maker to approval seeker was complete. Somehow, on Stanford's prestigious and beautiful campus, egotism didn't seem so dangerous—even though that was the very place where it was at its most dangerous, its most normalized. He'd gotten sloppy, that was it. Returned to his twisted roots when his guard was down, far more concerned with his reputation than the good he might do with it.

Franklin would say he was being too hard on himself. Maybe that was what love was: teaching your beloved to see himself as he saw you. But would Franklin still say that, Gene wondered doubtfully, no matter what shape the inn might be in, whatever shape Franklin might be in? Just that morning, Franklin had dusted and returned his Japanese tea set to its corner shelf, closed the glass door on the transparent etchings of bamboo and plum blossoms before locking it with a tasseled key. The satisfaction on his face when he turned around would have made a more jealous lover uncomfortable. From a time long before they met to the moment they'd parted company that morning, all those small, careful actions Franklin invested in, creating a place where strangers might feel at home, had been laid knowingly in the path of not just likely but probable decimation.

Gene trembled as a wave of suppressed anxiety overran him. He crossed his arms and drew his knees toward his chest, but that only made him shake harder.

Before Franklin, love had always been more an idea than a possibility. That wasn't to say Gene had never been curious about it, but for most of his young life, he had held such curiosity deep in his chest, well out of anyone's immediate sight. As armor, he instead greeted people with his professional demeanor and intellectualism, always quick with a witty comment but never quick to smile. Franklin liked to tell their friends that the only way to Gene's heart was through his head, and Gene had to admit there was some truth to that. Franklin had certainly captured his attention by regaling him with tales of what it was like to actually be there the night Harvey Milk was shot. Barely eighteen, Franklin had arrived with nothing but a pair of ratty sneakers and jeans shorts in August of '78, thinking he'd go shirtless in California for the next several months. He'd been taken in immediately by a matronly tranny, fed and clothed for the chilly San Francisco summers, and by November was already entrenched in the first real community that had embraced him, marching arm in arm down Castro with a boyfriend whose name he couldn't remember, the street thick from Seventeenth to Twenty-Fifth with their fellow mourners. Sure, Gene had read about that night thousands of times, but Franklin made him feel it—all those candles and the cold, silent San Francisco night air—in a way that took Gene's breath away. Sometimes he wondered if he fell in love with Franklin so quickly and irrevocably because he was falling in love with the city he lived in at the same time, smitten by what the man and the place suggested about the possibilities in Gene's future.

He felt rather than heard the footsteps stop behind him. He turned and looked up at the slight, serious face of a young woman with a river of straight black hair running down her back. She was wearing fashionable glasses—cat's-eyes in thick red plastic—but the left lens had shattered, leaving a spider's web of glass covering one eye. Still, her one-eyed gaze penetrated him, ruthlessly demanding, as if he'd promised her an explanation.

"Is he?" she asked curtly, gesturing toward the body.

Gene nodded.

"And are you just going to leave him there? Like that?"

When Gene didn't answer, the young woman edged in beside him, slipping her hands into the nearest pocket on the dead man's coat. Gene was too startled to stop her. Was she looking for money? He glanced nervously over his shoulder. "He doesn't have anything in there," he said sharply. "No money, no food."

"Is he a friend of yours?" she asked over her shoulder.

"No."

She nodded, rummaging around on the other side before twisting around to inspect Gene. "You just found him?"

"Who are you?" She didn't answer. Had he missed something? Already, she'd turned back to the man and pulled out his wallet. Gene didn't move to stop her. With thin fingers and manicured nails, she deftly unfolded it and sought out its contents, pulling out the license that was still secured within its clear plastic window. She held it up to Gene and pointed at it like an impatient teacher before a slow student. He squinted, trying to see in the dark. It took him a minute to recognize the photograph as the person he'd been carrying, flush with health and smiling an uneven smile that squinted into his eyes.

"Guozhi Liu," the girl said softly, reciting the name aloud to them both. She hesitated, looking down ruefully at the man, as if she was thinking about something that she, too, might have done to prevent such an end. But before Gene could guess what that might have been, she started pulling off the dead man's jacket.

"What are you doing?"

She looked up at him as if he'd asked a stupid question. "You can't just leave him in this," she said tersely, as if Gene had suggested the wrong attire for a dinner party. "It's red," she went on impatiently, as if reminding a child of something he should have known. "He'll become a ghost. Here," she said and handed Gene the wallet and a wad of dirty tissues she'd pulled from the man's pocket. He winced as she struggled to pull the jacket off the stiffening corpse, not sure if he was complicit in something right or wrong. Unable to think of what else to do, he peered at the man's license: 843 Stockton Street, San Francisco, California.

"Stockton Street," he said aloud. "He lived on Stockton Street. I was taking him home."

The girl nodded as if he were reciting instead of relaying information. She'd collected a pile of loose change and lint, the detritus of anyone's life.

She worked him free of his one warm piece of clothing, revealing a thin, white button-down shirt, now stained with dirt and blood. "That's better," she said, sitting back on her heels. To Gene, he just looked too cold. Uncovered. But he didn't say anything. She tucked the offensive garment under her arm and gently plucked the wallet with the exposed license from Gene's fingers. As she folded the man's hands over it, whispering to him in a language Gene did not understand, the ground rattled beneath them, arresting them both. It settled, and the quiet after was as earsplitting as the noise had been.

After a moment, she dared to move again. "There," she said, smoothing the hair back from his forehead. She got to her feet.

"Wait." Gene reached out as she stood. She had somehow known what to do. A perfect stranger. "How did you know to do that? How did you know what to do?"

She met his gaze for a moment. Her eyes were rimmed in makeup that had smudged, he saw now, so that they were amplified and encircled, comically alluring. "You're not from around here, are you?"

Fresh off the boat, are we? How long had it been since someone asked him that?

"Not exactly," he said. But who, in San Francisco, was ever from around here? "I mean, I am. I'm just not originally from here." Why was he explaining himself? "But I've lived here for a while now," he added defensively.

"And you've never been to a funeral in Chinatown?" She smiled ruefully at him, as if the expression contained what he missed, and she didn't have the heart to tell him that the experience couldn't be explained. "Funerals are the main attraction"—he couldn't tell if she was joking—"after the food. My grandparents lived a few blocks from him," she added, lifting her chin in the direction of the body. "Probably passed him on the street a thousand times. Anyway," she said, taking a longer look at Gene, "you should get to safety."

His heart flipped. What could she mean? If he could get to safety, he would have gone there already. His eyes stung with smoke and tears. "Where are you going to go?"

Again, the rueful smile. The taste of regret. He *had* missed something. Or someone? Something more than missing the chance to help others with what he knew, as she had done. Was the key, maybe, knowing when to help instead of how? Was that it? He felt like the kid who was too young to understand, the one who'd missed the joke, the punch line that drew everyone else together. "I'm going home," she said kindly, as if that were the simplest explanation and also the most difficult to understand.

Gene looked involuntarily north, toward the fire. He wanted to tell her that her home was probably gone or a danger to her. That she wasn't heading into safety. That he knew exactly what sorts of dangers might lie ahead for both of them. Instead he stood up, too, though his legs were stiff and painful. "I thought I was taking him to a hospital," he said apologetically.

She scoffed, a laugh playing at the corners of her mouth. "No," she said, "he would never have wanted a hospital, that far gone."

"Oh," he said. Of course. The man had seen death differently. Gene would have, too, if he'd taken a moment to get out of his head and pay attention to what was in his hands.

"Don't worry," she said, "you did the right thing."

How could she know he'd done the right thing? Was she really as free of doubt as she seemed?

Sirens sounded in the near distance, evacuation warnings amplified through speakers so powerful that the windows trembled in their frames. When she told him to get to safety, she must have meant the evacuation zones, the places where people fled when they had nothing else to lose. From a corner of the largest window facing the street, Gene could see the fire a few blocks to the north, temporarily occupied with a multistory apartment building burning from the inside out. *In Chinatown, someone is always home.* The echo of an old lecture came back to him, the chief of police speaking to the unavoidable dangers of fire after earthquakes. In a big city, the most vulnerable to fire were the ones who kept homes and cooked, who were alone during the day with an assortment of ignitable hazards that could jump quickly from surface to surface, room to room, apartment to apartment, building to building.

"I knew," Gene said suddenly, blurting out his confession. "About this. The earthquake, I mean. Or at least I think I might have," he said quietly.

"Where did you say you came from?" The girl's voice lifted skeptically.

All at once he saw himself as she must see him: dirty, bloody, unshaven, harrowed, harrowing. He would have fit in perfectly among any crowd of deinstitutionalized homeless citywide. Well, it wasn't exactly wrong to say that he was on his way to becoming deinstitutionalized, and, for all he knew, he might be homeless as well.

"I didn't," Gene answered. "But I'm on my way home, too. North Beach."

"Oh," she said. She took in his trousers and button-down shirt and patched together an uncanny guess at the truth. "No one knew about the earthquake. I don't know who you think you are, but if you'll pardon my French, bullshit." She smiled with kindness and good humor, the warmth entering him like a laser that only drew attention to the cold.

He nodded, unsmiling. A tiny, steel-haired woman ran between them as if they weren't there, knocking Gene in the knees with one of several thin pink plastic grocery bags stuffed to transparency with all the contents of her life that she could carry.

"North Beach, huh?" The girl looked cordially in that direction.

Gene looked in that direction, too, into the fire.

"It's an inn, actually," he said. "We live in an inn. Right across the street from Washington Square Park, so there are great views from every window." No, he'd never been to a funeral in Chinatown. All the funerals he'd attended had been formal, never occasions for celebration. Who would have thought death could be celebrated? Or that the parts of life that were lost could be remembered without pain? Recollected, even. The girl was waiting, listening to him like an animal temporarily tamed. He could see the desire to return to her nest in her eyes, not because it would be as she knew it that morning, but because it was where the meaning of shelter lived.

"On a clear night, you can see the bridges from the roof

deck, both of them lit up. If the wind is right, sometimes you can hear people laughing at the restaurants nearby. Sometimes there's music. Sometimes we invite a jazz band in, and the trumpeter always wants the window open so the whole neighborhood can hear."

A boy was crying, too tired to walk, and the pinch-faced woman who had been shepherding him along stopped, scooped him up, and kissed him irritably before breaking into a broken trot. "Did you know," Gene said after another luxuriously unhurried moment of thought, a suspension of time that sometimes materializes between two strangers who find an unexpected comfort in each other and cannot quite leave willingly from relief, transient though it might be, "that there are ships buried beneath the city's streets?" The girl turned to him, her mouth softening from a teasing smile into a more genuine one. "The Gold Rushers abandoned their ships and headed for the hills. When most of them didn't return, those who remained made a city over what they'd left.

"Anyway, someone once told me, or I read it somewhere," he said, letting down who he was, who he needed to be, as stiffly and carefully as he might lay a body to rest on a cold sidewalk, "that if a really big earthquake hit the city, the ships might just resurface, rising up through the streets. I'd like to see that, I have to admit, even now. That would be a pretty wonderful thing to see."

〰〰〰〰

24

Ellen had been brilliant to hold on to her nerd just a little bit longer. Their camera feed was uneven, but it didn't matter; every aerial news team within flying distance was competing to get whatever it could, and images just kept coming. And her city-planning expert proved himself to be interview gold. Platinum. Bringing back that soft touch when the footage edged into the dangerous territory of being too overwhelming, bringing the tragedy so close to home that people wound up turning the TV off. He was practically making her career for her with this interview alone.

As the footage unspooled and they watched it together, she saw aerial images of downtown with its usual spikes of industry tilting and leaning into and on top of each other like so many steel pins bowled partway over, and he spoke of the buildings that stood, the advances in retrofitting technology and the sincere, dutiful efforts on the part of the powers that be to take ongoing advantage of the safety mechanisms at hand; confronted with actual evidence of his prediction, grainy images of homes collapsing into themselves on the coast, he spoke of early evacuation plans no doubt in effect; at the sight of the patchy acres of lake that had once been Golden Gate Park, he spoke of the animals nearby in the zoo, how well their habitats had been designed; and when the aerial cameras panned to their finale, the city from all angles, small fires too numerous to pinpoint, he spoke of efficient evacuation plans and FEMA's many-levered, resourceful responders on their way.

Ellen listened dutifully and nodded somberly, asking all the right questions. But as the interview wore on and she steered her ship steadily, she could feel the waters beneath her begin to rock, then churn. She was human, after all, and there was only so much she could stand to witness.

During a commercial break, Ellen sneaked out the back door, but it slammed loudly behind her. Damn. She pulled a cigarette from the pack she'd stolen from the cameraman and lit up, her fingers trembling with the cold. It would be so cold in the city. She began trembling all over. At least Si couldn't see her.

The door behind her slammed again.

She didn't need to turn around. A once-in-a-lifetime opportunity, and here she was about to lose her shit. Did he guess? Could he smell fear in the water?

A few moments passed before she put a cigarette into his outstretched palm.

"Beautiful night," he said after lighting up. The smoke from his mouth came out in rings. She hoped he couldn't see how much she shook, furious with herself, desperate to pull herself together. She wondered if she should explain. How much he'd noticed.

"When'd you move?" he asked casually.

"What?"

"In the broadcast. You mentioned you used to live in San Francisco."

"Last April," she replied. "To Marin." She stomped out her cigarette. He'd been one of her references.

He inhaled deliberately. If he'd learned anything about women, it was not to look at them when they got emotional. "Too bad. Must be worth a pretty penny now." Had he even been listening to the broadcast, or was he being deliberately dense? "You miss it?" His tone was casual, but the weight of the question hung in the air.

Did she miss it? The café underneath her apartment that brewed fresh coffee every morning so she woke to the fragrant smell, the sun slanting in through the picture window that led out to a tiny strip of grass and a modest garden she'd shared with the other tenants, though they were always the ones tending it. Nicely, too. They'd probably been too nice, often inviting her to join them, though she never went. She'd meant to, even bought a pair of gardening gloves, but she was always at work, then exhausted when she wasn't. Then someone new moved in across the hall from her, and the only other unit on her floor was sublet, leaving no one she knew anymore. It didn't matter. She probably wasn't ever going to be the homey type. "No," she said, remembering herself, "I don't," but she spoke too sharply, and she'd been lost in thought too long.

Several more moments passed, hours in news time on a night like this.

"You ready?"

No, she thought, still trembling, but she nodded, filling her lungs with cold air.

"El." Si waited a moment. "You sure you're OK? You want me to call someone else?"

"No," she said immediately. Absolutely not. "I'm fine. I just needed a little air."

~~~~~~~~

25

The earth rumbled and muttered, waking Max, or at least keeping him from resting peacefully. Max thought he might be able to see something, now that his eyes were used to the dark. He strained to make out the structure of the things that surrounded them even as they held him so tightly that he could barely turn his neck to see.

"Tell me more about her," Max said softly, "tell me about Anita." He knew that saying her name would keep Vashti's mind off the unthinkable. But he also knew that meant they'd have to talk about her death. "How old was she?"

"Eighteen months," she replied softly. "Eighteen months, two weeks, five days."

He tried and failed to imagine eighteen months of a life he'd once hoped to know.

"It's too much to tell you all at once."

"When else would you tell me?"

"After. Later."

The quiet was so powerful, it buzzed. He wondered with a sort of detached curiosity if they were going to die there, and if they would die peacefully or painfully, together or alone. He wanted to try the experiment several times so it wouldn't seem so frightening.

"I always imagined," Max continued, "that we could look for a place to live somewhere in the city. Not where we grew up. It's too foggy in the Sunset, and everyone sticks close to home. Somewhere closer to the city center, maybe over a nice café we could go to in the morning. Somewhere small, but with a few big windows so that when we did get sun, it would warm the front rooms."

"Are you sure we're not asleep, Max?" Vashti asked, wondering. "Are you sure we're not dreaming?"

"It does sound like a dream," he agreed. "Seems like one, I mean."

"I thought about leaving him, you know," she whispered. "Many times."

"But you didn't," he said, finishing the thought for her.

"No."

Once, on a hot, hot day, when the acres of vineyard hung limply and lifelessly together and the lizards scurried between stones and the summer sun scalded the back of her neck as she lifted the stroller out of the car and strapped in her fussing daughter, Vashti had driven without a thought of anything but leaving that breathless, overly fragrant, yawning acreage and the man who had come with it. But Anita was soon shrieking, and Vashti had to stop the car in a small, nearly forgotten town on the 128, leaning her arms against the steering wheel with her head in her hands, her own shaking sobs drowned out by the sound of her daughter's. After a while, she'd wandered into the cool, dark grocery store near the gas station, letting the chemical coolness dry her cheeks, marveling at the dense miasma of things that shouldn't hold together but did: vodka and Nutter Butters on the display marked *Sale!*; fresh produce lovingly displayed in the window and out of reach; trial-size packages of razors and condoms and laundry detergent by the register; dusty back shelves filled with beer and caulk and hammers and cheap paper towels stenciled with blue flowers. It was a place that held no identity, frequented by the dusty, aching poverty of the immigrant vineyard workers and their families; the clean white shorts of women passing through on their way to weekends in Calistoga or Napa; the regular, everyday middle class that America forgot: slightly bland, slightly bloated white families who lived there in the miserable conviction that the world held no other place for them. Vashti came to love this town, to return regularly, anonymously, to escape in the car and drive the winding roads to a place where no one really knew her and a store where she didn't really need anything and where there was a cashier who noticed new things about Anita every time and smiled at her without needing to know her name.

"Max."

"Yes."

"How long can we last down here?"

"Who knows? A while, I'd say."

She considered this. "Are you hurt?" She made herself ask the question.

"Nothing too bad," he lied, the pain in his leg becoming a voice of its own. "My leg. Maybe my shoulder, or my collarbone, too. What about you?"

"I don't know," she answered honestly. "It's hard to breathe or move. Max?"

"Yes."

"Maybe it's better that we never got that apartment."

He laughed a little.

She smiled, her face breaking its stiffness. But the levity was short-lived. "Do you hear something?"

"No," Max said. It was agonizing, to wonder if any sound was the sound of salvation, if it was even coming. All that talk of hope made him understand why she'd imagine the sounds of help before it came. He might have done the same thing. He was glad for it. Glad for her again. "But don't worry. They'll come. The city didn't just collapse. Cites are like people. They don't just disappear into thin air."

"Yes," she said, her head suddenly pounding.

"And it's San Francisco!" he added with false hope.

"At the very least, I'm sure they'll come for those girls. And find us when they do."

"Of course." Then he remembered that he had promised to get help. What made him promise such a thing?

The priest was trying to find a way to make the awful space of their shared tragedy into something that seemed bearable, an act for which he had no props. He had managed to elevate Ally's lower leg on a stray board. On close inspection, it seemed to no longer be broken, and he drank in his own tonic, smiling with pleasure at what he could.

But to Tia, her sister's seemingly insurmountable brokenness and pain suddenly over, everything seemed even weirder and thus worse. Ally had started asking stupid questions again, and now the priest was trying to act like he was feeling normal, too, like nothing had happened, like they hadn't just turned over the trust of one of her sister's limbs entirely over to him. Tia didn't know whether to laugh or cry at what had come and gone so quickly, so she held herself stiffly, even more unsure.

Ally stopped midsentence, catching her sister's expression. "What?"

Tia just shook her head.

Ally looked back at the priest, biting her lower lip almost comically. It was clear she'd been at least temporarily silenced. He sighed. She was a nice little thing, easy to talk to. A few minutes passed with no words exchanged among any of them. The priest cleared his throat. What on earth had people talked about on a winter's night before they were able to turn the lights on? Maybe they'd just learned to sleep more. There wasn't that much to be said, after all, once the sun went down and voices became odd echoes of the dark.

"Do you have a family?" he asked Phil politely, the question as awkward in his mouth as it had been in his head.

"In Bernal Heights, yeah," the boy Phil replied. "They know I'm here."

"Well," the priest replied vaguely. "That's good."

"How about you?" Phil asked Tia, finally working up the courage to speak directly to her.

Tia glared at him. She reminded the priest for all the world of a bulldog his elderly mother had owned just before she died: the animal had taken up residence in the front yard and by her chair as she grew closer to death, in a constant stance of hostile vigilance. It had been oddly endearing, the clumsy way in which the creature had devoted itself to the cause of protecting his indefensible mother. But what was Tia protecting? Both sisters looked too well and neat to be neglected, certainly not abused. But he had mistaken such things for better scenarios in the past.

Tia tucked in her chin but answered Phil. "Our mom's at work."

"And where is that?" the priest asked, keeping his voice light.

"A grocery store."

"In the Mission," Ally added. "That's where we live."

Her sister jabbed her with an elbow, a reminder that she was holding them both in place, that she was in charge of their borders.

"I remember her," Phil said softly. "She came to drop you off one day."

"That was our cousin," Tia replied curtly.

"Yeah," Ally agreed slowly, looking at her sister's closed face for confirmation. Her sister broke her scowl for a second to shoot her a glance. "What?" Ally squeaked. "I didn't say anything!" Tia glared at her, her body rigid with warning and fear. "I wasn't going to say anything!"

The priest had seen that expression hundreds of times before, the shut-down misery of a dog too naive and small to protect anything in actuality, despite what it felt called to do. The expression of a kid who realized she was a better parent than her own parent for whatever reason, and who wears the pride and shame of that fact all over her face. It was funny how you could sustain the worries of your life, even when they were threatened.

"But why . . ." Phil blurted out, concern written all over his face, unable to heed the warning signs because he cared more than he should have, because he'd seen these girls for months, and he'd watched one of them too closely. Was that why he liked her so much? Because he could know her so well just by watching her? "Why doesn't your mother come?"

Tia didn't answer. Or she did, but it was wordless. There was a great story about her mother's return to Mexico in a frenzy of grief after their father died, about the aunt she'd left them with who didn't see them as anything but a burden, who drank tea spiked with rum and glared at them if they came near her after she'd slapped some microwave dinners down for them and turned on the TV. A story about the aunt who'd decided they were big enough to take care of themselves at that age because girls did such things when she was growing up, and their cousin down the street who rolled her eyes whenever they needed a ride somewhere, and about how their share of the rent was paid by envelopes from Mexico that didn't always come, though their aunt's threats always did. A whole story too awkwardly terrible to share with anyone, it made Tia feel that her family was a failure she could not separate herself from. But the external tragedies around her had shaken her protected ones loose so that they rose to the surface. As the others watched, Tia's face changed, the fury peeling away to reveal another, deeper level of grief, something too raw and close to the bone to be finessed into words, and although she never cried or looked up, she told them of her heartbreak without admitting to a thing.

〜〜〜〜

26

Gene hustled through the dark streets, his head down and his hands in his pockets. With nothing in his arms, he felt oddly light, like a man stepping back onto shore after being at sea, newly desperate to get home, to get to Franklin. As he continued his walk north on Taylor—the fire to his right an approaching beast he could sense but didn't want to face—he thought of the girl who wanted to reach her home no matter what she might find when she did.

The closer he moved toward the heart of the city and the makeshift fire evacuation zone—black *X*'s spray-painted on tilting buildings, cones, handwritten signs on folding chairs—the more hollow it was, devoid of people and activity, though the hollowness was so still that it had its own energy. It echoed in Gene's chest, an emptiness he wouldn't have thought he could sustain. All the things he thought he'd done, invested in—Franklin, and the desperate belief that he would stick around just because Gene needed him; the carefully charted maps of the world, as if lines on paper could be as powerful as the global foundations they represented—had proved easy to upturn, spinning uselessly on their sides.

At Sutter, he paused at a cute little red pub with striped awnings and iron arrows on the door. There was no visible sign of damage, but it projected abandonment, a yawning, black emptiness. It was just the sort of place he would have wanted to try had he passed it any other day. Could buildings sense their fate? A fresh gust of wind tore through, whipping open the door to a vacant sushi restaurant, tripping its bell. He tried to tell himself that all would return to normal, eventually, this was a city that could, in fact, rise from its own ashes—had done exactly that before—but he couldn't shake the sensation of walking through an abandoned set, the structures only cleverly designed props for a play that had suddenly been canceled, a play that had, until this afternoon, included his life among its plot lines.

Involuntarily, he looked up. Then, hypnotized by what he saw, east. Several hundred feet down Sutter, a fire surged behind the high-rises like the monster in a bad horror film: defined, inescapable, a hopelessly obvious villain. His lungs registered the smoke in the air. It hadn't just been fear creating the tightness in his chest.

He began to run. What if he couldn't get home? What if he didn't reach Franklin in time? He had been taking a dead man home. That girl was going home. Homes disappeared in the blink of an eye, the bad fate of an afternoon.

Now nearing Nob Hill, he was surprised to find crowds again, people trying to save valuables from their $2,500-a-month studios. Maybe the wealthy were the slowest to sense their own danger. People were running around with their belongings or their loved ones, hands clasped, too close to the fire and too attached to what it consumed; those who hadn't already run seemed hypnotized. He wanted to stop one of them, to shake him and point the way to safety. But he didn't know the way. Out of the corner of his eye, he saw a flutter of bright blue come to the ground.

He turned expectantly at the cheerful color, but the blue had been the lightness of a coat on a girl who had jumped from the upper floors of a brick-walled apartment building. To a person, the crowd around him began to surge, moving like a school of fish, cautious but determined, avoiding the body or assessing it. A few broke rank, darting toward it, compelled to help long after help was an option. Staring dumbly up, Gene saw that nearly every window of the building was blackened or consumed by fire. A man near where the woman had jumped was weeping into his arms while voices from the crowd shouted up to him, begging him to hold on a little longer. Promises of salvation calling up to him like balloons released with no one to catch them.

Gene turned right to run down Post, but there was the wall of fire. He spun back onto Taylor, his lungs burning, his mind jammed, thoughts tumbling together and then ceasing entirely; fire down Bush and then down Pine, every eastern path he fought his way toward blocked by fire, the north sure to follow soon.

He tried to talk himself down from panic's ledge. If he could just stay on Taylor and get over Nob Hill, hook over into North Beach after that, the fire might be contained by then in the east or have traveled elsewhere. *Surely it couldn't have spread through the entire northeastern quadrant of the city by now*, he told himself, even though he knew exactly how likely it was that it had. He knew he was being stupid, unsafe, doing everything he would have laughed at a man for doing on any other day before this one. But the voice within that steered him toward safety had been quieted first by shame and was now muted by love.

As the wind toyed with the smoke clouds, Gene could see the moon behind them, full and bright. When he was younger and would grow fearful at night or during other dark times, worrying about death and other tragedies, he'd become obsessed with ways that his own life might suddenly be snatched out from under him, that death could come without warning. His mother would tell him people didn't die that way. *You don't die from a cold. You don't die from climbing a rope at school, Gene. You don't die from a little teasing; a little of this, a little of that.* But as he grew older, those reassurances were chipped away like the layers of paint on the old things around their house, around the house itself, smooth layer upon smooth layer, so that you could see that, underneath, the house was only some old wood and nails, that even your home could take in water and warp. That it could burn. Gene knew that what his mother was really trying to tell him was that being gay wouldn't kill him. Except it might. Homosexuals were killed all the time, violently and impersonally. People died all the time in countless ludicrous and unexpected ways. People were found dead in the most inane places and ways—on airplanes midflight; beside a ladder used to fix a lightbulb; in their bathtubs with toppled appliances. Children ran into the street, blithely forgetful in the middle of games and laughter.

The thing was, he already knew that his time with Franklin was coming to an end. He'd known for months, he realized, now that he was awakening to it. It was a knowledge he'd come to without knowing how, in the same way the music shifts near the end of a movie and you know the story is almost over. Except it wasn't the music that had changed in their life together, it was the silences—horribly musical in their own right—the quiet spaces delivering the message no one knew how to say aloud. Midway through the Sunday paper, Franklin took his glasses off and closed his eyes, leaving Gene to read the Bay Area and advice columns aloud to him. And even though the days were getting longer again, Franklin's afternoon naps still extended until dusk. He took longer in the shower, too, though Gene couldn't hear him doing anything different in there. And the pauses between sips of wine or bites of food had grown agonizingly longer.

The smell of smoke was stronger than ever, thick in the wind.

Gene trudged doggedly up the final block on Taylor, the climb so steep that California in front of him looked less like a street than a path to the edge of the earth. Catching his breath at the vacant corner outside the Masonic Center, Gene wondered how far this city could fall, how it was both comforting and awful to dwell and die in a place where any one person's life, no matter how important, was insignificant compared to the place where he lived it. He'd felt the strangeness of this before, when traveling across the Golden Gate Bridge or taking in a movie at the Castro Theatre— how odd it was to see the particular details and memories of his life shimmering before legendary buildings and streets like an intricately woven, private silkscreen over a larger reality. Before he'd moved here, he'd seen the Golden Gate Bridge only in movies and pictures: a great, luminously sunset-colored mirage of a thing, giving off the impression that it hadn't so much been designed as willed into existence. Now he knew it as the bridge he and Franklin took to go for ice cream in Sausalito on summer weekends when the city was too cold, sitting outside and licking their cones while they watched the poodles and shih tzus march by, Muppet held close on Franklin's lap, the cloud cover over San Francisco looking from a distance like a beast with a body that could be touched. The Castro Theatre was plastered into the background of thousands of photographic moments in the gay rights history class he couldn't quite believe he was lucky enough to be allowed to take when he started as a graduate student at Berkeley, but it was also where they'd gone to the San Francisco Gay Men's Chorus sing-along *Messiah* every Christmas they'd been together, because Franklin's old neighbor Steve was the director and it didn't matter that neither of them could sing. It wasn't Christmastime until they'd hopped on the bus on a night when it got dark too early, and shown up in their scarves to warble along with the virtual nation of an audience Steve had assembled in his doomed but contagiously optimistic effort.

Maybe the city was a living thing in its own right, an entity that had never wanted to be settled. A sort of bucking horse of a metropolis. How many times had it burned down already? Six? Seven? And that had been almost a hundred years before the study of plate tectonics explained why and where big earthquakes occurred, when most people still thought the shaking of the earth was an act of the gods, a spiritual scolding.

Cutting across the lush greenery of Huntington Park was as strange as walking across the moon, familiar in a disproportionate sort of way. Gene knew it as a wide, empty expanse, dotted with children playing and old women practicing tai chi. Now its order was out of place, unsettling; the tidy playground, the fountains miraculously still running, the groomed fences and walkways inviting a leisurely stroll. But overhead, the sky was full of smoke and the fire was close enough to ruffle the tops of the trees with a hot wind. The whole place had a look of open surprise; a place meant to be filled seemed all that more ominous when it was empty.

When he'd first begun to study the earth, Gene had been entranced by the idea that the ground beneath his feet stretched farther down than one man could ever hope to go, no matter whether or not he was a disappointment to his father. Inside the thin eggshells of tidy laboratories and stuffy lecture halls, Gene first learned to trust in something larger than he was. It hadn't exactly been a religion, but it had been a belief system. Science had been a siren song to his trusting soul. And now Gene couldn't shake the feeling that a great trust had been broken, though the earth had never promised anyone anything.

Though he had made promises, hadn't he? He'd promised himself that he would find a way to help others live in an unsteady place more steadily, would ease worries that the promised land was just an illusion, too good to exist, sure to disappear in a puff of smoke. He could still recall the thrill he felt when he first learned that, while earthquakes couldn't be prevented, there was a good chance that they could be detected in time to secure the lives they'd upend. He'd felt the same strange tingling as he had as a child emerging unscathed from a Kansas basement after a tornado had passed, amazed that even someone small and weak could escape forces capable of shredding an entire city.

He'd loved geology once, he realized suddenly, simultaneously wondering if he didn't still love it now, if he hadn't for some time. So much of his scholarship had shifted into professional priorities, the desire to be considered learned slowly crowding out the desire to continue learning. When was the last time his research had made him feel half as excited as that morning's conversation with the dean? He'd grown complacent, too, focused on his future after years of living on ground that seemed as likely to hurt him as he did to hurt himself.

Gene suddenly understood exactly how well he fit into this, his chosen city. He was a man running so far from his own suffering that he'd both climbed an ivory tower and set his sights on the last possible place on the continent where one could build a life without falling into the ocean. As if a beautiful house in a wealthy city was a defense of its own against haunting memories and a foundation built over water. And it had only been getting worse now that Franklin was sick. Gene suddenly wanted to hold tight to some mythically constant thing, to some path that would never alter. He was no different from his parents in that sense, so desperate for things to be a certain way that he was developing a myopia around the way things were. And it hadn't been enough to believe he could escape his own suffering; he'd become obsessed with being the kind of hero who could help others escape their suffering, too, a sort of Pied Piper destined to rid the world of rats and children, suffering and vulnerability eradicated in one act of terrifying magic.

~~~~~~~~

27

As the fire that had already eaten most of Chinatown climbed steadily, now feasting on the meat of those buildings and gaining strength before making the leap toward Max and Vashti and everyone and everything else on Nob Hill, they talked as they had when they were teenagers, unwittingly detached from the sort of obligations that demand a sense of what a life might hold.

"It's so quiet," Max whispered. He had to remind himself that her ankle was still in his hand, that he was still touching her. "Like snow."

She thought about that. "What is snow like?"

He smiled. "You've never seen snow?"

"Not real snow. No."

He had to close his eyes to bring the memory back. His mother was good in an emergency, he reminded himself. They'd lost their lights a few times in winter due to power outages or unpaid electricity bills, and she'd always been quick to jump for the candles and the blankets, to make a game of difficulty. And then there had been the years-long emergency of how to survive without his dad. He wondered how she would be faring, trying not to let the ache of not knowing get to him. Surely this stillness was temporary. The world would soon be back on, the lights and power and heat and warmth and help—it was so much more likely that everything that had been would be again, quickly covering up the lapse in civilization.

"It gets really quiet just before it snows. It's like a blanket goes over the sky, you're looking up at the underside of it from down on the ground. It's sort of grayish, but also white with the lightness of the snow itself. And it's very cold, but not too cold. I liked it best when it snowed at night. It made it easier to sleep."

"How?"

He thought about that. "It hushed everything, I guess. In a real snowstorm, it falls in these fat flakes that muffle everything they land on, and the more they pile up, the more muffled everything gets. You can walk through it and not even really hear cars passing on the street. But the quietest part is after it falls, just after. I wish you could see a field of new snow. It's like staring at the ocean or the sky. But then you get to walk out into it."

"Why did you never go back, Max?"

"To New York? I don't know. I guess my life was here."

It was true. The life he had in San Francisco had sneaked up on him, becoming essential without his consent. There was his mother, of course, but it was also that he could lead a life that was both achingly lonely and joyous at the same time, and that he could see reflections of these emotions everywhere he went, in the city itself and the people it attracted. It would never feel like a home, exactly. It was a beautiful place, but it was too busy being beautiful to feel like a real home, much like a woman in a magazine whose expression insists she would rather be looked at than held. Still, he felt comforted surrounded by people who accepted beauty with its barbed edges, so many of whom had come to this spit of a city on the edge of a continent in search of new lives and opportunities, people who didn't let how much they missed their hometowns and countries prevent them from reveling in the foreign beauty around them, the endless days of mellow weather and wide spaces beckoning to be explored. He remembered again those early bus rides he took when he first moved to the city, how some of their greatest thrills lay not in what he saw around him, but in the vistas that unfurled when they crested the tops of San Francisco's many hills.

"Do you remember the first time we met?"

"On the bus? Of course I do. How could I forget?"

"No," she said, smiling to herself. "It was before that. I had a job that summer. Selling tokens?" She knew he wouldn't remember, but she wanted him to take the time to try. She had waited a long time to unravel this particular memory before him.

"That couldn't be," he said slowly. "I would have remembered."

"But I was behind glass! And you barely even looked up," she added triumphantly.

He thought of how her lips looked when she spoke, the dimple above her top lip that made a dent there before she laughed.

"But we didn't talk. I would have known if we talked. That doesn't count as a meeting."

She laughed. "You had a bandage on your chin. Were you

learning to shave? And you had your trumpet case. And your nails were bitten down so far! You looked so, so sad. I wanted to know you. I wanted to make you look at me."

He closed his eyes, seeing her hands, small and deft, plump but defined, the fingers knowing how to do so many things without preamble, without thought. His own hands, with their wide-spread and long fingers, always seemed so ungainly in comparison. His father had told him once not to be so frustrated with them. "These hands have been passed down to you," he had said and frowned, tracing their palms. "Think of what your ancestors would have done with them had they your opportunities." He thought of his father, but he was no longer angry about the letter. He wasn't even all that interested in being angry about his father anymore. Not really. Anger was boring, after a while, a nurse with no milk. All it did was mask pain. But pain's sharpness grew old, could grow brittle and be sloughed off.

"Vashti?"

"Yes."

"What did I say?"

"When?"

"When you sold me those tokens. What did I say?"

"Nothing," she said, as if it were a confession.

It was so quiet, he could count the seconds between the times that they spoke as if they were ticking aloud. "Hey, do you know what my mom's latest obsession is? Chocolate ice-cream sodas at Bi-Rite. How long has she been in this city? And she's just discovered them. I swear, the woman is going to waste her pension on chocolate ice-cream sodas. I have to take her there at least twice a week just to be sure she has a little pocket change left over."

She meant to laugh, but it was getting harder to breathe. The smoke had changed into the smoke that precedes the fire itself, whispering in and around them, examining its target before pouncing. But it hadn't changed the cold. "Javi's coming home," she said suddenly, realizing that she'd fulfilled her end of the bargain.

"Where is she?"

"Away. She'll be back at Passover." Her sister. They had both been flies in their father's web, and now they could feel each other tugging across so many invisible silk lines. Javi would be worried. Was worried. What could she do? What could any of them do?

"Vashti?"

"Yes."

He had been thinking of how he used to imagine the mother she rarely spoke of, a matter of such foreignness to him, given the fact that his mother was the only steady presence he'd ever known. He used to stare into Vashti's face and wonder if the frank kindness in her eyes—certainly something she didn't get from her father—was an inheritance or a happy accident, if the way she laughed, throwing her head all the way back, was the way her mother had.

The summer she turned seventeen, they'd figured out that she could sneak out of her house and climb up the fire escape and through the window of his bedroom, a fact so exciting—not least because she landed literally on his bed—that they'd make love until they were exhausted and fall asleep with the blinds still up and the moon shining through. Max would wake with Vashti asleep on his arm, or with her hand on his belly so he didn't want to move. He'd stare out the window as the night faded and wonder about everything, sometimes his mother, sometimes hers, wondering if he would love her as completely—or she him—if they had been completed children, without missing parents.

"Do you remember any of those stories you used to tell?"

It took her a moment. "You mean my mom's stories?"

"Yes."

It had been so long since she'd even thought of them. "Once upon a time," she said quietly, "there was a time when there was no one but God." He waited what seemed an eternity for her to continue. "I wonder if all Persian folktales began with that line, or just the ones my mother knew. What do you think it was like, the time when there was no one but God?"

"Hard to say." He didn't want her to stop talking.

"Mmm," she said and was quiet. "I forgot. You don't believe in God. Or anything. On principle, is that right?"

He smiled to himself. "That's right."

It was astonishing how easy it was to lose your way to the simplest of wants, to resist even the most obvious of joys. Food. Love. Max. What had been in her way? Was it still there? It must be. It couldn't have just disappeared overnight.

~~~~~~

28

As the deeper night settled in around them, they held themselves like creatures in a cave, listening to the strange noises settling and shifting around them, petrified. The girls, tucked in around each other, drifted off together before long. Sister Coco had succumbed to the clonazepam while still sitting up in one of the few front row seats of the auditorium that were within reach and not demolished. Now, worried about his lover's back, the priest had Phil help him slide his lover's blissfully drugged body to the floor. "Call her Willie," the priest told Phil affectionately after they'd arranged her as comfortably as they could. *As if she could answer to anything, knocked out like that.* Phil frowned. But the priest ignored Phil's doubtful look and proceeded to tuck himself in beside her as merrily as if he were in his own bed at home. Then Phil had found his own lonely spot near the girls, his back against the base of the stage. The priest opened one eye and thought Phil might be cold, but also knew he wouldn't say he was. Poor boy. The priest did not envy him his age, the creeping doubts and incessant desiring, the unmerciful and unreasonable demands of adolescence. Thank God for middle-aged love. He rolled over and into Willie—his very own saggy, sweet, high-strung addict—and for a few brief moments experienced that delicious surety that he'd be asleep in minutes.

Instead he lay awake thinking of the girls, how mother-less they seemed. Fatherless he could take, but motherless seemed like a far more excruciating condition to navigate. He closed his eyes, praying for sleep.

"Shouldn't we be doing something?" Phil asked, suddenly at his side. He'd crept over and squatted down beside him, insomniac urgency written all over his face.

The priest took a breath of patience. "It's pitch-black, my dear boy."

"Not that black. There's a little light. I'm used to it by now. I could just—"

The priest extended a hand toward the boy, feeling sud-denly tender toward him, willing to state the obvious with-out making it sound like an insult. "Let's just wait until morning."

The boy's body, poised to do anything but accept its im-mediate fate, sat back awkwardly on his heels. "I'm not sure I can," he confessed.

The priest sat up a little, trying to explain things as sooth-ingly as he could. "If you move any of this without know-ing what it's under or over," he lowered his voice, suddenly not wanting the girls to hear, "more could come down. Or you could be crushed." *The earth has shifted underneath you,* he wanted to say. *These are not the blocks of your boyhood, moved without consequence. Go back to sleep. Enjoy sleep while you can.*

But the boy was young, relentlessly so. "What about climbing over?" he went on. "Away from the girls? I could see what I could climb over. And if anything fell, it wouldn't fall on them."

The priest sighed. Did he not know the value of his own life? Was he going to have to break the boy's heart to teach him? "Do you hear that?" he asked Phil after a moment.

"What?"

"Exactly. No sirens. No helicopters. Nothing. When the rest of the world is still, it's usually for a reason."

"That makes no sense," the boy said, ready to go without permission.

"It makes perfect sense, actually. If one cannot see and one is in danger and no informed help has come, it is best to proceed with caution." He put a hand up to the boy's cheek; such simplicity in the face of such unimaginable complexity. "Of course you may try, if you want to," he allowed, "but I am sure that such a capable, intelligent young man as yourself knows the difference between dark and light. That people lie low at night for a reason." Phil tried to interrupt but the priest silenced him. "I know, I know. You dream of saving her."

"I don't . . ." the boy began. Then, after a moment's pause to consider, "I'll be quiet. I won't wake the girls."

The priest sighed again, the boy's tone a child's begging for permission, as if the only obstacle to risking his life was an adult's approval. The human condition, he decided, was practically fatal before the age of thirty. He sighed. "I don't know why you ask when you know I can't stop you." Who was he to save youth from itself?

He closed his eyes after the boy skulked away, trying to ignore the sounds of his futile attempts to ascend the treacherous debris all around them. When the boy paused for breath, the priest's ears rang with the silence. He guessed it wasn't just that any sound coming in from outside would be muffled, but that the city was unnaturally quiet. Even Willie was snoring softly for once. The priest lay for some time with his eyes open, listening as the boy's attempts grew fewer and more frustrated. He wanted to call out to him, comfort him, avoid the silence that would soon be complete again, filling his ears to bursting. He didn't, figuring with no inconsequential amount of affectionate acceptance that he was probably just a selfish old bastard. Moments later, he slipped gratefully into sleep.

〜〜〜〜〜

29

"I'm going to have to stop you right there, sir." Gene looked up at the voice that stood in his way. A young police officer in a dusty uniform held out his walking stick, his face a block of its own. Gene had just crested Nob Hill and was heading down its back side, no more than a dozen blocks from home. "This is a fire evacuation zone."

"I thought it was to the east," Gene stalled, taking his measure. "I'm headed north."

The officer looked at him as if he hadn't said a word. Though it was more likely that nothing he said would make a difference to his instructions. "Sorry, sir. It's not safe this way. Please turn around."

Gene felt the heat flush his face. "And go where, exactly?"

There was static on the man's receiver, which he wore near his collar. He leaned down to mumble something into it in the jargon of his trade. "Cross over Sacramento . . ." Something on his receiver kept squawking at him; he pulled it off and turned around swiftly, as if Gene might try to escape if he divided his attention a moment longer than necessary. He probably would have, given the chance. Gene took the interruption to gather himself.

"I've got to go home. You can stop me if you want, or you can just pretend you never saw me." He hoped he was calling the young officer's bluff. What was he going to do? Beat him? Shoot him?

"I can't let you do that."

Had he really come this far just to be stopped by a rookie cop? Gene nodded, as if he was about to comply, then shoved past him, already at a run. Much to his surprise, the officer's hand shot out and grabbed Gene hard by the collar, bringing him down to his backside. The impact only fueled Gene's primal desperation, the urgent feeling that if he didn't get to Franklin now, he somehow never would. He struggled, ready to bite, ready to kick, fighting back for once. "Shit," Gene heard the officer swear as he struggled, a new message shouting through on the receiver, louder than before. "Shit!" He held Gene with one hand and fished the device off his shirt. "Go do whatever the hell you want," he barked, suddenly shoving Gene off. "The Masonic Center's caught fire," he said, his eyes glittering in the orange light of a sky growing eerily brighter. "Nob Hill's as good as gone." Without another word, he turned back in the direction Gene had come from and fled toward the disaster.

30

"Max."

It had grown so quiet that her voice, reaching only between them, startled him.

"Yes?"

"Do you still play the trumpet?"

"Not too often," he admitted. "I rented a practice room for a while." But it was hard to go back to it after he'd turned in a different direction.

"You should go back to it," she said.

Max could smell flowers in a garden. White flowers. What did white flowers smell like? He wanted to shake his head to clear it, but there wasn't room even for that.

"Max?"

"Yes."

"Do you remember that afternoon on Strawberry Hill?"

Yes, he did, though for the life of him he couldn't think why. He had been brooding over how he was going to pretend he was glad that his mother took a second job to pay the gas bill, even though they'd see each other only two days a week; wondering if there was a way to live without things like gas and electricity, if he would like such a life. Then Vashti had found him. He lied and told her he was upset over something at school, then tried to distract her when she started sniffing him out by saying he was looking at the clouds for pictures, but she had pointed out that there was nothing but fog overhead. Then she laughed at him, at them both, until he did, too.

"You were such a grump that day."

He laughed aloud.

"I used to think of you like that when I missed you the most."

The quiet descended again, enveloping them, so that minutes later Max began to wonder if he had just laughed aloud, if he had missed some response he was supposed to give, something he was supposed to say. He drifted into the memories of playing the trumpet, the blare it gave off, a call that could be heard across mountains. When the world used to be like this all the time—with empty, great spaces ready to fill with sound—those animal horns must have been like foghorns, calling out to others whose existence the eye could not confirm.

He thought he heard Vashti's breathing change into something more even and deep, and he hoped she was asleep. He lay there for a long time, listening. He wondered how long they'd been there. Maybe it was already morning, or near it, but he guessed it probably wasn't. There was a weak lurching in his stomach, an emotional vertigo created by the rise of what he thought he should know against the descending spiral of what he didn't. Their surroundings kept up an uneven percussive dropping and settling, constant disturbances of sound that even the densest soul would find unnerving.

Max squinted into the blackness, wondering about bats

and blind men, both of whom could see with their ears. He
had forgotten how stubborn darkness was. Not since he was
a kid living near the northern woods had he experienced
such total darkness. It almost had a texture, that thick absence of light, as if it not only contained hidden things but
was a thing itself.

Before long, he began drifting in and out of a waking
dream. Images he hadn't summoned introduced themselves
as passing thoughts. First the few photographs he kept
in his apartment on the table beside his couch: one of his
mother and him in front of a cable car outside the Masonic,
snapped by a tourist; one of Vashti from high school; a fading, stern shot of his father that reassured him he was no
one worth missing. Then his old refrigerator, his kitchen,
his apartment. Had he left the lights on anywhere? He
turned away from that line of thinking, but there were so
many equally niggling ones waiting to take its place. Then
he thought of the problems he'd left behind in the everyday
life he was ripped from indefinitely, feeling a curious de-
tachment mixed with terror as to whether or not he would
find his way back into that life or another like it. He thought
of his mother again, lost the war with the part of himself
that insisted he believe in her well-being, had a nightmarish series of visions in which she was struggling, trying to
get to him, his father standing by holding out a letter. He
thought of how prickly she could be. What if she started
complaining and turning people off and didn't get saved in
time? The thought seemed so very real and possible, it took

him a moment to realize he'd been clenching his jaw with the anxiety of it.

He exhaled sharply. The breath reminded him that he was still alive, a fact that amazed him. He always thought that if his life were threatened, he might panic and make the wrong choice, a choice toward struggling. But here he was, much closer to death than he'd ever been, and he could still feel his heart beating steadily in his chest.

Then he must have fallen more deeply asleep, because he remembered closing his eyes before he started hearing seagulls chattering overhead. Seagulls or some other birds. What kind of birds? His mother would know. What was his mother? No, where—where was his mother? Was that her, or someone else's mother? Maybe Vashti's? Yes. She was a lost mother. Vashti's mother was lost.

An old memory visited from when he was a young boy: they had taken a rare vacation to try to mend the rotted-on-the-inside marriage between his parents. They had gone to a motel on the Saint Lawrence River, near Barston, a forgotten town on the Vermont-Canada border where his mother had been born. Max remembered the taste of a horribly bitter chocolate his father had called pure; and he remembered his mother standing against the window, looking out at the river. Most of her small family had died or left by then, but he could tell that she had come home. When she showed him around, she dropped her shoulders and talked to him instead of watching the streets and shadows for things she didn't expect. He remembered the curious way she stood by that window, leaning into the frame itself, as though it wasn't just the view she was experiencing but her place on the earth.

Why hadn't she just moved them back? Certainly they could have made it there on their own, together. Maybe he wouldn't have met Vashti, wouldn't even know that impenetrable layer of heartache. Wasn't a familiar place as important as a familiar person? Maybe one could even take the other's place. His mother had been as disappointed, as devastated by this city when they first moved. In those days, she seemed to have only glimmers of hope—they would live by the ocean—which were shortly extinguished by new practicalities—the coastline along San Francisco was almost always fogged in.

His father really had been the one who embraced upheaval, the dreamer, the one with dreams so big they could include a new place for all of them, or so Max had thought. Sure, his father had had the capacity to dream—but big as his dreams were, they hadn't been big enough to include his wife and Max. Max remembered a letter he should have read, though he wasn't sure what it was about, or if he was glad that he never got around to it.

Suddenly, he knew why they'd never gone back. They hadn't believed they could make the trip. Wasn't California riddled with cautionary tales of people trying to go home or make a new home or new life or find each other by crossing mountains or currents or parched valleys, only to die trying? Were poverty and discouragement any less insurmountable? There was barely enough money to buy food and pay bills and maybe go to the laundromat before they ran out of clean clothes; barely enough energy in his mother to get up in the morning after working two jobs and sleeping alone, never mind having enough to think of a new life, never mind having enough desire to find a way back to a town that had once been full of family and now was not. But just because a person—or even a place—is lost doesn't mean it can't be found again. Somewhere else, maybe, in slightly different form, but rediscovered all the same.

~~~~~~

31

Half-asleep, Ally opened one eye. A pair of silvery ones stared back at her. She yelped, trying to sit up and back away, but the movement made her screech in pain.

"What? What is it?" Her sister's hands were cold and she shrugged them off, unwilling to be consoled.

"A dog," she cried. "There was a dog! Right there!"

Everyone turned to look in the direction where the girl was pointing. There was nothing to see.

"It was there, Tia," Ally insisted, weeping now. "It was there."

"Maybe it was your imagination."

"It was not! There was a dog."

The words were barely out of her mouth when the ground trembled slightly, the feeling of a train passing by. Everyone held their breath. Willie stirred, as though about to wake. Phil held his place, and when the earth settled again, leapt to his feet, sniffing around the place where the girl had pointed.

"If it was a dog," the priest said, thinking of his mother's bulldog and its constant need to be around at least one other soul, "it wouldn't have run away. Or at least we'd hear it sniffing around. Come," he said, trying to take the little one's hand, "let's listen. Phil?" Reluctantly, the boy held still.

But although they heard nothing, Ally kept her face

pressed into her sister's chest. "She's afraid of dogs," Tia explained unnecessarily. Together, she and the priest remained quiet, listening still on her behalf. Phil watched them both, waiting until he could move again.

"I don't hear anything, Al," Tia whispered into her ear.

"It was there," the girl insisted, crying now, but softly, as if afraid to wake someone.

"We'll keep watch," the priest said. He rested his hand on her back. "We'll stay up and look out for it."

"I'll help," Phil announced. "I'll take the first watch."

"I can," Tia said sharply. "I will. You don't have to do that."

Phil ignored her, settling in near where he thought the girl had seen whatever she'd seen.

"No," she corrected him. "There. A little over, yes, there." She beamed at him when he lit upon the spot and sat down, crossing his legs and checking with her to be sure he was exactly where she wanted him.

Her sister looked away pointedly during this exchange. The priest held back. For a while, no one spoke. The younger girl began to fall back asleep. Her sister curled around her again, trying to warm them both, trying not to think of the boy keeping watch instead of her.

When Tia was a little girl, she had a terrible habit of climbing into things, of hiding. She could get into spaces only the lithest and most timid of animals would think to fold themselves into, and the anxious moments her father spent looking for her during these escapades seemed to drain him as if they had been days. After he died, she wondered sometimes if she had contributed to his shortened life. She hadn't felt guilty, exactly, or at least she didn't place any more blame on herself than she did on the rest of the people in his life—all of whom she blamed collectively and thoroughly—but she did see herself in the odd, complicated equation her imagination had created to explain why he'd lost the battle with what they'd all been told was a relatively simple cancer to cure. At first it had looked so simple, too, just some spots on his arms and back, but then instead of healing, they'd become angry and vicious, and her father's face sunk in on itself from the pain. Closing her eyes, Tia let herself travel to her hiding days, that blissful state of sheltered anonymity, the peaceful power of withdrawal. But not for long. She was cold. She tried to wrap herself even more tightly around her sister, but she couldn't get warm. And she was hungry. Terribly hungry. It was like something tugging on her sleeve, not letting her rest. She wanted to yell at it, yell it away.

Ally shouted, sitting straight up from her sleep.

"What is it?" Tia demanded, but Ally pushed her away, crying.

"The dog," Ally choked out, weeping.

"I'm still here, Ally." Phil's voice broke through the dark with a gentleness that made it sound as if he were sitting right by her. "On lookout."

Ally tried to right herself, sniffling and wiping her eyes. A light scrabbling interrupted her work. She went rigid with fear.

"That was nothing," Phil said, lying, looking nervously at the hole he guarded. A single silver eye this time. He shifted his body to block it. "I was just making myself more comfortable."

Tia and the priest held their breath, watching Ally for signs that she might have seen through Phil's bluff. There was a sickening moment when she started to frown, but her tired young mind took over, protecting her from seeking the truth, and she turned and relaxed once more in her sister's arms.

The rest of them, though, were left with the adrenaline of looking out for her, the new knowledge that what she had seen was real.

Phil wished he hadn't volunteered so quickly, but he had. He pulled his knees up to his chest, resigned to an untold number of sleepless hours. The priest saw this and crawled closer to the girls, sitting by Tia to keep her company while her sister slept. For a while, the three of them were quiet, almost comforted by the uninterrupted nearness of one another, listening to the girl's sleep sounds, the gentle scratching of whatever it was in there with them settling into its own makeshift nest.

"Do you think she'll be cold?" Tia asked a while later, looking at the nun.

"Nah, Willie?" he asked, surprised she'd even noticed her. "She's thick as a horse."

He could see Tia smile in the dark, the way it drew her lips up and pulled her forehead back.

"Are you really a priest?" she asked him, the voice in the dark seeming to come out of a younger, softer child.

"Well, no," he said carefully. "I can't perform any rites or blessings. I'm not ordained. And this getup is really for show more than anything."

"So you're not a real priest?"

He closed his eyes. "No. More of a mascot, really, especially in this order. But if a priest is someone who helps others to live a fulfilling life, no matter what that might look like on earth, then I'm a priest. But the terminology doesn't matter much, my dear. It never does." He thought a minute before saying something else that had been on his mind, "You can call me a brother instead of father. I never liked 'father,' anyway. A brother in the Sisters of Perpetual Indulgence."

She seemed to accept his concealed apology, or at least be willing to let her curiosity take over. "What's that?"

"It's an order, I suppose. A local institution."

"So it's not a real religion."

"Of course it isn't, my dear. This is San Francisco."

She seemed to consider this. "My grandma was Catholic," she offered.

"Right. The sisters take care of anyone who isn't Catholic. And I help take care of the sisters. The novice ones in particular."

Tia thought about that. "That's a lot of people."

"True," the priest admitted. "And we even take care of some Catholics!"

"So you haven't explained anything."

"Tia, my dear." He had grappled with this sort of child before, one who, as the result of one extreme of parenting or the other—neglect or its opposite—had managed to enter adolescence without losing her childish ability to recognize and call bullshit. And he chose what he wanted to say next to suit her rare strength and delicacy. "How old are you?"

"I just turned fifteen."

"So she was the first person I took care of." The priest looked over at Willie, still sleeping soundly. "But when I met her, she was a year younger than you are now, kicked out of the house, earning money by selling whatever she could. And all she had was herself, you understand, or the boy she used to be but didn't recognize as herself. She sold him so she could get food and a warm place to sleep. Then she earned enough to have the care she needed to become the person she needed to be. And now she's forty-four. Thirty years of struggle, and she still wears a pink wig to work. That's who I take care of, Tia. And the fact that the minute she got her feet under her she turned around to help others like her—well, that's what I call a miracle."

Tia was not accustomed to expressing what touched her. "Doesn't sound so hard. It would be easy to sell yourself, if you didn't want to be the person you were anyway."

The priest thought about that. "Maybe. Or maybe it's even harder, because you know that it's all you are at the time, and that it would be all too easy to just let it go. Sell it away until there was nothing left."

"It must have been awful," Ally said. They hadn't realized she was awake. "I can't sleep anymore," she added. "I'm scared."

"Don't be scared."

"What's going on out there?" she whispered.

They all considered the question, finally asked aloud. "I don't know," Tia said honestly.

"Why doesn't anyone come? Where are the police and the fire trucks?"

"They'll be here soon," Tia said shortly.

"Do we still have a home?"

"Of course we do."

"It didn't come down? In the earthquake? The earthquakes?"

Tia shook her head vigorously, crowding out the thought. "Of course not."

"Why do you always say that?"

"What?"

"Of course?"

Tia didn't have an answer. She did always say that.

"You don't really know, do you?"

Tia sat up and pulled her sister back down with her, trying to warm her to sleep.

"Please go back to sleep."

"Sing to me."

"I can't sing, Al, you know that."

"Doesn't matter. Sing anyway."

"Go to sleep."

"My leg hurts too much," she argued. "Pretty please?"

"No, *mija*." The word echoed a tenderness someone Tia's age would not have come to on her own. It must have originated elsewhere, in someone else's voice. Tia had been loved. Was loved. Had it been their father? Whatever it was or had been, that person was gone. The priest could see that the word hung in the air between them, too important for a single utterance. After a moment he crept away, thinking that he, too, might try to close his eyes.

But sleep eluded him. He continued to wonder, the longer he felt separated from it, about the outside world; though he knew it was best to fight wonder just now, to suspend disbelief for as long as he possibly could, no matter how unreasonable doing so felt. Reason had no place in preserving sanity.

He'd been through earthquakes before. But he didn't have to be on the outside to know the difference between a tremor and a real, honest-to-goodness shifting of the earth. He knew he should be glad that the kids could not possibly be aware of this. So why was he hounded by the desire to rouse them, prepare them, protect them for or from something, anything? How could you prepare anyone for the possibility of starving to death? Or smoke, the very real likelihood that they might just fade away into headaches and nausea. Death preceded by suffering, being hurt and trapped or thirsty and starving, not just facing fear but watching its slow and agonizing approach.

He sighed, turning on his side, something hard digging into him as he did, making tears spring to his eyes. His own childhood was rising to the surface in the midst of such muted deprivation. The least he could do, the best, was to keep it together and remain an adult for them. Wasn't it? He was no longer quite sure. *What an inheritance*, he thought, picturing the vulnerable city around him. What did its ancestors mean to teach their children about starvation and fear and loss and certain death? What had possessed them to bring children here in the first place?

〜〜〜〜〜

32

Finally, *finally!*, the usual communications began to blink awake, their sparks seen and reflected locally and then nationwide. The newsroom was a flurry of short phone calls, each one exploding before long into a cacophony of story collecting. Si forced Ellen into a ten-minute nap on the grimy newsroom couch, then came in seven minutes later to stare at her until she woke.

"Do I need to call in Jerry?"

She opened the other eye and sat up. "No." She put her hands over her face, waking up. "I slept, actually. I feel better. What's up?"

Seated, he pressed his palms into his knees. "They can't contain the fires."

She shook her head, trying to clear it. "Where?"

"North Beach. Chinatown. And spreading."

She was awake now. "What do you mean, they can't be contained?"

Si stood up and shoved his hands into his pockets. "I mean, the streets on those hills are blocked with God knows what, debris and people and worse, the dams are out and the cistern supply was limited as it was, and the fire department is currently operating, as it has been for the past several years, with a twenty percent reduction of personnel. Not that it matters, really. Even if they had a hundred percent, they're fucked up there. Where the hell would they even get the water?"

"I don't understand." She did, but she needed time to process. No matter the news, Si was so quick to deliver it, never imagining that she might have trouble swallowing it.

He acted as if he hadn't heard her. He knew the difference between her real questions and hedging. "They say, the experts say, that with all that wind and all that fire, the firestorms are bound to be starting, El," he said, dropping his voice. His comforting tone only put her more on edge.

"Firestorms?"

"Fire-generated wind, storms of wind and fire." He sat down heavily, as if he'd been pushed.

"Are they getting this from the sky?"

"Some aerial," he said, rubbing his index finger and thumb together, studying them intently as he did. "Helicopters still can't get low enough for details. Or to help. And the increased wind only makes it worse for them."

"What about the bridges? Can they get through?"

"Bay Bridge, eastern span only partially down, no one hurt, but no one can get in. And the Golden Gate, well, you know the news on that."

She'd kicked off her heels and her arches ached, but it was her hands that were shaking, trembling. She made fists of them and pressed them to her thighs. "So what's the plan? What are they going to do?"

Si shrugged, rubbing his eyes. Under the bright lights from above, the bald part of his scalp shone. When he took his hands away, his bloodshot eyes had turned from a faint pink to an angry magenta. She wondered if the rumors about his having been a drunk were really true. She could understand it—anyone in this business had every reason to turn to alcohol. He'd been her mentor for two years, constantly in her face, but he'd been at KSRO for fifteen years, and the rumors came from those who'd been there just as long. She hid her trembling hands behind her back.

"Boats. Whatever the hell they can do, I guess."

She felt sick, but kept it to herself. A journalist has to be like a doctor, Si once told her, able to remove herself from the situation when there's a job to do. The knot in her stomach wrenched in on itself a degree tighter. *Think*, she demanded of herself.

"Anyone get hold of the mayor?"

Si shook his head.

"Damn." She sat down across from him. "You would have thought that with all the planning, all the warning . . ."

"What do you expect?" Si insisted. "When you build a city within shouting distance of major fault lines, then crowd it down to the square foot, there's only so much that preparing's gonna do."

"Right." She stood up, smoothing her trousers and shooting her cuffs. He didn't need to see her doubts. "What's our plan?"

He shifted back into go mode. "We're going on air. Well, you are," he said, glancing up at the clock on the wall, "in about six minutes, once we get makeup in for a touch-up." He frowned. She must look like hell after her nap. She tried not to squirm under his stare. "We lead with a few lines about the firestorms, but keep the emphasis off the stuff that creates panic. Make sure to play up the poor suckers fighting up there, lay a good firefighter story on thick, emphasize the evacuations that are sure to happen—somber but not desperate; you know the drill. At this point, you've got to win their trust with how you spin the story: they want to feel like they're getting the truth but not drowning in it. Information's what catches their attention, but a good story's the way to keep it."

She nodded slightly, mechanically, efficiently. "Got it. No panic, bookend with the firestorms, zoom in on rescue efforts. Not too scary. Anything else?"

"That'll be good for now. We'll manage the rest as it comes in. Don't want to plan too far ahead. People like it when the news seems spontaneous."

〰〰〰〰

33

For a few more blocks, Gene struggled forward through the heat and undeniable impassability; the wind and the last people fleeing the neighborhood surged through and past and around him. Where to now? All he could see was fire and escape from fire, people running every which way, heads down, the things of their lives in their hands.

The wind changed direction and ripped violently down the hill, stinging his eyes with its thick lace of smoke. Struggling down the last block he could manage, he stood upright, catching his breath. But it was hard to get the lungfuls of air he wanted, and the pain of breathing hit on a primal nerve that spasmed, releasing a backlog of tears.

Blinded by smoke and tears, Gene dove into a stairwell out of the wind, surprising a fusty but kind-faced man sporting a collection of rags, a pyknic belly, and a sleeping bag. "Welcome," he said, clapping Gene on the back, "welcome to the SS *Sacramento*! I'm the Sea Captain. Leading sailors over rough waters for forty-nine years." He extended his hand as if gesturing to the sea around them. "Come," he went on, "get yourself out of the wind." Gently, he put his hand on Gene's shoulder, urging him deeper under the stairs. In another city, in another world, Gene would have feared for his life if an unhinged wanderer tried to coax him into a dark corner, but he could feel the good in that touch, see the man's blankets and bed in the corner. Yielding, Gene pressed his palms to his face. He could never and always find his way home. If Wichita was a respectable Episcopalian priest, San Francisco was a wild-haired goddess, as likely to destroy her subjects as to bestow them with ethereal gifts. It was why he had come there, why so many who hadn't found a home anywhere else did: the city wanted the homeless, it wanted those who could embrace the sorrow and ecstasy of living at the whim of a vibrancy greater than anything they could ever invite or invent. Maybe that was why the people of San Francisco were so generally welcoming, knowing that the only real home they could ever hope to establish would be one they could create together, even if their former lives lay in ruins.

"Hey, hey," the man pleaded soothingly, "it's OK. Don't cry." And then, swabbing at Gene's face with his own dirty sleeve, "Hey! You've got blood on you! You're dirty!" he exclaimed, surprise taking over his face like innocence.

"I was carrying someone, a man, he died, well, he died on the way, or earlier, and I had to take him . . ." He couldn't find his way to the words he knew would explain who he was and why.

The Sea Captain nodded sympathetically. "Ah, yes. I've been a corpse taxi myself more than once. Carried a dead woman through these streets in broad daylight from Howard to Jones, and nobody stopped me!" He wore a ragged series of cloth pieces, none of which could be described as anything so specific as a shirt or pants. "Of course, no one saw us." He paused, picking his front tooth with a thick nail. "Good for the soul, that sort of errand. Good karma." He squinted one hopeful eye at Gene, searching for a far greater degree of potential than he obviously had. "Do you maybe have any food? Water?"

Gene admitted he had neither. The two of them were quite a pair, trapped in an urban mecca of progress and innovation, miracle drugs and messiahs, and not a drop of water between them. The Sea Captain walked toward the opening Gene had come in through and stared philosophically out at the scene. Gene joined him. The heat was so searing, they might have been standing under a full sun.

"It's gone, isn't it?"

"Eh, maybe," the Sea Captain said, tipping his head thoughtfully. "But who knows? Either way, I wouldn't worry about it." He grinned at Gene's expression. "Oh, come now. A city is nothing more than an idea, my boy! We'll rebuild. It's not the first time it's gone down, and it surely won't be the last."

~~~~~

34

Max woke suddenly. "You forgot to finish your story," he said.

Vashti made a sound of recognition.

"What happened after God?" Max persisted.

"It's such a strange story, Max," she said softly, "they all are, now that I think about them." She paused. There was less air to speak with, the choice of words more important than ever. "About goats and monkeys—I think they make no sense."

"Doesn't matter."

"No," she said slowly. "I guess it doesn't. They were probably just the sort of thing that parents tell their children to get them to fall asleep. If they made sense, the children would have stayed awake."

Max didn't say anything. His breathing was shallow and soft.

"My favorite was the story of the baker and the fish." How strange, she suddenly realized, that she was not hungry. Perhaps cold and fear had stolen her appetite. No doubt she would be hungry soon. Unbearably hungry. But it was nice to have a break from it, a break from need.

"Once upon a time, there was a time when there was no one but God," she began again. "When people believed more than they could explain."

"A good baker lived in a small house with his wife, spending long days devoted to his trade, considering the person who might eat each loaf of bread as he made it. A baker of this kind rarely exists anymore, a man who brings such tenderness to his work! At the end of the day, if he had any bread left over, he could not bear to throw it away, so he tossed it into the river for the fish to eat."

Max imagined a younger Vashti, needing only dessert and stories to be happy. Simple things. Easy to replace if they were lost, easy to hold in the palm of one's hand if they weren't.

"One day a wealthy merchant came and offered him forty days of pay for one day of work, as long as no questions were asked. The baker was a poor man with a wife to feed, so he figured he had nothing to lose. He took the wealthy man's offer, and the next morning showed up on the man's doorstep as promised."

"What did she look like?"

"The baker's wife?"

"Your mother."

"Like Javi," Vashti said after a pause. "Or maybe I've confused the two of them. I remember her voice more than her face."

She waited so long to keep going, he wondered if she'd fallen back asleep.

"Go on. I want to hear the rest. It's a good story."

"The baker was led into a home of such surpassing beauty, he could never have guessed the things he saw there even existed! And the kitchen! It was a cook's paradise. Pans and dishes of the finest materials, acres of marble just for rolling out pastries, the finest ingredients lining the shelves and larders, and an oven so tall it could fit a man. The baker began to get nervous, wondering what his place could be in all this finery. He was only a humble artisan, after all, unfamiliar with such materials. 'That is where you are mistaken,' the wealthy man confided. 'This is a task for a true bread maker.' Here he paused to be sure the other man understood his desperation, frowning deeply before he continued. 'I have had a hundred talented pastry makers and cooks of the finest reputation in to do this job, and not one could complete it.'

"The baker was very curious at this point, and not a little eager to prove his mettle. He told the merchant the job would be done, and well. The wealthy man smiled, quite pleased, and produced a bread pan that could fit in the tallest oven and was of the most intricate design, the shape of a bird and its feathers carved into its massive surface with exquisite detail. The baker was honored to have such material to work with, and he set out happily to complete his task.

"When the bread was done and had cooled and the baker marveled at his work, he called to the wealthy man to say that the job was done. The merchant was satisfied, but when the baker asked for payment, the merchant only smiled and pointed up to the sky. 'The sun is not yet set on this day of work!' he exclaimed. 'And your task is not complete.'

"The baker was tired, but he was an honest man, and he

saw that the merchant was right. A group of servants suddenly appeared and began to carve into the bread, hollowing out its tender core with knives so sharp that only the very outer layer, the crusted bird, remained."

Max was breathless, waiting to hear of the baker's fate, cushioned in the world Vashti was spinning so artfully. He wanted to tell her how good she was at telling stories, but he was afraid that if he interrupted, she would stop.

"The sun had almost set, and the baker stood nervously with his hat in his hands. Finally, the merchant turned back to the baker and told him he must climb inside this crust to see if it could fit the shape of a man. Nervously, the baker did as he was asked, though he did not know why. As soon as he had stepped into the bird's wing, a flock of real birds swept in and lifted the man and the trap he had made with his own two hands into the air, flying them together to the highest aerie, where he was dropped into a nest of jewels. He lay there, swimming in riches with no way out.

"Before long, the merchant came to the bottom of the mountain and called up to him, 'If you throw the jewels to me, I will tell you the way home!' Having no choice, and knowing the jewels would be of no use to him in his present condition, the baker threw them from the aerie, jewels too beautiful to describe, so that when they were out of his sight, he could not have told anyone about them."

Vashti paused, reliving the childlike fear this part of the story always left in her. *Maybe stories are memories, too,* she thought.

"Don't stop, Vash," Max said. "Please. Keep going."

"It's a silly story, Max."

"No," Max insisted, "it isn't. Please. What happened next?"

She felt that if were she to speak again, the ghosts would certainly pull closer. "The baker threw himself off the mountain," she whispered hesitantly, "and landed in the sea."

"And the fish saved him."

Vashti smiled. "Of course they did. I told you it was silly."

But they'd made a raft of themselves to save him, she remembered. How clever those fish were! She and her mother had remarked on it.

Outside, the silence began to lift. The sound of sirens could be heard.

"But what happened to the man who tricked him?"

"Something. I'm not sure." She closed her eyes. "Let me see. I think, yes, I think the baker tricked him back!" He heard a smile in her voice. "He disguised himself so that the next time the man came looking for a dupe, he hired the baker once more, not realizing it was the same man. And instead of climbing into the bread bird after it was baked, he asked the man to show him how first."

"Like Hansel and Gretel."

"What?"

"Gretel asks the witch to show her how to test the fire in the oven the witch made to cook and eat her brother. God, these stories are terrifying!"

Vashti's laugh resonated in his own chest. "Yes, they are. But we loved them anyway, didn't we?"

"So what happened? Did the wealthy man fall for the trick?"

A flurry of movement was taking shape, something nearby and purposeful, the sound, possibly, of help.

"Of course. He crawled in, and the birds carried him away, and he landed on the jeweled mountaintop."

"But the fish wouldn't save him."

"No. He jumped into the sea, but he drowned there."

"Do you hear that?" Max asked, listening.

And now my story has come to an end, but the sparrow never got home. All her mother's stories ended the same way. Javi and Vashti didn't know why until their father sold their old house and moved to Sonoma. When they were packing up all his old things, they found a book of Persian fairy tales, dog-eared, the pages wavy and stiff with age. Each one began with God and ended with the sparrow.

The warmth and the smoke and the sound of her voice had finally helped them both relax. *Javi will be so glad I finally came to see you*, Vashti wanted to say as she dozed off again. *And she'll be here soon for a visit. She moved away a long time ago. I don't know where she's been.* In her sleep, Vashti watched a sparrow gliding through the air, searching the ocean below for her missing nest.

〰〰〰〰

35

"A fox, I think," Phil said into the dark.

"What?" Tia asked, barely awake.

"I've been watching it," he said, his voice coming from a faraway place but articulate and alert. "I think it's a fox, or a pair of them."

Tia closed her eyes.

"They're not dangerous," he said.

She nodded. "OK," she said.

"You know what?" Phil asked. "Tia?"

She didn't answer.

"I think you're a really great sister."

Nothing.

"Tia?"

Still no answer.

"That's OK," he said. "I was just going to say, I think the foxes are a pair. They look like they're working on something together." He leaned forward into the dark, as if doing so would help him see through it and into the debris all around them—just enough to see the animals he was no longer afraid of seeing, feeling his borders ease to include them. "A family, at least," he said to himself. "They're smaller than I thought," he added casually. "Can't see what color they are. Probably red or silver." An image of a small, orangeish creature rose to the surface of his mind, something he couldn't remember seeing before. "No, probably red." He yawned, lying down near the opening. *They remind me of you guys a little*, he told only himself. *Sharp eyes. Pretty ears.* "They're working together," he commented reverently out loud, a little sadly. He was falling asleep. "I'll keep watch. I know she's afraid of dogs." He'd always wanted a dog. A little one, smart, with a sharp bark, whose hair smelled dirty and sweet. Finally, his body relaxed into sleep and he was dreaming of a creature running so fast through an open field that all four of its feet left the ground at once.

FEBRUARY 15, MORNING

~~~~~~~~~~~~

After the first storm, a little sunbeam stole down the steps and made a bright spot upon our floor. I sat down under it, held it on my lap, passed my hand up and down in its brightness. I gathered up a piece of it in my apron and ran to my mother. Great was my surprise when I carefully opened the fold and found that I had nothing to show.

—ELIZA DONNER,
Winter 1846

〰〰〰〰

36

The morning was lifting the night away slowly, all around them a gray light coming in where there had been no light at all.

"You must go very, very carefully, do you hear me?"

Tia eyed them, raising an eyebrow.

Phil tried to walk away casually. The priest frowned at his back, upset.

"What are you doing?" Tia was suddenly behind him. Phil didn't answer. She walked over and looked boldly up at him. "What," she said, "are you doing?" She was almost a foot smaller than he was. He hadn't realized how small. There wasn't much light, but he could see her well enough to take in her developing beauty, the soft angles of her nose, the deep color of her black-lashed eyes, the skin on her cheeks still smooth as a baby's, the tiny breasts budding. She took his breath away even when she was glaring.

"I'm, well, I was just going to . . ." Her stare penetrated his as effectively as a needle might a balloon. He began to deflate rapidly.

"Tia," the priest said. "Let the poor boy alone."

"I'm going in there." He indicated over his shoulder the space he'd been babysitting all night. "I was just thinking, that if the animal came in. I just thought . . ." He threatened to wilt again.

"He's going to help, Tia!" Ally exclaimed persuasively.

"That's right," Phil said, daring Tia to contradict him. "I'm just going to go in there a little farther and block its way while I'm at it."

In there? Tia tore her eyes away from her sister's hopeful face and peered doubtfully into the small crevice.

"I really did see something," Ally went on. "A dog, I think."

"You can't fit in there."

Phil shrugged. "Don't know if I don't try."

"No," she said. "It's stupid. Don't go in." Her hand was on Phil's elbow before he could speak. "You'll get crushed." He looked down at her helplessly. "Don't be stupid."

If he leaned forward just a few inches, he would be able to smell her hair. "I'm not," he said. "I won't be." Phil lifted her hand gently. "If I don't go . . ." he said, looking to the priest for confirmation or a challenge. Now that the daylight had come in through the cracks in everything, they could see some of what had trapped them. But the smoke was also creeping in. He lowered his voice so Ally would not hear, ". . . we might not get out, Tia. You know that."

"That's not true," Tia insisted, turning to the priest. "Tell him. They're coming for us."

Their earnest faces were waiting for his answer. He took a breath.

"Tell them the truth, Jon," Willie said, suddenly awake, her voice as startling as a prophet's or a ghost's, so that they all turned to her expectantly. "You're right," she said, gesturing with her chin toward Tia, "they'll come for us." She locked eyes with the girl, who did not look away as she continued. "It's just a question of whether they can come in time."

37

"Wake up, Max," Vashti said. "Do you hear that?"

He didn't.

"I'm sure I heard something."

"You probably did," he said, wondering if he thought he'd heard something, too.

"You know," she said a moment later, "I do have another story, but it's not a made-up story. It's a true story."

"Tell me." He no longer felt pain, just cold.

"When I was about seven years old, my family and I went to the beach in August. Ocean Beach, I think, for a family reunion. What a ridiculous idea! Ocean Beach in August. It was windy and chilly, with a blanket of fog so thick, I kept trying to reach out and touch it. We met what seemed like a zillion relatives when we went there. I guess it was my father's family. It must have been. God, there were so many cousins, Max! I wonder what happened to them all.

"Anyway, there were too many people around for anyone to really watch the younger kids, and I ended up climbing out onto the rocks, much farther than I meant to. I played for a while. It was nice. There were things to find out there. Nothing anyone but a child would think was treasure—just colorful rocks and shells the ocean had turned up. It was only when my pockets were full and I looked around for a place to put another shell that I realized I was much farther out than I'd thought. I think it was just at that moment that my father noticed I was gone.

"The truth is, I hadn't been scared until my dad started yelling, but as soon as I heard him, I was totally petrified. When I could move again, I stumbled and got cut. It hurt so much and the wind was so bad and I was so afraid of my father shouting that I thought to myself, *Maybe it's better if I never go back. I could just disappear when the waves come, like a fish.* I used to pretend I was different animals after my mother died. Animals with abilities I could never hope to have. Gills. Wings.

"Then, from out of nowhere, Javi was next to me, looking at me as if I'd already left her. When I told her I was scared, she knew I meant of our dad, but she was still so mad to have almost lost me that she didn't say anything, just walked me to shore, rock by rock, showing me how to come back."

"Vashti," Max began. The smoke had gone from being a scent to being a quality of the air itself, hard to breathe and thick with heat.

A moment before the small tunnel he'd managed to forge collapsed on Phil, he was marveling at what he'd found: a fox kit, dead at his feet. He narrowly missed stepping on or beyond it. He tried to ease himself into a crouch, but the space was too close. From where he stood, he couldn't see its face, buried in its belly. Maybe it was only sleeping, curled so well into itself, as if its last posture had been intentional. But he knew that a small mammal would never have chosen such a dangerous place to rest. He was bending down farther, trying to know for sure, when the careful balance over his head creaked and tilted. He froze, holding himself as still as possible, as if to reverse the charges of accidental movement. He heard a scream, possibly his own, before it came down on him.

~~~~~~

38

"I can't read this, Si."

"I don't get your meaning."

She held out the copy he'd handed her. "It's all about the president's state of emergency, all the rescue efforts. It's just a bunch of acronyms: AMR, FEMA, HHS . . ."

And? his expression said.

"What about the fires? All the buildings going down? We have good footage of the city now. Where does that fit into all of this? You want me to talk about fixes before the damage is even done?"

Si frowned at her. "When did you last eat?"

"I'm sorry?"

"Eat," he said loudly. "Put something in your mouth that isn't coffee or cigarettes."

It had been . . . she didn't know how long. The realization made her feel dizzy.

"Come, we'll talk while we walk."

She followed him down the sand-colored hallway—everything here was the color of sand, every wall and floor and upholstered chair—toward the vending machines.

He fished a bill out of his pocket and fed it into the brightly lit machine, taking a second to choose peanut butter crackers for her. "You aren't allergic, are you?" he asked, his finger on the button. She shook her head.

Her mouth was so dry that it was hard to chew.

"Listen, Ellen," Si said, unwrapping the Snickers he'd selected for himself and leaning against the machine, "lots of young girls—I mean women—think they want to be a star until a day like today comes around. A story like this one? It isn't for the faint of heart."

"I'm not backing off, Si, you know that. If anything—"

He held up a hand to stop her. "How badly do you want this, Ellen?"

Her look told him he shouldn't have asked that. He, more than anyone else, the one who signed her time sheets and answered her 3 a.m. e-mails, knew how badly she wanted it.

"I thought so. So I can't emphasize this enough: we have a responsibility to uphold here, to give people the information they want. That's what gives us a job, Ellen. You're not just a talking head, there to spit out what's delivered to you. You're there to deliver a story, a good story, one people think they need to hear. We can't just front-load with the fires and expect them to stay with us. People turn the channel when they see too many bodies. You know that instinctively, El. You guided Peter right into that spin, and he danced beautifully." The chocolate smeared on the side of his mouth, and he used the back of his hand to wipe it away.

"This is no different. If anything, the right spin is more important than ever, considering the magnitude of what we're dealing with. What you say might mean the difference between getting the people in San Francisco the kind of support they need and encouraging a mass exodus from Washington to Cabo San Lucas. You don't start with fire, with Americans losing their lives in real time, unless there's a better story behind it. That's not the case here. It's just a free fall, and it's our job to find that better story to latch on to. So you start with the president and the powers that be, let people know they're being taken care of, that the guys in charge are on top of it. Then we can ease into some of the footage, but most of it we keep off the screen until the city's looking better." He wadded up the candy wrapper and tossed it into a sand-colored garbage can.

"I'm sorry, Si. But aren't we here to tell people the truth?" she demanded, an uneaten cracker still in her hand. He gestured toward it, and she took an obedient bite.

Si smiled indulgently. "We both know there's no such thing, ever, as the truth, Ellen. There are truths, plural, in the news world maybe more than anywhere else, and they need to be selected judiciously. If we lead with the worst of the worst, sure—it might be the most immediate truth we'll come across today, maybe in our careers, but people will tune us out if we don't filter it. They'll change the channel. And don't think for a minute that they won't find what they're looking for on one of the other networks scrambling for ratings right now. If it's not you delivering what they want, it'll be someone else."

She shook her head, hesitant, about to object.

"Let me ask you this: Why is every other news story on global warming or the Middle East crisis or organic farming, for God's sake, so goddamn important?"

"Because they're current events?"

"Wrong. Only people who live under a rock don't know that global warming is a problem. Jesus Christ, you think we're actually here to wake people up? Hell, if we had footage of a burning bush and Moses coming down Mount Sinai, we couldn't wake people up. People take the information they want and do what they want with it. Ever notice when a group of girls goes missing we hear about it for only a few weeks, whether or not they're found? Ever seen something terrible happen with your own eyes that never makes it to the nightly news? When was the last time you saw a major network lead with the shit that's still going on in Darfur? Or Congo? Or eastern Chad? Hell, there are enough human rights violations going on every day in *this* country to fill a year's worth of airtime, and hardly any of it will make the news. People don't want to hear about things they can't or won't do anything about. They don't want to be terrified by the real water situation in California, or the truth about the state of education in this country. Things none of us can probably do anything about. And you can bet your ass that they don't want to see someone's grandma trapped on the twentieth floor of the Mark Hopkins with no one in sight. They don't want to see the dogs people had to leave behind, the abandoned fire trucks, policemen shooting first and asking questions later because they're panicking about crowd control. People only say they want to know everything because it makes them feel good about themselves, eyes wide open and all that. So we make them think they're getting an edge on information without bringing them too far out."

He jabbed money into the machine and pulled out a soda for her and then one for him, handing over her can to pop and swallow, letting her wrap her head around what she needed to do.

"Let me ask you this," he continued. "How much do you love this job?"

"You don't need to ask that, Si."

He nodded. "Right. So if you want to keep it, you've got to bide your time, ride the waves. You've got to get people to love you as much as you love this job, Ellen, and they won't love you if you scare them shitless. They don't want the truth half as much as they want a face they can take information from and walk away feeling like they've got someone in their corner out there in news land, someone who gives them what they want when they want it."

"So we lie?"

"We shape the truth appropriately. We don't lie. We never lie. But the facts can be told in lots of different ways. We just choose the way that will keep viewers with us."

"But all this time . . ." she said.

"Different ball game, different plays."

"Jesus, Si. What about objectivity? Integrity?"

"Objectivity's a myth." Si slugged back the rest of his soda. "Or rather, it depends on how you look at it. You choose the object to present, and you do a damn fine job of it. Integrity isn't just about speaking your mind. It's also about looking out for the folks who'll be listening to what you have to say and take it to heart. C'mon." He gestured to her food and the garbage before steering her back down the hall. "Let's get you back on air, then in for another rest. I'll make sure you get thirty minutes, twenty at the least. It'll make more sense to you once you've slept."

At the news desk, another layer of makeup freshened up the old, and Ellen scrolled through her iPad, confirming her notes. *How had it come to this?* she wondered. Si was now staring at her.

"You ready?"

She nodded.

A spot of makeup near her eye stood out. Si reached over and smudged it in gently with his thumb. "San Francisco's not any safer if people feel it can't be saved. In fact, a miracle's much more likely to occur if folks have a little hope. With every good story, there's a little hope, Ellen. You've just got to help people find it."

She nodded again.

"On in ten!" the PA shouted. She'd stopped making eye contact hours ago, exhausted herself.

The on-air light was on a full five seconds before Ellen began all over again.

〜〜〜〜

39

"No!" Tia cried out, the word strangled with weeping.

"No," the priest insisted, holding Willie back. Her makeup had run overnight, making her look as though she'd been smeared with paint.

"Let me go, Jon."

No, the priest thought to her back, *no, I can't, don't go, you're weak, you're tired, it's been a long couple of hours, days, a long life.* But Willie was already moving things aside, her great height and strength enabling her to lift from the top where Phil had tunneled through.

"What's his name?" she asked without breaking stride.

"Phil," Tia answered, swallowing tears.

"Phil? Philip?" No answer, the shuffling of things moved aside.

"Phil?" Tia called.

Nothing.

"Please, please," the girl started. The priest had her in his arms. *Please, please,* he begged silently. Tia was now crying into his chest. Ally watched, dumbfounded, from the floor. How could someone who had just been so asleep be suddenly so awake? Maybe Ally was sleeping. Maybe she was asleep and awake at the same time, or they all were, and this— everything that pained and scared her—was just a nightmare.

Like a great, giant doll, Willie lifted first the things over Phil—a seat back, a heavy iron strut, miscellaneous crumbling remnants of the building—then found Phil himself and lifted him, too, bodily, by the armpits, up and over the things that had crushed him. As they watched, Willie's long, elegant arms and her face awash in color and dirt and sweat made her seem like a massive puppet pulling a smaller one out by its strings, or a matryoshka doll finding its smaller mate, collecting him with the intention of fitting him back into place. With one more mighty heave, she lifted all of Phil free. Once in her arms, his body looked much lighter.

"Stand back, sweetheart," Willie instructed Tia gruffly, laying Phil down by Ally as carefully as she could. He was blue from cold or not breathing or both. Tia wanted to touch him, but she also wanted to be as far away as possible.

"Is he dead, Tia?" Ally asked.

"Shh," she demanded.

The nun bent her still-pink lips down to the boy's face as she pinched his cheeks to open his mouth. He lay there looking like a strange thing without a soul. Tia hadn't realized how thin he was, how much hair he had. She crept forward, finally summoning her courage to get close. Willie's mouth on his looked as if she were sucking the air from him. She leaned back to press on his chest, then returned to his mouth, and then to his chest once more. She sat back on her huge heels, staring into Tia's baleful expression.

"Is he a friend of yours?" Willie asked quietly.

No, Tia wanted to say, but her voice didn't come out. She scuttled forward a bit more, taking his hand. *No.* She looked up at the nun, not ready. Dutifully and hopelessly, Willie followed Tia's silent request, leaning forward and breathing again into Phil's mouth, knowing one more press on that rib cage could break it, that there were some lives too small or short to respond to rescue, that a graceful death was better than one broken by desperation.

But Phil wasn't dead. He was returning from the nether regions of his mind, envisioning things he knew were there but had never seen before. A dog with a girl's heart. A bird with eyelashes for feet and a snake so gray, it was silver. No, that was light. His eyes flew open, and the silvery thing was gone. How disappointing. He looked up at Tia. She'd never believe him. Never believe what he knew he'd seen.

〰〰〰〰

40

Gene convinced the Sea Captain to leave the SS *Sacramento* and come with him as he headed west toward the safety of the Presidio. He tried not to think of how difficult it would be for him and Franklin to track each other down in this mess, now that home was no longer an option. As they were making their way back up Taylor, Gene saw the policeman who'd stopped him earlier, talking into the receiver on his shoulder. He spotted Gene and scowled at him before calling out.

"You done being an idiot?" He took in the pair of them before addressing Gene again. "I could use an extra set of hands. There's a fireman and some kids stuck under a shitload of debris in the Masonic Center. They need manpower, fast." He was already turning on his heel, looking over his shoulder scornfully. "You got it in you?"

Gene opened his mouth to shout back, but the Sea Captain stopped him. "Go help the little prick," he urged gently. He put out a hand to keep Gene from speaking. "You can't leave people to die. Whoever it is you're trying to find is either dead or alive, and whether you start wandering around the city searching for him now or in an hour isn't going to change that. You think he wouldn't want you to save a life? You think I wouldn't leap at the chance, if I could?"

Gene opened his mouth to object again, then clamped it shut, already running after the policeman, who had a few seconds' lead. The heat at the top of Nob Hill was searing and awful, but there was no time to think. There was just the compulsion to help, insecurely and clumsily, with a truer purpose than anything Gene might have found if he'd had the good fortune to keep searching according to his best, most thoughtful plans.

~~~~~~

41

He'd been angry, hadn't he? She had made him angry. About something. But what had she done? Perhaps his mother would know. She never forgot a slight. But now they were together and warm. Finally! He felt as he'd always imagined he would, distantly amazed that it had finally happened, incredulously grateful.

As he slept, his dreaming mind made short work of the sounds drifting in from the distant outside: the howling wind was the sound of ambulances, the flapping of the roof overhead a searching helicopter, the pop and rush of fire vehicles making their first successful attempts up the road. For a while, this trick led him to sleep in comfort, his mind willing to be soothed into oblivion.

The priest lay with his head in Willie's lap, looking up at the haze around them, the sunlight that was coming in now; dusty, lit particles. He could hear noises outside, of things moving, men's voices, a lot of yelling, and that made him happy. But mostly he was happy because although he couldn't breathe very well, he was still comfortable—and help had begun to come, even if it might be too late; it didn't seem to matter. It had come. Ally's head was on her sister's lap, at rest, and Tia leaned against the stage, something slipping from her fingers. Phil looked to be sleeping peacefully in front of them.

Gene took a quick step backward, looking up as the construction crane dug into the partially collapsed side of the building. It was the first real rescue effort he'd seen, and it felt as if he'd stepped into a revision of a nightmare, one equally terrifying but threaded with hope.

"Careful!" a man shouted at the crane operator as Gene jogged toward him.

"How did they get that up here?" Gene wondered aloud.

"Already here. Construction at Huntington Hotel. I'm Rafael." A man stuck his hand out for Gene to shake, a displaced gesture. "I work here," he indicated with a tilt of his head at the massive building. "There's kids in there. People stuck inside." His face was grim with purpose.

Gene's stomach lurched.

"They'll never make it," Rafael spoke aloud what they were both thinking. "If anyone's even alive in there." He turned and looked over his shoulder, at the fire making inroads on the other hotels and the cathedral, the buildings and the park.

The priest heard the crane first, opened his eyes in time to turn his head in the direction of the noise and see its open, iron-toothed mouth breaking through the debris. He sat up, almost falling over, Willie already sitting up beside him.

Ally woke and raised her head as she saw a man come through the rubble. "Tia!" she shouted. She might have been sleeping, but finally, a good dream. "Tia," Phil said, close by. "They're here. They came." He smiled at her, and she was distracted from her own rescue, realizing she'd never come so close to kissing a stranger.

Gene thought of the woman in blue falling to her death so beautifully, the others who called up to those who remained, begging them to linger for just a few, indefinite minutes more. He thought of Franklin, wondering if he'd get to tell this story, as one of the building's sides was successfully ripped open. He and the others who had collected to help stood watching, their hearts in their throats, as several agonizing moments passed while the rescuers sifted delicately through indelicate materials, looking for life. The fire behind them was a dull, ear-buzzing roar. Still they watched, standing in the middle of the street, as if their own lives depended on what might emerge from the wreckage.

Gene was certainly no ascetic, but for much of his life he'd been a man with a partially hidden, tightly wound heart. He did not really know this about himself, but he was surprised to feel his own expansiveness when that first person emerged whole and limping from the rubble, like a lid lifting off a music box.

Together, the evacuees made their way out and over the path the rescuers had carved from ingenuity and sheer willfulness. "You're lucky," the smaller of the two firemen sent in there to pull them out said grimly, "you had a fireman call in trapped children on a radio that still transmitted. We lost him." Unconsciously, he put a hand near his heart. "But we could hear you in there. Not well, but we didn't have to, did we? And thanks to the city's official bird"—he gestured toward the crane that had helped them dig—"we got to you." He shook his head, as if he didn't quite believe it himself. Ally wrapped her arms around the other fireman, who held her against his chest while shepherding her sister, Willie, Phil, and the priest out. They were almost at the door when Ally let out a shriek, freezing everyone in their tracks.

"Max!"

The smaller fireman turned, startled. The girl was pointing at nothing.

"He's still in there!" she cried frantically. "They have to find Max, too!" she pleaded with the priest.

"What is she talking about?" the fireman demanded.

The priest followed the line of her outstretched arm, pointed, trembling, toward the balcony rubble. The fireman tried to collect her in his arms again, but she squirmed and cried, refusing to be soothed.

"Ally," her sister said, stepping forward, her body rigid with determination. "He's dead."

Ally met her gaze with a steely one of her own. "No," she insisted, matching her sister's calm. "Tia. He's not dead."

The two locked eyes for a long moment while everyone held their breath. There was no other sound of movement nearby, only the eloquence of the dark cave they'd just emerged from, wide and waiting.

"Can you just check?" Phil asked unexpectedly, breaking the spell. The priest shot him a warning glance. He met it without flinching, "I can do it if you won't," he said, not daring to look in Tia's direction, though the whole of his attention was trained on her.

"Jesus," the smaller fireman swore, the one in an oversize jacket instead of a full uniform—a volunteer by the looks of it, though he was so torn up and frazzled that it was hard to tell how he'd wound up where he was. "Someone's gonna have to give me a hand."

〰〰〰

42

"Sir." There was a man's hand on Max's shoulder. He could feel the meaty, warm weight of it and opened his eye. "Sir, can you tell me your name? Can you tell me where you are?"

The man had an arm around his back and was lifting him and helping him, though his body and mind lingered in pain. Like a miracle, a section of the southeast-facing aisle had been cleared. Max felt like he was looking into the Red Sea, but the waters were dense and still with dark materials, piled higher than Max himself. Up ahead, he saw the priest and the nun and the children, the little girl waving.

"How did you—"

"No time for that," the man advised, examining his leg. "Looks like your right leg got sliced up pretty good"—he gestured silently to his companion—"we'll have to form some kind of tourniquet." He went on. "You're one lucky shit, you know. One of those kids remembered you were here. We were sure you'd be dead."

"Vashti," Max looked back at where they'd been.

"Quiet, now, this might hurt."

Max looked down as the smaller of the two tied something tightly around his throbbing leg, watching the whole procedure as if they might have been doing it on someone else.

"What about Vashti," he asked, as they tried to get him to move and the pain in his collarbone jolted him back to his senses. "Where is she?"

The first man's face pulled in quietly on itself. "I've got to help carry those kids, OK? Let's get you out quickly. The fire's on its way. Thank God we got to you in time. With some help, I think we can get you to safety."

"Where is she?" Max demanded.

The man didn't answer.

Max's heart leapt into his throat. "The woman beside me. Her name is Vashti. You got her out already?" He hadn't even noticed them come get her. Why hadn't he woken? With his good arm, he tried to push past the other fireman, standing in front of a view he meant to block. As Max struggled he saw her, lying right next to where he'd been.

"I can wait," he declared, gripping the man's shoulders, begging. "You can't see in here to help her. You'll have to go in after her."

The man dropped his gaze. "We can't retrieve any more bodies now, sir. I'm afraid we have to gather them only after we've dealt with all the living victims. I'm sorry. There are only so many of us."

"But," Max said, dizzy, wondering why this man spoke like his father, "she's fine. I was just talking to her." Max shoved at his immovable chest. "You didn't even check on her, you idiot!" he shouted.

"I did," the fireman said steadily and not unkindly. "She probably died sometime last night, I'd assume, given the state she's in," he added gently. "It was a bad injury, probably left her with an internal hemorrhage." He searched Max's face, trying to find the right words. "She would have gone pretty quickly," he said. "I doubt she suffered very much."

"You're wrong," Max argued, his voice building in his eagerness to explain. "Just check again! For Christ's sake," he cried out, the urge to run to her greater than his awareness of pain, "how can you just leave her there?"

"Hello." Max opened his eyes to a man crouching quietly beside him on the street outside the building. It was lighter outside, but the light was wrong. The man put a hand to his chest to introduce himself. "I'm Gene." Max looked into his face, which felt familiar. "I'm going to help you get to the emergency shelter. But I'm afraid it's quite a few blocks away. Can you lean against me with your good arm? Give me the weight you can't carry?"

Max was sure he couldn't move, but still Gene managed to hold him up and coax him forward and down the street before helping him to descend into the shifting, blinking city, coming alive under the rising sun. All around them was a purgatory of souls shifting in and out of fear and fighting. Gene felt Max pulling toward them, because he also knew the horrible limbo of anguish instead of finality, that sickening state that felt nearly like drowning if you were unable to give in and go under. Two children ran by them, followed by a third, the first with light sticks, the second without. There was squabbling and screaming. Were they hurt or angry or lost? It was impossible to know. Max had always thought of hopelessness as a great emptiness, but it wasn't, it was a steel core running through the chest, cold even though blood pumped in from the heart surrounding it.

"Tell me," Gene said after they'd negotiated a rhythm of Max leaning against Gene with his right arm, his right leg dragging along beside them, his left arm useless beneath the collarbone and his mouth busy spurting its nonsensical grief. "Tell me what she said to you in there," because he did not doubt that she'd said many things. Just as he no longer doubted that if he found Franklin again, the nearness of death would no longer be a matter worth discussing.

And so they joined other grief-stricken creatures stumbling through empty streets and parks and past partial buildings, hollering, stealing, accompanying each other home. Everywhere, the normal boundaries between things blurred indeterminably. Birds soared and called excitedly, a cornucopia of seafood and fresh meat suddenly at their disposal, the air confusing with foreign smells. The only sameness was on the faces of strangers, crowds of people and their pets confused or bullish, desperate to reattach. Deep among them, the city's rescuers worked where they could, mute with understanding. The hospitals that stood from the grace of generators were filled beyond comfort, and the caretakers within prayed for the dying to die, if only to create some space, if only to not have so much impossible healing crowding in on them. High on the windiest hills, the firefighters battled each blaze as it came, knowing as they did that they had their backs to ten more, that without relief from the outside world, they would be like ants fighting to support a slipping hill, each grain of sand they pushed back up making no difference whatsoever to the whole. And while the police kept what order they could, they were overwhelmed in the confusion of disorder. Who can name a villain when nature is to blame?

AFTERWARD

~~~~~~~~~~

I tell you that on the right-hand side of the Indies there was an island called California, which was very close to the region of the Earthly Paradise. The island was made up of the wildest cliffs and the sharpest precipices found anywhere in the world. [Its people] had energetic bodies and courageous ardent hearts, and they were very strong.

—GARCI RODRÍGUEZ DE MONTALVO,
Seville, 1510

43

Max opened his eyes. He was staring at a sheet of white. A sail? Maybe a curtain. He turned his head as a woman in uniform walked in. A nurse. He opened his mouth, but his throat was too dry to speak.

"Hello there," she said warmly. "Welcome back to the land of the living."

He turned his face to the ceiling.

He heard her fussing around. "You've got a visitor, today, Mr. Fleurent." She fluffed out a sheet on an empty bed nearby, lifting it up and out to float before landing. She smoothed it with the flats of her hands. "You up for it?" She straightened up, indifferently cheerful.

He didn't answer.

"Cat got your tongue?" She was clearly the sort of steely person who could chat through anything. Max hated the sound of her voice. "He's been waiting for two hours already. I told him he'd be lucky to get you awake, but he wanted to stick around. Anyway," she said, tilting her body away, offering him a last chance, "do you want me to bring him in? Seems a shame to send him away after all that time waiting."

Max shrugged with his good shoulder.

She muttered something far less pleasant to herself as she left the room.

A moment later, Gene appeared at the door.

Max looked at him for a long moment before turning his face back to the ceiling. "Where am I?"

"Presidio. Makeshift hospital." He took a folding chair from the wall and unfolded it, winding his long legs around it. "I'm sorry." He smiled forcefully. "I mean, the New San Francisco Hospital at Crissy Field. They had to give it a proper name. We're supposed to call everything by its new name." Though Franklin refused, even when filling out paperwork. Gene had left him in their government-subsidized room on Geary with Muppet, Esmerelda, and a bottle of rescued 2008 Harlan cabernet by his side, making a list for the insurance company the way other people make a guest list for a wedding. "I'm touched, sweetheart, born under a lucky sign," he said when Gene remarked almost reverently on his ability to sally forth unharmed through a sea of disaster, "always have been, always will be." Though he was now calling Esmerelda by her given name, and he'd put the wild poppies she'd plucked for him in a paper cup by the window.

"How long have I been here?"

"Little over three days. You can thank a major puncture wound, a fractured collarbone, severe dehydration, and shock for these sweet digs," he said, patting Max's cot. "The rest of us are stuck in a bunch of block buildings built too unimaginatively to fall. That is, those who aren't well enough to camp out or flee."

Max closed his eyes.

Gene tried again. "If you eat something and pee on your own, they'll let you out."

Max's eyes shot open. "My mother," he said, the panic startling him. "Can we call her?"

Gene reached out and steadied him with his arm. "She's OK, Max," he said. "You mentioned her while we were walking. I checked in on her for you. She's fine. Buena Vista was fine. Had a few cases of heart trouble and panic attacks, but your mom was good. Rattled, but good. Glad to know you're out of harm." He had the grace to look away while Max broke down in relief and despair.

Gene stood and walked to the camper's window, plastic cut into canvas, for a watery, muted view of the light outside. It was a bright day, sunny, everything blooming in the mud. It was spring in California. Spring always came early in California.

"How long were we in there?" Max's tone was soft and searing.

Gene turned around. "Not too long. Less than twenty-four hours."

"But she was dead that whole time."

Gene watched Max carefully. "Don't know. Most of it, I guess."

Max's face was white, his eyes red. "Have I lost my mind?"

"No," Gene answered.

"I swear she was there." Max met Gene's eyes for the first time since he'd walked in the room, though he whispered.

Gene scraped his chair over to sit by Max. "I've been thinking about this. Well, I started thinking of this while we were walking. You know how everybody argues about when life begins? Who's to say the same arguments can't hold up at the end? Who says when death begins?"

"Doctors."

Gene smiled. "Do doctors know everything there is to know about life? You said you loved her all those years, even when she was away. You said you loved her like a fool. But you loved her, so who cares if you were a fool? Who cares if you held on to her longer than anyone else might have? Most of us tend to lose each other too easily, anyway."

"You're telling me what I want to believe." Max's face was contorted by grief.

"It's what I want to believe, too, then. Death and love— they're just ideas anyway. They change depending on how we think about them. Don't get stuck in ideas. Ideas aren't real. Even the best ideas—ideas about love—aren't real."

Gene stood and picked up a brown envelope by the side of the bed with Max's name on it. He handed it over, and Max took it, studying the handwriting on the outside. It was vaguely familiar. Cautiously, he opened it.

Inside was a photograph with a note taped to the back.

Dear Max,

I'm only in town for the day to take care of a few things for Dad, and you were sleeping. Sorry I can't stick around. It took me three days to get here, and I'm heading back out tomorrow. I'd say I have work, but the truth is, it's just too hard. I keep thinking that if all of San Francisco had burned

*down but she survived, I would consider myself lucky. Please
forgive me for not sticking around.*

*I'm attaching a picture of Anita I took shortly before her
first birthday. I thought you'd like to have it.*

She really wanted to go see you. I'm so glad she did.

Love,
Javi

Max studied the photograph. It had been taken outside,
and his daughter's hair was fluffed by the wind, her smile
crooked. He closed his eyes, then put it back in the envelope
and set it on a tray by his bed. Some things were just too
beautiful to bear.

As if on cue, the nurse chose that moment to bustle in and
take Max's vitals, grabbing the tray and balancing it on top of
her equipment on the way out. Max's eyes were closed again.
"Here, let me." Gene helped her with the door, grabbing the
envelope as she walked past him. "This isn't trash," he said
casually, slipping it into his pocket.

After she left, he took a seat again by Max, wondering if
he'd fallen asleep.

"Thank you," Max said after a while. "I never got to say
that. You helped save my life."

"You're welcome," Gene said, smiling a little. He turned
around and gestured to the window. "You have quite the
view from here. The bay and all the rescue ships, the
cleanup efforts." He stood up when Max didn't respond and
walked over to the window. "Did you know," he said, "one

of the reasons why Alcatraz was so effective in crushing the spirits of its prisoners? You could see the lights of the city from your cell block. It was so close, a good wind could bring in the sounds of tinkling crystal and laughter from the yachts moored at Hyde Street Pier. Sometimes you could even hear the women's voices. All that lay in the few miles between you and them were a score of armed guards and some frigid, shark-infested waters."

"It must still be standing, at least," Max finally spoke. "An island out in the water."

"It is," Gene said, smiling wanly. "I hear they're thinking of building it up. Condominiums. You know what's weird about old pictures of San Francisco?" he continued. "Except for the high-rises, the city doesn't really look that different. The spacing between the buildings is the same, you can see the same kinds of gables and porticos and long windows and quirky doors and sun-splayed streets. It's like the city is seeded. What's aboveground can't last for long, but it also has this way of growing back, pulling itself back together into a patchwork of its former selves, oddly familiar but never the same. Anyway," he said and paused, going over to help Max sit himself up in the bed, "isn't it better to admit—even if it's just to yourself—that the things worth loving the most will never last?"

≈≈≈≈≈

44

"Oh God, Jon, I'm too old for this."

"You're fine. Just pull yourself together."

Willie picked up another pillow and fluffed it relentlessly.

"Leave the upholstery alone. There won't be any stuffing left."

"Jon. What if they don't like it? Don't like *us* anymore?"

"I'm not sure Tia ever liked us, honey," the priest replied, going to the door, "so you can scratch that off your list of concerns."

She'd grown taller by at least three inches. Ally was still thin but there was color in her face.

"I made this for you," Ally said, stuffing something indefinable and crafted into his hand.

"Come in," the priest said.

"Let me show you your rooms! We have rooms for you!" Willie exclaimed.

"It's only for the month," Tia said.

"For now," Jon reminded her. "We still want you to stay for good."

Tia shrugged.

"It's the beauty of a half-empty city," Willie explained, Ally's hand already in his as he led her down the hall, "acres of space, just acres of it. A room for you, a room for me, a room for your sister . . ."

Jon and Tia followed them down the hall.

"It's a little girlie," Tia commented, peeking her head into Ally's room. "But nice, I guess." It was the nicest room she and her sister had ever seen.

"And yours," Willie said, "I made it special. Perfect for a girl your age. Oh—I was thinking! We can plan a sweet sixteen!"

Tia scowled darkly at her. "I'm still only fifteen. My birthday's not until December eleventh. Do I need to write that down for you?"

"But you didn't get a quinceañera, you prickly little thing, now did you? So I was thinking sweet sixteen, American-debutante style. We'll need all that time just to plan it!"

Tia sat down glumly on the bed, putting her bag on the floor beside her.

"Hey!" Jon enthused. "We were thinking of inviting Phil over to dinner one of these nights. He's working on reconstruction only a stone's throw from here. Wouldn't that be nice?"

"Don't bother," Tia muttered, refusing to meet his eye.

The two adults exchanged a glance. "I'll just leave you two alone," Willie announced, leading Ally away for the rest of the house tour.

"Did your aunt get off to the airport OK?" the priest asked mildly, sitting down in a chair across from her. "Guadalajara's a long trip. I don't envy her that flight."

But Tia didn't answer. She was crying into her hands.

"Come here."

She did. "Sweetheart," he said into her hair, "you just let as much of that out as you want. Trust me. If you don't, it clogs the soul. And don't you worry. Just because people gave up on you doesn't mean you're going to give up on you, too. Not on my watch, at least." She moved to wipe away her tears. "Don't be afraid to be sad," he said, reaching for a box of tissues on the nightstand. "I'll let you in on a little secret: if you don't fight it, it always leaves a gift or two behind."

Ally and Willie were back, standing in the doorway. Willie stepped in, tentative with concern in her new cobalt wig and yellow silk kimono with elephants on the sleeves. *Elephants!*

"I've got just the thing," Willie said somberly, stepping into the hallway to retrieve glasses of milk and sandwich cookies on an ornate silver tray she'd polished for the occasion. "Oh," she said a moment later, frowning as she reappeared, "forgot about the dog again." A spectacularly ugly mutt with a milk-soaked muzzle and a crumb-filled tongue hanging out of its mouth followed on her heels. Taking one look at it, Tia laughed aloud, surprising them all.

45

Max was watching the news when his front doorbell rang. Some newscaster had replaced the one he was just getting used to—Ellen Sanchez? Sarducci? No, Santiago—who was now a hot item, had moved on to national news, no longer went near anything as pedestrian as a local station. He took a minute to listen before muting the set:

> *When we return, we'll take a look at the ongoing debate*
> *about whether or not to relocate the peregrine population*
> *that has exploded in upper Market following the*
> *earthquakes. And we'll be asking Mayor Benioff if hi-tech*
> *communes really are the answer to SRO restrictions in the*
> *Tenderloin. Stay tuned.*

It was a beautiful day, so instead of buzzing his visitor in, he made his way down the stairs, his leg still stiff but functional, and opened the door himself. A man stood there. He was wearing a brown jacket and jeans, his bald spot wreathed in gray, his hat in his hands.

"Hello, Max."

His voice had not changed, though the rest of him had aged significantly, most of his body falling off into curves where there had been strength. He was smaller than Max remembered him, too, though he wasn't sure if that was only a function of his father's age.

"Your mother told me you'd be home."

He'd gotten so old. Somehow, in Max's mind, he'd always stayed the same age he'd been when he left. "Yes." His mother had mentioned his father's intention to visit, but that didn't dampen the shock.

"I'm only passing through," his father said, clearing his throat. "But I wanted to see you." His voice trailed off. Then, "May I come in?"

If he'd had time to think about it, Max might have closed the door and walked back up as deliberately as he'd come down, but instead he found himself showing his father up the stairs in a moment of courtesy that felt like someone else's moment, the moment of a civilized adult making a stranger comfortable, not a man welcoming his estranged father into his home.

Max found something for them to drink while his father took a seat. When he returned with two glasses, his father took a deep breath. "Your mother seems well," he said.

"Yes," Max said. "Considering what she's been through."

"She was lucky to come through it unharmed. She was always very strong."

Max considered that she had never let him see her otherwise.

"This isn't your apartment?"

"No," Max said. "It's temporary. My old apartment is on the list for restructuring, but it's a long list."

"Your mother told me what happened. With your friend."

Max looked away. Four months later, and the nerve was just as raw. Though now he was dreaming of her as if she lived. That was some comfort. To know how well she stayed with him even when she wasn't there.

"You look like my father," Guy said after a while, regarding Max with curiosity. "I see it now, in your profile. I used to think you only took after your mother."

Max's expression turned inward. "You could have called, instead of just showing up on my doorstep. I'm not even really sure why you're here in the first place."

"To be truthful, I wasn't sure you'd see me."

"That's fair."

His father rubbed his hand across the back of his neck, an old, familiar gesture Max had completely forgotten about until that moment. It sent a chill down the back of his own neck. What else did he have the capacity to forget?

"Listen, Max, I know a good father would say he was sorry right about now, be tucking his tail between his legs and all that. But I've never been a good father, and I won't insult you by pretending otherwise."

Max couldn't even summon the anger he knew he should be feeling. Or he was just still too sad, too overwhelmed by all the loss. The old grief was atrophied from his memory's disuse, the new one so muscular it shoved out all other concerns, bruising everyday pleasures and choking them like a bully. "I don't want an apology," he said. "It's hard to ask for anything from someone who chose God over the people who loved him."

"I guess that's true," his father said. "God is really the greatest love story ever told."

Ever the philosopher. Even when it came to love.

"Why are you here?" Max asked.

His father held his gaze. Max clenched his fist involuntarily and didn't look away.

"How long do you have?" he guessed.

"Six months, a year. I'm told I won't see another spring."

"You know what?" Max said after a moment, surprising them both with his honesty. "In all my wondering about why you were getting in touch, it never occurred to me that you were dying and wanted to say good-bye. The simplest explanation."

"It's hard to imagine a parent dying," his father said and shrugged. "Even one who hasn't been much of a parent to you." He twisted his glass around in his hand. "I'd like to make one thing clear, if that's OK with you."

Max waited, listening.

"I would never have been the father you wanted, Max. I know it sounds like an excuse, but it really isn't. I just wanted to make it clear to you that even if I had stayed, I would have disappointed you. I know that for sure. I was already disappointing. For a while, I wanted to believe something about myself that wasn't true, I guess, but it never worked. At first I thought marriage would do the trick. But your mother and I married late. And then, well, you were somewhat of a surprise."

"One you never wanted."

"Maybe. Yes."

They were quiet, letting the long-hidden truth between them get some air.

Outside, a truck rumbled down the street, carrying surplus produce from Salinas to the volunteers working in the thick of reconstruction. It took a left down New Columbus and headed toward Fort Mason, the driver rolling down his window as he drove so he could rest his elbow in the sun. A few blocks down, he stopped his truck in the middle of the road to greet a family moving in, passing them a bushel of blackberries, welcoming the new and wishing it luck, sympathies extended in the greeting.

"But I did love you, Max. I loved your mother, too. But once you really started to grow up, I recognized that nothing would ever happen to change me into some kind of great parent, as much as we all wished it would."

"So you walked out on us?"

"I couldn't figure out how else to leave you."

Max looked up at his windows, realizing they needed to be washed so he could see better. It was almost summer, and the sun would be warming the south-facing room. He could get some plants, maybe. Something hearty, easy to keep alive. "You couldn't have sent money? Anything?"

"From a Benedictine monastery?"

Max dropped his gaze, meeting his father's directly. "Right. It was always all or nothing with you. I assume they let you out to make your worldly peace before you go back to them to die? Or are you hoping they'll heal you?"

His father gripped his knees with his hands, anxious, irritable. "Look, Max, I won't mince words. I'm a selfish man. Arguably a pretty cold one, too. It's why I was always attracted to God. I needed someone to guide me toward being good.

You can't imagine what a mess I was around you. Right out of the gate, there were no answers to you, and then you only grew more complicated. Eventually, there came a point when I realized that leaving you was better than staying. I saw how closely you were watching me. Like boys do, I guess. But you needed someone different." He paused, something soft or sad awakening in his expression. "Or something different, at the very least. I guess I loved you just enough to see that."

Max let a silent moment pass between them. "Did you know you were leaving before we moved?" he asked. "Why uproot us and then take off?"

Guy passed a palm over his face before speaking. "I knew you weren't like me," he said after a while. "I used to watch you and worry that you were, but the minute you picked up that trumpet, I knew I had nothing to fear. Your mother said you're teaching music now?"

Max shrugged. "Volunteering at the school until they can pay me."

His dad nodded. "I can see why you've been hit so hard by your friend's death. I have to say I'm not surprised; I wouldn't have expected any less of you. You were always so different from me that way, able to go so deep and feel what needed to be felt there, instead of always skimming the surface. I'm sure it's a better way to live." He paused, lost in thought.

"So, Max, there's your answer, God help me, I got you to a place where you could be the person you needed to be, and I gave you over to your mother. If a man can't raise his son the way his son should be raised, maybe he should step out of the way. Let God, the world, whatever do the work. When the opportunity came to go to San Francisco, I figured it was God's work."

"That's why we came to San Francisco?"

"Yes and no."

"Bullshit."

His father didn't blink. "Then why did you stay? Why haven't you left?"

"I don't know," Max said, though he might have been lying. "I don't know why any of us are here. Especially now. But we are."

"Eh," the old French Canadian in him came through, a million memories in that voice, a father, a preacher, a man Max once hated. "Bad things come and go quickly, and then life sucks you in again. People aren't designed to dwell on dangers. It's not healthy. That kind of thinking alone could do us in." He watched Max stand up and clear the glasses away as if preparing for one of them to leave. "We're no different from animals that way, and animals are built to think of two things: immediacies and inevitabilities. An earthquake doesn't fit into a life."

Max sat back down. In recent months, he'd seen so much softening, so much breaking away of the old. He wondered if softening was the only way to get rid of so many stiff, lonely layers of strength. "You're right," he said at last. "You are a cold man, and love is always more interesting. It makes for a better story, at least."

"Yes," his father agreed, "it certainly does."

〰〰〰〰

"Just go. The fog's coming in, and you'll lose daylight. Stop fussing over me."

"You'll freeze down here."

"I've got my flask and my stool. I'll be just fine." Franklin frowned, gesturing to Gene to hand him Muppet after he unfolded the chair they'd brought. "Look," he gestured across the street, "I can watch the kids trying to plant a community garden." A bunch of twentysomethings with spades and rakes were earnestly clearing a vacant lot. "Though someone should tell them the soil's too uric on Castro. Unless they want asparagus."

"Are you sure you'll be OK?"

Max tucked a blanket around Franklin before his lover shooed them off. "Go. I didn't wait an hour for a bus with you two to have you dillydally around me."

He was already calling across the street as Max and Gene trudged up Liberty. Max was grateful for the excuse of his weakened leg. It made the emotions already brewing in him look like strain.

At the top of the hill, Max found the number he was looking for, pulled out a key, and let them both in after figuring out the trick of the lock. Once inside the door, neither one of them said a word. Gene put a hand on Max's shoulder. "Do you want to look around alone?"

It was as beautiful as he might have expected, and it still held her scent. As Max walked across the front room, the sun-soaked wooden floors creaked under his weight. The windows looked out in three directions. Her father hadn't left many of her things, but a love seat and a table remained by the windows facing south. The best view.

"She didn't specify furniture, I see," Gene said, trying to sound practical. "Franklin will help you with that."

Still Max didn't speak, staring out at the city, one hand on the sofa, another on the window frame.

Gene joined him. "I can see why she left it to you."

Max nodded. "It was her home." And now it was his.

Gene smiled, spying a sign in the distance directly in their line of sight: San Francisco Brass and Winds, Since 1886. "Huh." He was grinning. "Hard not to believe she didn't buy it with you in mind."

Max had seen that, but his throat clenched when Gene saw it, too. It's one thing to dream privately, another to have someone dreaming beside you.

"Here." Gene fished something out of the Franklin Supply Bag he carried everywhere these days. He placed a framed picture on the table by the sofa. "I rescued it from the hospital." Anita looked like her mother, Max decided, taking in the dimples, the wild hair.

"I wish," Max started, finding it difficult to continue, "I wish I'd met her." Seen her. Smelled her. Held her.

"It's not too late," Gene said.

"Maybe it isn't," Max agreed, thinking of how Vashti stayed with him long after he would have expected, how sweet that staying was.

"I mean, for a child."

Max looked at him blankly.

"I'm just saying. This would be a great place to raise a kid."

Max stared back out the window at the city, half-alive and half-dead, but still more alive than it had been a few months ago, even a few days ago. "You think I could be a father?"

Gene shrugged. "Hey, anyone can adopt these days. Even brokenhearted, gimpy bachelors."

Vashti had wanted him to be a father. It was the one thing he wouldn't give her, because he was afraid. He was still afraid. But he didn't think it would stop him anymore. He looked around the apartment, knowing she could have given it to Javi, or her father, or just left it to be sold. But she'd left it to him. That whole, huge, beautiful place. A place that was never designed to be lived in alone.

"You know," Gene said when Max was quiet for too long, "someone's going to have to teach you how to use that kitchen."

"You're going to teach me how to cook?"

"God, no. But Franklin's been teaching me. On a hot plate. In the Richmond. Maybe he could teach us both here. If I know anything about a good kitchen, it's that it needs to be used."

Max considered Gene's advice. "I guess a child will need a good meal at least once a day."

"At least." Gene looked like he might laugh.

"Hey." Max smiled. "You must know we're facing a steep learning curve."

"Good. It just so happens that I specialize in that very thing."

When the sunlight was almost gone, they closed up the house and walked down the hill together in the thick fog. Neither said very much, but what they did not say spoke to a rare peacefulness, a trust so solid that even if they could not see each other, they both knew the other was there.

ACKNOWLEDGMENTS

This book was lucky enough to have been shepherded by three extraordinary editors: Maya Ziv, who was equal parts tireless champion and brilliant coach from start to finish; Jillian Verrillo, who hit the ground running and proceeded to knock it out of the park; and Emily Griffin, who stepped in at the eleventh hour to contribute her invaluable advice and expertise along the final road to publication. Endless thanks must also be offered to Lisa Grubka, my agent, who always goes way above and beyond the call of duty to guide, encourage, and promote me.

There are always extraordinary people working behind the scenes on any book. Cindy Achar, Nikki Baldauf, Victoria Mathews, Melissa Chincillo, Sylvie Greenberg, Gregory Henry, Gregg Kulick, Fritz Metsch, Laura Maestro, Diana Meunier were instrumental to the production of this one. Thank you to each one of you for your unique and indispensable talents. And many thanks to Jonathan Burnham, who makes such a difference in the world of literature and the lives of its devotees.

Pages of thanks could be written about each of the following, but space allows for only the briefest of mentions:

Adam Kendall and Brian Montone at the Nob Hill Masonic Center; Joan Baranow; Cheryl Barton and Meghann Dubie; Meg Waite Clayton; Jennifer Chung & Friends for translation assistance; Vickie Chang; Keith Ekiss; Robin Ekiss; Barbara Hoffert; William Kenney; Mia Lipman, copyediting superwoman; Susan Elia MacNeal; Rosie Merlin; Timothy Peltason; Captain Ron Pruyn and the tireless firefighters of Station 41; Zachary Schulz; Patrick Stull; Lisa Taner; Susan Terris; Julie Vance; Liz Whaley; Marilyn Yalom; and Dr. Mary Lou Zoback, geologist and reader extraordinaire.

And finally, my nearest and dearest: Aurora Serna, who takes care of my beautiful babies when I cannot; Dawn Wells Nadeau, whose constant friendship defies reasonable expectations; my in-laws, Tom and Judy Percer; my beautiful sister, Shayna Schulz; my other beautiful sister, Rachel Wachman; my amazing brother, Gabriel Wachman; and the two people who somehow managed to raise us all: my father, Amnon Wachman, and my mother, Ann Wachman. Finally, my greatest stories are inspired by my children, Aidan, Arielle, and Liam, and my husband, Adrian, who teaches me every day more about love than I could ever imagine.

ABOUT THE AUTHOR

ELIZABETH PERCER is the author of *An Uncommon Education*. Her poetry has been published widely, she has twice been honored by the Dorothy Sargent Rosenberg Foundation, and she has been nominated three times for the Pushcart Prize. She received a BA in English from Wellesley and a PhD in arts education from Stanford University, and she completed a postdoctoral fellowship for the National Writing Project at Berkeley. Her academic publications on art, the education of the imagination, and writing have been published and presented internationally. She makes her home in the San Francisco Bay Area, right above the San Andreas Fault.